# WHIPPOORWILL CHRONICLES

A NOVEL BY

# TIMOTHY STRONG

Black Rose Writing | Texas

ISBN: 978-1-68433-507-7 (Paperback); 978-1-944715-75-5 (Hardcover)
PUBLISHED BY BLACK ROSE WRITING
www.blackrosewriting.com

Printed in the United States of America
Suggested Retail Price (SRP) $20.95 (Paperback); $25.95 (Hardcover)

*Whippoorwill Chronicles* is printed in Sabon

*As a planet-friendly publisher, Black Rose Writing does its best to eliminate
unnecessary waste to reduce paper usage and energy costs, while never compromising
the reading experience. As a result, the final word count vs. page count may not meet
common expectations.

## Praise for Timothy Strong's last published work:
# *All the Echoes*

"A kaleidoscopic adventure with powerful insights into the longings of the heart. There are glimpses of nature here that would make even Henry David Thoreau take notice."
                    - Peter Corodimas, Professor Emeritus, SUNY Plattsburgh


"It's a legacy, an epic. It does, in wild and unique prose and poetry, what every good story does... it took me on a journey with you."
                    - Chris Shepps, Chief of Staff, *The TIA Group*


"In *All the Echoes*, Timothy Strong writes alternately rough and beautiful, articulating the desperate roller coaster rides of mental illness and romantic love. This is unsettling poetry, tender and blunt."
                    - John Berbrich, Editor, *Barbaric Yawp*

*To my mother, who gave it all to me.*

Special thanks to Eric Alan for his computer expertise,
and general editing advice.

# WHIPPOORWILL CHRONICLES

# CHAPTER 1

We played in the river as if summer wasn't almost over and school ready to start. George, who was fifteen, squirted water at me through his two crooked front teeth, then took a dive to the bottom among the smooth round river stones. I dove toward shore, then with my head barely above the water, smacked two small rocks together. That brought him to the surface like a trout starving for mosquitos.

"Dammit, Sam, that hurts." He came toward shore knocking the right side of his head against his palm to remove the water. George was smaller than me, but feisty and quick. Before I could stand up, he dunked me under, before I'd had time to take a breath. I thrashed, then stayed motionless to fool him. It did and he let go.

As we spread out our towels and rested on the hot sand, George said, "You'll have 'Big Lips' for homeroom this year."

"Queer old prick."

"School sucks. I'd like to be in San Francisco with the hippies smokin' dope and screwin' all the time." I pushed the back of my hand along my forehead as if moving away long bangs.

"Sure you would," George said, and laughed up toward the sky. "Why not?"

He said then, "How many twelve-year-old hippies you suppose they have out there? As a matter of fact, how many of 'em you see on the news?"

1

"I don't give a shit," I said. "I could fit right in if I put my mind to it. Anyways, I'm half a head taller than you, and you're three years older."

"Your father would kick your ass as soon as your hair touched your ears. Remember what he said when he saw The Beatles on Ed Sullivan?"

"Yeah. Doesn't make me want to do it any less. Wouldn't bother me if the old man called me a mop head." I sifted a handful of sand through my fingers.

"What's it like not knowing your father?"

"I hate the bastard." George sat up and chucked a stone across the river, and I wished I hadn't asked, not on this blue-sky hot day so near the end of summer. "You know that," he said.

From where I sat beside him, his scowl looked very mean.

"Sorry I asked," I almost whispered.

"It's for Ma that I get so mad. The sonofabitch hasn't paid nearly nothin' since he ran off with that whore."

"What a bitch." That's what we always called her since we finally found out four years ago. They'd run off about three years before that when George's brother Albert was still a baby and George only eight. Until then, George's mom had always told him the story that their father had just up and run off one day, leaving out that it had been with a woman I'd since overheard my father and mother say was a tramp.

"Forget it," George said. "He'll get his turn and so will she." He threw a handful of sand at the water. "Christ, Mom had me stay home from school most of that first year after they ran off. All she did was cry and sleep."

The tree-fort was behind my house in a huge old pine tree on the edge of a brushy field. We hid our bikes in the woods and walked down the stone wall that marked the north side of my parents' property. Way up in the tree you could see off to the east, to hills that lined the Hudson River, and that high was where George had wanted to build it. I'd almost cried convincing him how scared I was of height. We'd argued every day for almost a week, and finally he'd said, "I'll nail a couple wide boards across those limbs way up high, then at least I'll have a place to sit sometimes."

Lower, maybe twice as tall as me, we built what we thought was a palace of a tree-fort with old boards we got at the dump. Every time either of our mothers took out a couple of weeks' trash, we rode along and filled the car trunk with boards and anything interesting we found.

Inside the fort we shared another cigarette from the pack we had stashed in a baggie wedged in a crook of the tree. Darkness descended quicker this time of year. A whippoorwill sang from under a cedar bush near our tree, its eerie chant another reminder of day's end. We sat closely and passed the glowing tip back and forth, each of us so aware of each other, and that the long summer was at an end. I wanted to tell him how much he meant to me, that I was glad he was my friend, even though so many years separated us.

After a while it seemed the smoking and silence had brought us closer and we climbed down from our fort and walked back to our bikes. The whippoorwill flew up in front of us and George said, "I wish that bird would fly away for good. Every night the same dreary noise." He mimicked the voice, "Whippoorwill, Whippoorwill."

# CHAPTER 2

In the middle of the hill I hollered a long drawn out, "G-e-o-r-r-r-g-e," and by the time I reached the bottom he was in the road pedaling to beat the band, as my grandfather might have said. I glided right on by, arms crossed against my chest.

"Ten o'clock tonight, George," I said, when he rolled alongside.

"No shit."

"Yup."

Mr. Ross, the head of the social center, came in, nodded at me, then stepped into an alcove where he dropped a stack of forty-fives on the record player. "Paint it Black" by the Rolling Stones came softly out of the speakers located high in the corners. One of my favorite songs.

"Last dance of the summer tomorrow night, Sam," Mr. Ross said.

"That's right."

I broke the balls so hard the cue stung my back hand. Years earlier my Gramp had taught me to play. He died three years ago, but at times it seemed I remembered everything he told me. So serious, then completely funny.

By the time George came in I'd cleared most of the table. He stuck his head around the corner and had a look toward the same two girls I'd seen. He looked at me and made an ugly face.

"Rack 'em up."

He won, as usual, then said, "Let's take a ride. Must be somethin' goin' on someplace else." He pushed back his hair along the sides from the center part, then glanced in the mirror over the fireplace.

"Irresistible," he said. I laughed, even though I figured if we ever did find some girls I was sure to end up with the less attractive of the two.

"Dance tomorrow night," I said.

"Yeah. I know."

We stopped on the bridge near the center of town and stared into the shallow water. Trout finned to hold themselves steady in the current, and one occasionally came to the surface for a bug. George stretched out his thumb and forefinger like a pistol and fired a few shots. Then, "Where the hell is everybody? Shit. It's Thursday. Let's see."

"It's early," I said.

"Not that early. Bet we're missing a party."

He took off across the bridge, veered left down a side street, then he steered off the sidewalk behind a thick, tall cedar hedge. "Listen." He held up one finger.

"Yup," he said, then turned to me. "Dandelion wine, Sam! I forgot."

In twenty minutes, I was drunk for the first time and knew the true meaning of the words: gut rot. The stuff was sour and coarse—piss yellow and watery with strands of junk floating in it.

I stood up and didn't feel good at all, and the next thing I knew I was bowing to the cedar hedge that ran almost all the way around their house. My guts seared, and I couldn't imagine anything worse. I heard laughing behind me and reached my hand around, middle finger extended. After minutes of retching I closed my eyes, and quickly knew that wasn't the thing to do. I burrowed into the hedge and sat down, staring out into the dimming light at the others, most of them just as drunk as me. Why weren't they sick? George was stumbling and weaving, swearing about something. I wished this never happened.

The next day I called George around noontime to ask about swimming, and we agreed to meet right after lunch. I kept burping up that wine and my whole body seemed dull like a worn butter knife. I took my time crossing the field, enjoying the long soft grass against my legs and the breeze all over. A tiny coolness meant the end of this summer. I dreaded school. On the edge of the woods I waited for George, and a few minutes later he came into the field. He couldn't see me from this far away and I imagined him as a stranger I'd never seen before and tried to decide if I'd like him or not. But I couldn't fool myself enough to decide. He meant everything to me, and I wanted to be like him, in most ways, at least. I couldn't imagine not having a father.

"How'd you like that dandelion wine, Sam?"

"Probably I drank it too fast."

He laughed. "You weren't the only one to get sick."

"You?"

"Naw. I know when to stop. Something you better learn." He said it like a big brother.

We dove right in as soon as we got to the beach. I treaded water on the edge of the strong current, its tug a drag on my body. Then I sunk my lower lip under water and tried to drink the whole river. It tasted flat, not like in the spring. I started choking and closed my mouth, but that didn't help, and when I opened my mouth I swallowed what seemed like a pail full. I tried to stand up in the too deep water and went under. When I came up, George was laughing, and my lungs felt like bricks. Then I went under again and pushed off the bottom. In the open air I screamed, and that was when George knew I wasn't kidding. Different shades of grey heading for black passed in front of me as I stared toward George, then mostly black as I went under and the current grabbed and held me. It pushed me down. I was paralyzed, pushed against the round bottom rocks. Bumping. Bumping. Then George grabbed a handful of my hair and with the other hand reached under my armpit. My lungs were bursting, and I opened my mouth only to swallow and gag on more water. George finally got me half out of the water and onto a sand spit fifty feet below our swimming hole. I raised up on my knees and puked and choked while he pounded my back hard. He was scared.

"Jesus. Jesus," he said, over and over. "You weren't kiddin'. I'm sorry, Sam."

After I could breathe a little better he helped me stand up, and I hugged him like I don't remember ever hugging anyone before. "Thanks, George. Thought I was a goner." I hoped he understood all those things I couldn't put into words.

We walked through the shallows, arms around each other's waists, and I stared upstream where I had gone under, only a small ripple visible to indicate where the strong current began. Stretched out on my towel I felt all slack, like the skin on an old dog.

"Jesus, Jesus." George stood facing the river logs. "I thought you was foolin', Sam." He whistled low between his teeth. "What happened?"

"Just that I was treading water and having a big drink. I'd never been that thirsty. As a matter of fact, I kinda feel drunk now like I did last night."

"You weigh one hell of a lot underwater, I can tell you that. Pullin' you against that current was unbelievable." He stepped closer to the water, then turned and came back to where I rested on my side. "Sam," he said. "I thought you were dead. Honest to God. No shit."

"You saved my life. I'd have never gotten out alone."

George looked down river for a few seconds. "You won't ever know." He reached down, picked up a handful of sand and let it trickle through his fingers. "Look." He pointed downstream. "Another thirty feet and the river is knee deep shallow."

"I dunno," I said, and sat up. Now it almost seemed like it hadn't happened.

"Let's agree on something," he said. "We won't ever say nothin' to nobody about it."

"Well . . . why?"

He turned, took a step toward me. "Can't it be enough that that's the way I want it?"

"Sure, George." I stared up at him and he looked a lot taller than five-and-a-half feet, his reddish brown, Beatle-length hair fanned out a little behind his ears. George stared at me, his dark green eyes seemed sad, like we'd both lost something.

He leaned toward me and placed his hands on his scrubbed knobby knees. "Forget it. I know you can't shut up about anything without a reason. Here's one. Your mother would never let you come swimming here again. And if everybody in town knew, they'd always say you owed me. I don't want that between us. Do you get me?" He stood and took a step away.

"Why are you mad? Won't it always be between us?"

"I'm still scared that I almost didn't get to you in time. How'd it be living with that?" We didn't speak for a minute or two, each of us looking everywhere but at each other. Above, the mountains clouds piled up, and it looked like we might have a shower. That's what this whole thing seemed like: clouds rushing in, thunder and lightning, a downpour, and then everything back to normal.

Finally, I said, "A thank you don't seem like much, George."

"What would you expect if things were reversed?"

That idea puffed me up. If I could have saved him it would guarantee we'd always be close, at least that's what I wanted to believe. I didn't tell him that.

"Nothing," I said.

"Don't bullshit me, Sam."

"Okay. I wouldn't expect you to owe me."

"Good enough," he said, then he walked to the water's edge and skipped stones downstream.

I fell asleep or passed out. When I woke up George had gone. I called several times. No answer. We'd always gone home together. The river gurgled against its banks and a slight breeze ruffled the surface. Goosebumps. Things had changed for sure, and I didn't want to think about the glimpse of death we'd shared. I don't think either of us had ever thought about death before, not seriously.

A shiver ran through me, and I stared at the sun trying to figure out how much time had passed. I could see Gramp lying in that coffin. I hadn't really seen that as an end. I did now.

All the way across the field those images of grey to black reminded me of death, how close I'd come—and life. It will pull and push us for as long as we live, I thought, trudging my way up the hill, lungs aching with even this small effort.

# CHAPTER 3

The next week George told me he was moving to town.

"When?" I asked.

"Next Saturday."

"I'll help."

"Thanks."

After a minute he said, "Christ, Sam, you'd think I was moving to Timbuktu. Grow up!" He stood and shook the sand out of his towel, most of it falling on me. "Sorry," he said.

I knew he was exactly right. Except I also knew I was losing the best, most fun thing that had ever happened to me. When we were together it was like all the great things we'd ever done had just happened: the tree house, our first cigarette, bike rides, cooking out in the woods, and everything else—happiness. Alone, they'd only be memories. Maybe it's dumb, but I felt the same way about him that I did Mom and Dad, sometimes. Maybe it was because George was older, and I still had more growing up to do. I wanted to say this in just the right way to him as I sat there and stared up at him. He stood waiting for me.

We walked along the path and, in most ways, nothing had changed from the way we'd gone home almost every day that summer and the two before that one. Except, of course, everything had, and I cried on my way up the hill, feet poised on the very edge of the road, balanced, trying not to fall in the ditch. Damn.

The next week after school I moped around the house mostly. I'd been cut from the soccer team the second day of practice. George hadn't. Twice when I went to the river, I dove down among those rocks with my eyes closed, half hoping to knock myself out for good. But I always held my arms out in front of me.

I hated school. The homeroom teacher was a mean old bat who yelled if the legs of your desk weren't lined up perfectly on the linoleum floor. She was fat, and had witchy hair, always twitching the long pointer she held. "Big Lips" everyone called her. If you didn't answer roll call loud and clear, she'd humiliate you. The combination on my locker jammed half the time, and all the girls seemed smart and snotty. Everything made me madder than hell that first week of school. Junior high school sucked if ya asked me.

On Saturday Dad and I went down to George's early to help move. George had come up the night before and Dad had offered himself and the use of our station wagon, and Mom had said she'd watch Albert. George was excited about moving to town, even though he tried to hide it. I guessed I would be too and kept tellin' myself we'd still see each other and do some of the things we had always done.

While piling boxes in the back of the station wagon, George told me, out of the side of his mouth, that he'd asked Lorraine to go to the high school dance that night and she'd said yes. My eyes must've bugged out of my head when he said that. She was beautiful, one of the most, if not the most, popular girls in school.

"What's with you, Sam?" We walked in the house for another load. "Is it because she's a senior? So what? Big deal." He handed me a heavy box.

On the way out, over my shoulder, I said, "A senior, for Christ's sake! Tell me you're kidding."

"Yeah!" George laughed. "I like this high school stuff. I wish you'd made the soccer team, though. It's fun, except for the wind sprints. They're killers."

"I don't care much," I said, and saw the short, fall days stretch out long ahead of me. "Junior high is a drag. English stinks. We have to learn the eight parts of speech, take a quiz every day. Every day, George, until the whole class gets 'em right." I kept on bitchin' and complainin' as Dad,

George, and I took the first load into town. Dad pushed back a lank of his dark brown hair and tapped me on the shoulder.

"This guy your friend, George?"

"Usually." He poked me in the side. "Especially when he's not complainin'."

The new apartment was over a garage behind a trailer park not far from the center of town. It was easy to see that quite a few folks on welfare would be neighbors, and I wondered if George had said the truth about the reasons for this move. Maybe something had happened, and his mom couldn't afford the rent on the nice little house at the bottom of the hill anymore. This certainly had to be cheaper. Big rust stains in the kitchen sink, chipped, gray, painted floors, and it seemed the floor gave underneath our weight in places, and quick I imagined George starting to go through and my grabbing a door knob with one hand, pulling him back to safety with the other just as a big chunk of floor collapsed.

On one of the trips I rode alone with George's mom while George and Dad stayed behind to dismantle a bed. She said, "You'll still have to come over for Kool-Aid and cookies, Sam."

"Okay." Didn't she know I was in junior high now?

George's Mom was kind of lean and tough, and her hair the same thick dark brown as George's. And she never laughed too much, like maybe she had a weight across her chest.

"I wish you weren't moving," I said.

"Well, so do I." She turned right at the bridge in town. "George's father won't pay what's due us, and I don't make enough in that insurance office. So we're moving."

"Here," she said, and stopped in front of the apartment.

So I'd been right. Not that I could blame George for his lying.

By noon time we'd finished, and stood around the new, seemed to me, boring apartment for a few minutes, not knowing what to say. Except Albert who had come from my house with the last load. He loved the new place and ran around opening and closing the windows, tugging on George to come look here and there. Then George's Mom tried to give Dad some money, at least to cover gas, she said.

"No. Really. We'll miss having you as neighbors." Dad stuck out his hand and George shook it.

"See you at school," I said, as Dad started down the stairs and I followed him.

"Not coming to the dance?"

I stopped and turned. It must have been easy for him and his mother to see I was going to cry. "I'll be there."

I jumped in the car and Dad turned the car around and we started home. As we passed George's house the tears really began to fall, and I thought what a jerk I was. Dad patted me on the knee. "First of many, Sam. Unfortunately, they don't get much easier."

I swiped at my eyes as he shifted gears for the hill.

# CHAPTER 4

The next three years evaporated like hail stones on a hot fall day. By then I was fifteen, my sophomore year, and George was a big-time senior. It was my second year on the soccer team, but I still didn't have a regular girl; seemed to me I'd gotten homelier—long face with two big ol' ears, cow pie colored eyes, and of course, stray pimples like dandelions in late summer, and scars of the ones gone by.

I opened the medicine cabinet door and splashed on after shave, even though I didn't have to shave yet. George and I still did things together, not as often and mostly with a bunch of other guys. Now we swam out behind his apartment, in the same river, just a different bend.

And I thought of all the past summer evenings we spent in the treehouse. Sharing a cigarette watching the light fade. Then one whippoorwill sounded in the pine woods, then another answered.

George said, "Damn those whippoorwills." He'd throw a stone in its general direction and they stopped. "Every night that boring sound."

Later, with the stars out, we'd climb down and George would start for his house just down the hill on his old grey bicycle. He'd wave just before he was out of sight. Those nights sleep came easy.

I walked out of the bathroom, on my way to the kitchen and Dad said, "Look at that." I turned in time to see planes dropping hundreds of bombs, like salmon spawning, then the camera focused on them exploding. The war in Viet Nam. 1968 and the news showed war constantly, and the protests, and every once in a while, something about the hippies. That's what I still wanted to be. And here in this podunk town the soccer coach had threatened to kick a few of the guys off the team for pony tails. We didn't think he ever would though; those boys could be dead six months after graduation.

I'd started hanging around the gas station at the bottom of the hill in the center of town. Billy, the owner, had let me fill the soda machine earlier in the summer. I'd lost my dime in the machine that day and he handed me the keys and asked if I minded filling it. It was hot shit. Everyone wanted a job there. It took me a while to figure out how the inside handle worked, but I got it and was amazed at all the gizmos inside that took in the coins and spitted out the correct change. Billy, he'd looked me over pretty good that day after I finished filling the machine. "Like to fill it every day?"

"You bet." I handed him the keys.

"You're Paul Caster's son."

"Yes, sir. Sam."

"Call me Billy. Your pay is a free soda." He winked. "Two if it's real hot."

"Thanks." Billy, tall and skinny, probably near fifty, picked up the cutting torch he'd been using and ran the flame over a rusted tail pipe clamp.

Ever since then, for the last two months, I'd filled it almost every day. Now that school was open I walked down in the forty-five minutes between school's end and soccer practice; riding a bike was for kids. I planned to ask Billy for a job as soon as I turned sixteen next year. He hired guys to pump gas from five till nine week days and all day on Saturday and Sunday.

Billy was strict, and the floors had to be mopped just so, and the windows cleaned once a week at least, and the bathrooms spotless, always. He'd won awards.

Coach worked us hard at soccer practice. It was my second year and George's last; he played first string inside. In the last two games George had scored twice each time. I sat on the bench unless we were killing them.

After a home game we'd lost by one point, I walked home with George. He'd invited me to supper before the game, and I wasn't sure he'd remembered until I mentioned it in the showers. He'd missed a couple of fairly easy shots.

We took the shortcut to his house through a field used for a skating rink in the winter, and into the gardens behind the museum.

After a minute, I said, "Getting' older, aren't we?"

George looked at me kind of cockeyed. "What's that mean?"

"Well. All serious about stuff. Losin' a game, women, drinkin'. Lot different than swimmin' after school and buildin' a tree house. Don't you think?"

"Guess so." He kicked up a few of the orange maple leaves. "I graduate this spring, you know. Got to have plans."

"Such as?" I stopped in the path. He did, too. I said, "I damn well know one thing. If they don't draft me for this war they claim ain't a war, I won't go! No sir."

"Don't blame you. See, though, Sam, if only I knew. Letter could come any day after graduation . . . or maybe never."

"This is one time I'm glad to be younger than you. Maybe this will all be over before it's my turn."

George stared right at me, almost like that day after he saved me from drowning. "I damn well hope so, too." He turned and walked down the path. Then he said, over his shoulder, "Let's tie one on after supper."

"Sure. Where will we get the string?"

He stopped again. "Sam, if assholes could fly, you'd be a world class pilot." He punched me right in the heart, not too hard, and laughed. I did, too, though it hurt pretty good. I liked to be a wise-ass, something I'd been developing.

"I bought beer at that little store in Spott's Landing on noon hour. They'd sell it to a newborn."

"That must be true," I said, "if they're selling it to you."

"Holy shit!" George pointed behind me, then as I looked, he tripped and pushed me over.

I grabbed him behind the knees and we rolled over and over down the hill through the fresh fallen leaves.

We lay, out of breath. "We better get going," George said. "We're late now."

Just before we reached his driveway, George said, "I do miss those times down by the river, in the tree house, all those things. It's probably one of the best parts of life gone by."

"Maybe." I was surprised he said it.

"No maybe about it. I might be fightin' in a fuckin' jungle come this time next year. You still got over two free years left." He kicked a stone out of the driveway. "Don't you give me any of that maybe shit, Sam."

For the first time since George had saved me I saw fear in his eyes, this time for himself. Until right then, the whole war had seemed pretty far away, and those grisly scenes only nameless faces on a black and white screen. Now George could be the one flying in bits from a communist shell.

We walked down the driveway. Only one guy's brother in our school had been killed; he'd fallen on a grenade to protect his buddies, such a classic act—he was still dead, though. A town hero.

We didn't have much to say at dinner. George's mom and Albert did most of the talking.

After we'd cleared our places, George's mom said, "You stop by more often." George and I shrugged into our blue and grey letter jackets. "Sometimes I wish we'd never moved." She paused and stared out the small window above the sink. Then, "Oh, well."

"Bye, Mom."

We went through a brushy field, paper and broken glass cluttered, and headed along a rutted track used by loggers quite a few years back.

George had jammed two six packs against a log in the river. He popped open two bottles with his Swiss Army knife and handed me one.

"Thanks."

"Going to be a party later in the field. Supposed to have been a victory party."

We sat on the sand bank and stared into the cold water. A little later, when our first beers were almost finished, we heard a car coming, and it stopped a ways back, out of sight. We grabbed a couple of beers and walked back into the field. It was a car load: couple of soccer players, two other senior guys, and two girls, one a sophomore from my class and the other a junior.

One of the seniors yelled, "It's Friday," and the party began. They had two cases in the trunk, and said more people were on the way.

Bill, the guy whose brother had died in Viet Nam the year before, came over to me. "Howdy, Sam," he said, then stepped up real close as if to tell a secret. "Want to get high?"

"Huh?"

"Look." He half opened his hand and I could see a fat submarine-shaped cigarette roll back and forth in his palm. I wasn't sure why he'd singled me out, then he said, "George said you might like to try it."

I searched for George and saw him talking to one of the girls. He winked at me, then raised the thumb on his left hand. Something didn't seem right.

"Why all the secrecy, Bill?"

"This stuff is expensive and hard to get."

Bill had turned strange ever since his brother was killed. At first everyone kind of treated him like he was the hero in his brother's absence. Either it had gone to his head, or he just wasn't able to adapt to being the oldest boy in his family; no one was quite sure. Bill had seemed to shrink, literally, and he drank and smoked dope whenever he could. I thought he was on the verge of something, not quite sure what.

George came over, his letter jacket hanging on one shoulder and his green, checkered, flannel shirt tails hangin' out. "Think it's time you got high, Sam?"

"May be."

"C'mon, this is good shit," Bill said.

We walked down toward the river, and out of sight from the others. Bill lit the joint and passed it to me. I took a big hit, then tears came as I coughed and coughed. I gulped beer while George and Bill laughed. Next time I took just a little. I wanted to show I could party with the big boys.

After Bill ate the roach we walked back, my head a little light and a slight pressure in my chest. "Nothing to it," I said, and they laughed.

More people had shown up, mostly older, but a few from my class, and even a few freshmen. I noticed small things, like the noise of caps pried from beer bottles, and shoes shuffling around on the hard ground, and different, almost weird smells—combinations, like under arm deodorant and beer mixed. Then, as I stood off to the side, the smell of a hot car motor and stale pot and tobacco from my breath. The fall leaves were more brilliant, like on a sunny day, except it was dusk and overcast. Little chips of what was normal fell away.

Someone tapped my shoulder, then again, and I turned.

"Catch a buzz?" George wanted to know.

"Good stuff," I said. He smiled a big grin at me, and I noticed one of his front teeth was slightly chipped, then I remembered it was from when we'd had a stone fight not long after he first moved down the hill from me. I was only nine then, and George twelve.

I started to giggle. "What?"

"Open your mouth again."

I tapped the tooth with a fingernail. "I'd almost forgot about that chipped tooth."

He touched it with his index finger, rubbed it a little, then tapped those two crooked front teeth. "Never thought your aim would be that good for a little shit."

"You picked a bad time to stick your head out from behind that tree."

"More luck than anything, ol' buddy. Luck."

It must have been the marijuana that did it, but we got to laughing so hard that we had to lean on one another to stop from falling down. Bill and a couple of the other guys came over to see what was so funny, and all we did was point at each other and hold our stomachs. It finally quit, and we walked down to the river to rinse off our faces and get another beer.

On the way back to the party I said, "I like pot."

George made a face, and that's all it took to set us off again. The others must have thought we were already drunk. Pot was just starting to come into town then.

# CHAPTER 5

I met her the next spring. Finally. Already my junior year almost over; I'd begun to think no girl would ever want me. Seriously. And it was a girl lots of other guys were after, too. She was cute and cuddly, and warm and soft. And she could kiss. Winter was over, and spring had started. I was seventeen, had just gotten my night license. What a time to be in love. Delores.

George had graduated and for most of the last year had worked for the phone company all over New England. It didn't seem possible he was twenty years old and it was 1970.

But Delores. It wasn't as if she'd suddenly appeared out of the wood work, but I was a junior and she was in eighth grade, a kid.

I'd noticed some of the other guys paying attention to her, and thought I'd take a closer look. One day I sat across from her at the next table during study hall and gave her a real going over. Something about her was very different from all the other eighth grade girls. I talked to her a week later, Friday, in the library. I sat directly across from her at the same table, hoping the sweat marks under my arms didn't give me away.

"Hi ya, Delores," I said.

When she turned those hazel eyes on me and I saw those flecks of light in them like chipped ice in the sun sparkling, I almost got up and left.

"Hi there, yourself," she said. "Sam." She'd said my name as if testing it or tasting it on her tongue.

"How goes it?" I managed.

"Okay." She bent her beautiful neck towards her notebook and my heart fell with it. I want to kiss that neck, I thought. I wouldn't have gotten up if the principal told me to.

Her hair was parted in the center of her head, a perfect white line. I could hardly bring myself to speak, and figured it was all or nothin'.

"Delores, can I take you to the dance tomorrow night?" She raised her head and smiled. She's going to say she has a date.

"I guess so," she said. I loved that voice, a liquid flute in the middle tones. Goosebumps. I wanted to tell her right then that I loved her and offer my letter jacket and promise my senior ring which I'd get this fall.

"I'll pick you up at eight. Okay?"

Delores placed her elbows on the table, leaned forward. She said something just as the bell went off. I picked up my books and walked around the table, then leaned down, as if to hear words from a saint's lips.

All I said was, "It sounds like fun."

"Oh. Okay." The smell of powder, perfume, hair spray—didn't know what—filled my nostrils as she stood up and stepped beside me, hesitated for a second, then walked off in the opposite direction from my next class. As my knees tried to find each other, I walked down the hall to my locker, opened it, wanted to crawl inside its shadows, and close the door. In that blackness my senses would remain full, sharp, and content for a long time.

In Geometry, my last class, I doodled hearts and arrows, intertwined initials while the teacher droned on about parallelograms. I wasn't any good at math and didn't think the teacher was any good at teaching it, so we were even.

I walked out to the parking lot and wished I had a race car, at least something else other than my mother's dented, powder blue Corvair. I sat in the car and decided it was about time I had a date with someone like Delores. But the feelings were so intense, and I hadn't spoken to her for even five minutes.

The beginning of something. My stomach churned. I wanted to do all the right things.

Now that I had a girl, maybe, everything was right on schedule. I at least had a car to drive, the job I wanted at Billy's, and most importantly

George hadn't been drafted. And over the past year I'd come into my own sort of coolness, I think from my past of hanging around with guys George's age and older. Many of them had been drafted. The war cast a shadow on everything.

I raced the engine then pushed the lever into reverse, then drive, and drove out of the parking space. I didn't have to work till five. Usually I watched baseball practice, which I didn't play because I couldn't see the damn ball cross the plate. Not today. I drove around to all the parking places I knew; if the opportunity presented itself I wanted to be ready. Then I wondered if I should get something to drink, what I should wear, and half a dozen other things. It was still over twenty-eight hours till I'd pick her up. One thing, for sure, I would not push the sex stuff on the first date. Hell, I'd be happy just to slow dance with her, maybe kiss her goodnight.

I'd ask George some questions when he came home tonight, if I could think how to put them without seeming totally ignorant.

I found the perfect spot to park, in a grove of birch trees near a small brook that emptied into the river, the ground soft with a pad of leaves. Everything around so green. Then I said to myself, you idiot, what difference does it make, it'll be dark!

I changed into work clothes at home, ate a ham sandwich Mom had made, then went to work.

"Hi ya, Sam," Billy said, then glanced at the clock. I was a minute late. Billy squished hand cleaner back and forth between his fingers. "You look kind of dreamy, Sam."

"Oh, nothing." The air bell sounded, and I hurried out. It was ol' Mrs. Malin, in for her weekly five dollars of gas. "Hello," I said. "How much?"

"Five dollars, please, young man."

She could hardly see over the steering wheel, kind of all humped up, like someone diggin' potatoes, I thought, as I washed the windshield carefully, then lifted the hood to check the oil.

"Everything is a-okay, Mrs. Malin." She held a five out the half open window.

"Just a second."

21

I removed the nozzle, twisted on the cap, and put the hose away. "Thank you," I said.

"Nice to see you, young man." She drove off slowly. I rang up the sale while Billy put on his coat.

"You working tomorrow, Sam?"

"Yes."

"See you at noon, then." He waved and went out to his new red Chevy truck. After he left, I hoisted myself up onto the counter and watched traffic go by. How many hours now? I stared at the big yellow clock. Twenty-six and a half.

So I twiddled my thumbs and kicked my heels against the counter for a minute, not thinking very clear at all. I got a soda, all the while her soft voice, perfect lips, the tiniest cupid's bow, and those eyes kind of jumbling all around. Finally, everything came into focus, just as if she was standing in front of me.

A horn tooted. Jesus! Did I miss the bell? It was a stranger at the pumps. A fill up. I washed the windshield, then stayed back by the pump, the sensations kind of like the first time I smoked pot. Then I wondered if she got high. Just think of the fun we could have. Too young.

I topped off the man's tank. "Six-fifty, please."

Business stayed slow for a Friday.

# CHAPTER 6

The next day, Saturday, dance day, as beautiful as mid-April can be—the smell of everything new from recent rains, the sun a heater no fire could match, and the first mayflowers about to bloom. I swear every place I went that day carried a vision of Delores, related to her, would be perfect with her a part of it. I still had to wait ten more hours. I acted the date through a hundred times, and I willed more things to happen than ever would, ever could, and most of them were just pleasant wishes. I wanted to know her.

Work was very busy, and I made change wrong twice, something I never did. Then I decided I was a fool for all the dumb thoughts. And cursed the alien feelings in my gut, the future so uncertain.

When my relief came at six, I drove home and stopped at my spot and, from the car, stared at a big boulder by the side of the river and imagined all my thoughts had somehow sunk down into it through the years. I turned off the car, walked over, and sat, knees drawn up, and stared down into the sluggish, distorted reflection that stared back.

At home, Mom placed a plate of cube steak on the table just as I came in.

Dad said, "You almost missed supper."

"Sorry."

"Listen, young man," Mom said, a bowl of mashed potatoes in one hand, her index finger of the other hand accusingly raised. "Your father and I have been talking while I tried to hold your supper." She placed the bowl next to the plate of steaks.

"That's right," Dad said. "You may think because you can drive at night and use the car all the time you're free to do whatever you want."

"Not true," Mom said, sitting down.

"What?" I said. "Did I do something wrong?"

"Are you eighteen?" Dad asked, then answered, "No."

The drinking; then I knew what was coming: the drug and alcohol lecture. I listened while we passed the plates and they took turns describing the consequences: car wrecks, addiction, failure. I nodded and said they didn't have to worry.

"Make sure," Mom said, and Dad nodded.

"Okay." Then we ate our supper in peace. Lately I'd come to realize they thought they were losing me to something they did not understand, not that I did either. It was just a feeling more than anything else.

During dessert I said, "I have a date for the dance tonight."

"Do I know her?" Mom asked, her eye brows raised, waiting.

"Delores Prairie."

"You be nice to her."

"Yes, Ma."

They acted like it wasn't a big deal. Another hour and a half to go. I helped clear the table, then walked out back to the tree house. I didn't want to shower too soon; something told me this was going to be a sweaty experience, especially meeting her parents.

I placed a hand on the trunk of the tree, and a thick pitch bubble broke between my fingers. I swore and looked for something to wipe it off. Old maple leaves took the worst of it off, and I hurried back up the path to the house to scrub off the rest with comet. Black fingers for my first date.

First I shaved, then washed everything twice in the shower, cleaner than I'd ever been before, even between my toes. Dad hollered from the living room that I was wasting hot water, and I heard Mom tell him to leave me alone. Seemed there was more shouting lately.

I promised myself to spend some money on clothes as I leafed through the shirts four or five times, then the pants, and finally decided on a pair of sun-tan slacks I'd never worn before, and a dark blue paisley shirt—

for luck. I really hadn't grown much since my first dance in seventh grade, except taller. My hair was almost Beatle length, and I shook the bangs around, combed the sides over, then back of my ears, and splashed on a palmful of Timberline English Leather. I hoped she liked it.

"God, I can smell that stuff from out here," Dad said.

In the kitchen, I shined my penny loafers, checked the clock, seven-thirty, and wondered if I should be a little late. Back in my room again, I stared out the window above my desk, the sky a pale blue, the sunset more yellow than orange. I pushed hard against the window ledge and thought, "Shit, I'm seventeen and this is my first real date." Why was I so worried?

In the bathroom again, I cleaned my ears, combed my eyebrows, and splashed more cologne under my shirt against my belly. Christ, I was already sweating. I sprayed on more Right Guard.

"What are you doing in there?" Dad called, and I could tell he thought all this was funny.

"Nothing," I said. "Leaving in a minute." I walked into the living room.

"You look nice, Sam," Mom said, and pushed up the sleeves of her gray sweatshirt.

"Thanks." I kept on going. "Goodnight."

"At least he smells good," Dad said, as he unlaced his work boots.

Mom ignored him and followed me into the kitchen. "Home at midnight."

"Right." I closed the outside door behind me.

Sunset beams reflected in the car's spotless windows, and I quickly went over the whole car with a white rag, then checked to make sure the inside was still clean from all the work I'd done that afternoon in-between pumping gas.

Delores lived in a big house on a back road, two miles out of town. I drove through town, took a right past the Bistro, saw George's car out back. My hands had sweated up and I wiped them on my pants. Thoughts skidded through my head like a sled on bumpy ice; part of me couldn't wait to see her, the other part wanted to turn the car around.

The house sat back on a rise, and though I'd always known where it was, it was as if I were seeing it for the first time. I climbed the front cement and slate steps to the porch and knocked at the front door.

Her father opened it. "You must be, Sam," he said, and stuck out his hand.

We shook, then I stepped inside and looked over his shoulder for Delores.

"She'll be down in a minute," he said.

I stood and stared at the bowl of plastic fruit on the kitchen table. "Help yourself," he said, then laughed.

"They're plaster."

"Oh." Was he making fun of me?

"This is my first date, Mr. Prairie. I'm a little nervous." God, what had I gone and said that for? What a jerk.

He looked at me over his black half-lensed reading glasses, then took them off, and they dangled from a black cord around his neck. "That's all the more reason for you to drive careful and take good care of my daughter."

"Yes, sir."

Delores came down the stairs, her mother behind her.

Everyone waited for someone to say something, then we all smiled. "Hello, Delores, Mrs. Prairie."

Delores placed one loafered foot on top of the other, and I realized she was wearing the same dark blue skirt she'd had on the first day we met, except now, in this light, I could see there were purple and silver threads running through the material.

"I'm ready," she said, and her mother patted the frilly gray material around Delores' neck.

I turned, glanced at the plaster fruit, then stepped toward the door. Mr. Prairie held out his hand, and I wanted to wipe mine off first, but didn't, and we shook again.

"Have a good time," he said.

"Don't forget the time, Delores," her mother said.

Delores stepped out in front of me, and I let the screen door slam. "Sorry," I said, and they both stood there and waved.

"Dad always says he's going to fix that, but all he does is read."

I walked to the driver's side, opened the door, hesitated, and started to walk around, but she was already inside.

"Glad that's over," she said, and I wanted to kiss her.

"Me, too." I backed the car around.

"Did my father seem nervous to you?"

"I didn't notice."

"No one ever picked me up for a dance before."

"What?" I reached the bottom of the driveway and headed for town. She hadn't answered.

"Why?" I asked.

"Weren't old enough. Didn't drive." She shrugged her shoulders and moved maybe six inches closer to me. I rested my hand in the middle of the seat.

"Do you have any cigarettes?" she asked.

I reached under the seat and handed her the pack, then pushed in the lighter.

"So you might say this is my first official date, ever." she said.

I smiled inside and out and remembered what I'd said to her father.

"Put 'er there then," I said, praying it wasn't a big mistake admitting it was mine too. We shook hands and I wanted to hold on forever, then the lighter popped out and she let go.

We didn't say much for the next half mile, and I inhaled the smell of her sweet perfume mixed in the fresh spring breeze. Then I heard this flicking sound and couldn't figure out what it might be. I glanced in the rear-view mirror; it almost sounded like a stick caught on the frame, scratching lightly along the road. But it was too regular for that. Something in the motor? Oh, no. I began to sweat again.

"Something wrong?" Delores asked.

"That noise. Do you hear it?"

"No . . ." Then it stopped.

"That was me." She held up her right hand and flicked the outside of her long index fingernail inside her thumbnail. "Sorry."

"It's okay. I just couldn't figure out where it was coming from." Must be she was nervous. Why? I couldn't figure it out. We were almost to the school, and it was still early, no one showed up till almost nine, usually.

"Want to ride around a little?"

"Sure." She took a final drag on her cigarette and crushed it out into the ash tray. I wanted to ask so many questions that were none of my business.

"Does the tape deck work?"

"Yeah." I reached into the back for the tape case and handed it to her.

"Oh, let's hear this!" She picked out a recent Chicago tape, and I slid it into the deck.

"I love it," she said, and hummed along with the song "Closer to You."

Oh, her voice. I ached. It was almost as if I'd never heard a girl's voice before. All kinds of horns sang in the four speakers. I turned it up, and Delores rested her head against the back of the seat, and I stared until the front right tire bumped down onto the shoulder. I shifted a little, so I could see her and the road, too. She took a deep breath, then she opened her eyes. "Such a good band."

"This is fun," I said.

"Yeah, it is." And then she slid across the seat, her left thigh not six inches from mine. My breath caught. Delores flicked each finger on her right hand against the inside of her thumbnail, then she bounced on the seat like a little kid, turned toward me. "I like this car. Kind of cute, Sam."

"Doesn't go very fast." I floored it, and the sound of the motor didn't change much.

"Gets ya where you're goin'." And I heard her laugh for the first time. A sound higher pitched than her speaking voice. Her laugh soared as if she couldn't control it, then she did, and its echoes seemed to mingle with the music and die away.

We drove a while longer, and I thought of not going to the dance, of course, and heading for the birch grove. Instead I said, "Ready for the dance," and placed my hand in the small space between my right leg and her left. Chicken, I thought.

"Sure."

I did a three-point turn in the middle of the road and back we went. The band, from Spott's Landing, called themselves Clippers, because I don't think any of them had had a haircut since they'd started playing three years ago. They played loud rock and roll: The Stones, Doors, The Who, Led Zeppelin, and every once and a while a slow dance to keep the couples happy. "Us couples," I thought and looked at Delores next to me. Then the band began the first chords of L.A. Woman, and I asked her to dance.

Neither of us were very graceful, and I wished we'd had a few beers to loosen up. We slid around on the sawdust-sprinkled floor, now and then picking up one foot, looking at each other, then away, bending at the waist, hands describing arcs. When the music stopped we walked to an open section of the bleachers.

Delores took a couple steps to the side and spoke to several freshman girls, and I figured they were discussing me.

"Want to sit?" I asked Delores.

"Okay."

We walked up a couple rows of bleachers and sat. This whole thing so awkward. The music was a little less loud this far away.

"People are nosy," she said.

I didn't say anything, and she continued, "Two of those girls wanted to know if you tried anything in the car on the way here, or if we had beer, or smoked any pot. Do you smoke pot, Sam?"

"Once in a while."

"I never have."

We watched people dance, then a chaperone walked by, Mr. Bowman, the English teacher. I waved and he nodded, his goatee wagging up and down. He walked over to a group of chairs in the darkest part of the gym and whispered to several of the couples; they looked like one person till he said something to them, then they broke and moved apart.

"Sorry I'm not much of a dancer," I said.

"It's fun though, don't you think?"

"Oh, yeah."

In the dim light I couldn't see her very well but loved her perfume every time she turned toward me. Then she told me about a pony she'd owned and how sad she was when they had to put it down. I didn't quite see why she told me this.

"What was his name?"

"Boulder, because he was stubborn."

Ned, a guy on the soccer team, a senior, came over with his girl. He placed one foot up on the bleachers and leaned forward. He whispered into my ear, "Smoke a joint at the break?"

I glanced at Delores and remembered my pledge not to screw up this first date. "Better not. Thanks."

He stepped back, raised both thumbs, and winked. Then he put his arm around his girl and walked off.

Delores slid a little closer, "What's up with Ned?"

"Nothin' much."

We danced once more, then the band took a break, and we went into the cafeteria for punch and cookies, something I hadn't done since I was in seventh grade, unless I had the munchies from smoking pot. In the bright light, Delores' soft skin seemed perfectly molded to her face, and I imagined tracing all the contours of her face with the tip of one finger. She leaned against a bulletin board, and we looked at each other, then away, and back again. Neither of us very good at holding the other's gaze. The wall clock was at nine-fifteen. "What time do you have to be home?" I asked her.

"Eleven-thirty," she said, sipped her punch and red droplets clung to her upper lip. "Do you like being a junior, Sam?"

"I think I do. Another season of soccer and basketball, then I'll probably go to college."

"Do you worry about the war?"

"Some."

"What college?"

"Probably Paul Smiths up in the Adirondacks."

"I've heard of that. Will you study forestry?"

"Probably." I read the bulletin board behind her. One flyer advertised working on a ship during the summer. Then it came to me that she really was a full-grown woman; they always said girls matured earlier than guys. Shit, at fourteen she was probably my mental equal.

"The music is starting again," I heard her say, as if from far off.

She followed my gaze to the advertisement. I took a step toward the gym. "You have a good summer job," she said.

"Yup."

She slid her arm through mine, and we walked toward the gym entrance. Then, for the briefest part of a second, that sensation of no air, a gulp of water and air, drowning, came over me as my toe caught on the metal threshold of the entranceway. Delores gripped the inside of my elbow to balance me, her fingernails dug in a little, just as George's had the day he saved me. All this happened so quickly I had taken only two steps past the doorway when everything seemed normal again. Had it really happened?

"Whoa, there," Delores said.

I glanced behind me. "Damn thing. If a chaperone saw that they'll accuse me of drinking. The one time I'm not."

We kept walking, slower, a little more together, maybe.

# CHAPTER 7

I had another date with Delores.

In the shower after dinner I wondered what experiences Dad had with women. Kind of weird. I wanted to have lots of fun before I got married, at least that's what I'd thought before I met Delores. As I dried off, a strange feeling came over me, prickly, yet numbing, like Novocain, kind of radiating out from my rib cage, an undefinable center.

Delores came out before I'd stopped the car in her driveway. She slammed the car door and slid across the seat. "Ready," she said, her jaw set forward, cupid's bow more furrowed than I'd ever seen. I looked up the steps at the front door, its glass empty of her parents. "Let's go, Sam."

I backed around and drove down the driveway. "Anything wrong?"

She leaned forward, then sat back against the seat. "They make me mad sometimes."

I almost said, "Now what," then realized this was a first. Somehow it amused me that she was mad.

"Did you have a fight?"

"You could say that."

"Tell me."

"No. It's all right now."

I headed north at the main road, and the Corvair droned up the road, top speed about fifty. Neither of us said anything for a few miles, then we both started to say something.

"Go ahead," I said, pushed a Doors tape in, and turned the volume down.

"Well, if you want to know, Andrew Jenson called and asked me to his house for dinner."

"When?" I squeezed the steering wheel.

Andrew was the son of a lawyer, a sophomore, and a real goody, goody. But obviously she'd turned him down.

I could almost see the steam rise from her head. She moved over tight to the passenger side door. "I said no when he called," Delores said, her nose almost touching the window.

"You've been out with him before?"

"A couple times. No big deal."

"I'm sorry," I said. "None of my business." I shut the music off.

She turned toward me, then I looked at her eyes, the hazel color seemed shrunk and the white exaggerated. Still madder than hell.

"It's more than that," she said, and crossed her arms across her chest. I waited.

"My parents really like him." She paused. "What they really like is that his father is a lawyer."

"And mine is a carpenter. Right?"

"They didn't say that."

"Did they have to?"

When she didn't say anything, I said, "That's a yes. You're always judged in this fucking town by what your parents do for a living and how long they've been here and how much dirt has been said about them."

She still didn't say anything. I said, "It's like on the soccer team, one of the guys I'm friends with, his old man is a doctor, and every time I go to their house his mother is a haughty, condescending bitch." I took a breath. "Talk to me, Delores. What makes one person better than another?"

"I agree with what you're saying," she said.

Now she was calm, and I was the one pissed. How had that happened?

"Do you really want to go to a movie?" I asked. "I don't even know what's playing."

"Why?"

"Well, there's a keg party over in the hollow."

"Let's go." She slid over to the middle.

I did a U-turn, pushed Chicago in, and turned it up. Delores was smiling, and for some reason that reminded me of her temper, and I didn't want her mad at me.

Then she sang, "There's a diamond sky that's waiting for us just outside of town."

The field party was just beginning when I pulled in and parked beside George's car. He came right over as we got out, rubbing his hands together, then quick gave me a thumbs up, and tapped Delores on the shoulder. "Delores," he said.

"You know George, right?" I asked.

"Sure," she said. "I watched you play soccer when I was in elementary school."

George took a step back. "Man, I am getting old." We all laughed and walked to the keg.

A couple of guys were getting a fire started. Around the low, but steep hills surrounding the hollow the sun cast a soft yellow glow, and I put my arm around Delores. She smiled up at me. "Still cool these nights," she said.

"I've got an extra coat in the trunk."

"Okay."

We walked to the Corvair, and I opened the front lid. It was an old black and red checkered hunting jacket of my father's. I shook the dust out, then held it open for her.

"Thanks, Sam." She turned around and I stepped closer, then she lifted her heels off the ground and we kissed. Our lips parted, and we stared at each other, her head tilted back, lips parted, eyes clean like fresh washed glass. Light-headed, I kissed her again, then reached my arms around her waist, picked her up and set her down on the front fender.

"There," I said.

"Hand me my beer, please."

"Sure."

"Thanks. It's like I always thought a field party would be."

Our faces were on the same level now, and in the fading light of the sun and the growing light from the bonfire flickering off the windshield, I was more amazed at how large the whites of her eyes were, then we kissed again, and she closed them. We kissed for a long time.

"Wow." I couldn't help saying it when we stopped to take a breath. She smiled. "Likewise."

Then we really went at it, absolutely oblivious to everything else. Our lips searched, sent each other messages unconsciously answered, exploring, soft, hard, harder, soft again, and the next time I looked up the stars had come out, or I'd died and gone to heaven. Holy moly! Her light kisses as soft as I imagined the belly feathers of a whippoorwill.

We had another drink, then started again, hands up and down each other's backs, caressing, holding hands, then I began to rub her sides and she giggled, her lips tickling mine, and my knees weakened. I'd almost touched the side of her breast. Maybe the giggle was a warning. I reached for my beer on the roof, and handed one to Delores, not sure which was which, as if it mattered.

"I'm very ticklish, Sam."

"Oh. Sorry." I hugged her and loved the way the movement of her breathing felt against me. She took a deep breath, then let it go. "Let's have a cigarette," she said.

"Okay, I could use another beer. You ready?"

It was dark and more people had shown up, and music came out of the back of a van. I started to cool off, and all I could think of was the heat that her chest gave out, Christ, like a furnace. It went right through me now, away from it, I was freezing.

More than twenty people hung around the waist-high flames of the fire, and I held my hands to them for a minute, then went over to the keg. George stood off to the side talking to a blonde he'd graduated with. He came over while I topped off the second cup and poked me in the ribs.

"Been scuba diving, Sam? Thought you'd gone down for good."

"Nosy, ain't ya?" But I didn't care. I said, "We're talking about world problems. Boring stuff, really."

He laughed and said "Right."

I walked back, eyes adjusting to the darkness, and could see other couples, some in cars, others leaning against them. A beautiful night for the first field party of the year. I had a girl.

I handed Delores her beer, took a sip of mine, then placed it on the roof.

"Is that pot I smell?" she asked.

I sniffed the air. "Sure is."

"Oh," she said.

"Ever try it?"

"No."

"Want to?"

"Maybe. Not now."

I lit us each a cigarette, and after she took a long drag I reached up and touched her cheek with the back of my hand, a little nervous, kind of bold and shy at the same time.

"Not many others here my age."

She was right. Most of the people had graduated and worked in town, some for the grocery store, a few of the Viet Nam vets were there, the people from high school were mostly juniors and seniors. I'd seen two guys from Delores' class and a couple freshman girls.

"Does it bother you? We can go any time."

"No. It's just that if my parents ever knew they wouldn't let me out for a month, or more, and wouldn't let me see you."

"I can imagine."

We drank our beers and finished our cigarettes, listening to the loud music that bounced off the hills, distorted. Grand Funk Railroad.

"Let's go for a walk," she said.

"Okay." I kissed her, then lifted her off the fender and to the ground. We walked away from the campfire toward the trees. A narrow path led into a forest of cedar, and I went first. Ahead and to the left a steep bank, almost a cliff, blocked the way, and we stayed on the path that curved around the small bowl, Delores a half-step behind.

"This is a strange place," she said.

We heard noise from ahead and stopped. Delores gripped my biceps with her hands, and whispered, "What is it?"

"I don't know," I said, and took a step forward, then looked back over her shoulder.

Then the moaning noise was louder, and clearly human, at least to me. We could hear digging sounds, too. I knew it was two people really going at it. George told me one time he'd dug holes with the toes of his feet at least six inches deep, just pushing and pushing. The sounds grew louder and changed in pitch.

"What?" she said, obviously frightened.

"A couple messing around," I said.

"Sam. It is not." She let go of me and took a step back toward the fire.

"Listen," I said, and smiled.

"Let's go back to the car."

"All right."

She didn't say a word the whole way back and, after she finished her beer, wanted to go home.

On the road she said, "It sounded like animals."

"You know it wasn't. What's the big deal? Sounded like fun to me."

"Sam. You must know—you know—I'm a virgin."

"So?"

"Well."

"Haven't you ever heard your parents?"

"I guess. This is all so weird. Let's talk about something else."

"You won't always be a virgin, Delores."

"I'm only fourteen."

"Are all the girls in your class virgins?"

"No. I want it to be special. My parents would kill me."

"Do you think the other girls' parents know?"

I could tell she didn't want to talk about it. She stayed by the passenger window this whole time, and at the end of the road from the hollow I looked over and could see a pout on her face. She looked so troubled, and I kicked myself for asking all those questions. Her lip started to tremble, her lower one was pushed out and the upper one held in underneath it. I looked up and down the road, then back at her. Not quite a frown, more of a cute puppy dog facial expression.

"I'm really sorry," I said.

She came over next to me and pushed her face against my arm, like she might have hugged her pony. I headed down the road toward the birch grove. It was still early. After I'd stopped the car she looked up at me, in the dash light's glow, her face all red and blotchy, streaks of mascara stained her cheeks. "I won't be long," she said, and opened the door.

After what seemed like a long time she came back. In a calm voice, she said, "Yup."

I waited for more, confused. I didn't have any idea what thing or combination of things I'd said had led to this, only I was sure that 'yup' sounded certain, like she'd decided it was over between us. She turned the rear-view mirror so she could look at it and wiped away the mascara with a tissue she'd taken from her small leather pocketbook. I could see a crescent moon coming up over the birches and rolled down the window a little.

Suddenly she said, "Got my period," and stuffed a wad of tissues into her purse.

"Oh," I said, and wondered if I should offer congratulations or condolences.

"It's nothing you said or did, Sam. Honest."

"I couldn't figure it out."

"I'll be better tomorrow."

"Do you want me to take you home?"

"What time is it?"

"Nine-thirty."

"Hold me for a few minutes."

We sat quietly, the sliver of a moon back-lighting the birches' white bark and the blackness of their limb's silhouettes shivering in a light breeze.

Our second date.

# CHAPTER 8

It wasn't until the middle of the summer, almost three months later, that Delores and I went all the way. It was a very hot summer, in more ways than I could count. On each date Delores and I did something a little different, a little longer, always on her terms; I hated being a chicken, but not as much as I hated the thought of losing her. She was so kind and thoughtful—kind of complicated.

Sometimes we'd go to the hollow, and at others to our place, the birch grove. As the summer days lengthened, more and more parties were at the hollow; before and after them, we spent most of our time near the small brook at the birches.

I still worked three nights and two days during the week at Billy's, and Delores wasn't allowed out past eleven, so on only two week nights, Monday and Tuesday could we see each other.

In June Delores had turned fifteen and we'd gone to a restaurant with her parents, not exactly my idea of a good time; let's say my prospects as a forest ranger weren't up to their standards. After dinner, Delores and I went to the birches and drank champagne. We smoked pot now, too, when I could find it. On that night I thought sure we'd go all the way, and the excitement we caused each other fully dressed caused me to think the real thing must be comparable to heaven, but Delores resisted, and I didn't push her, believing it had to happen some day. We both began to recognize that she was hornier at certain times of the month, and finally, near the end of July, that's when it happened: we made love.

We'd never really talked about protection, and I'd made up my mind I would always wear a rubber—but only after the first time—that first time had to be natural and real. I guess I got that idea from all the flower power talk in the news, and lately a couple girls in town had really joined in. They went out with a different guy every week. I decided that must be free love.

Delores and I did believe we loved each other. Yet some moral, Sunday school lingering, told me it was wrong; she was too young. Maybe I was too young, but I didn't really believe that. Our desires were so adult.

We'd talked about these things since before school let out, slowly insulating ourselves from every other opinion except our own. We believed that we lived for one another—no one else, especially our parents, could understand us. Finally, like a pact between two gamblers, we justified the sex, even though Delores had the last say.

We'd gone to the birch grove, spread out our blanket a few feet from the small brook, now really a trickle at the end of July, and we'd drank some champagne, our favorite drink, and smoked part of a joint left from the night before. Earlier in the month, Delores had bought a couple fancy juice glasses on a shopping trip with her mother, and, like a housekeeper, each night before we left she rinsed them in the brook, put them in a plastic bag and hid them under the edge of a boulder.

Tonight, before the first bottle of champagne was half gone, we were in each other's arms; my hands up under her shirt unhooking her bra before we'd ended the first kiss. Her skin soft and smooth, a thin layer of baby fat all over, made it all seem so forbidden and dangerous.

She said, "Oh, I'm so glad we did it, Sam. Aren't you?"

"Naw. I wished we'd waited."

"Oh, you," she said, and gave me a big lick up the side of my cheek.

"Yuck." I rolled off and we held hands for a long time, staring at the stars, listening to the slow trickles of the brook.

We toasted to love and happiness, then rolled up in the blanket and shared a cigarette.

She hummed the words to Yesterday.

"What time is it?" she asked after a while.

When I stood up to pull on my pants my knees popped, and off the edge of the blanket at the bottom in the moon light I could see where I'd dug up the dirt, at least six inches deep. My socks were black with birch leaf mold. I went over to the car, the dash clock read nine-thirty. I told her, and she asked me to put on some music. In the dark I picked the first tape I touched and turned it on low, a collection of Rolling Stones.

Away from the car I stood beside a tree and gazed at the sky, stars bright off to the west on this half-moon night. So much to try and remember, my first sex now a memory.

Delores called, and I whistled toward the bright stars to let her know, hoping a star would fall and I'd make a wish. A whippoorwill, very close, answered my whistle, and Delores thought it was me. She came over and wrapped her arms around me. A star fell, and I pointed to it, a slight twist in my stomach, as I wished she wouldn't become pregnant.

"We're okay, aren't we, Sam?"

"Yes. For sure."

We walked back and folded the blanket, then I kicked dirt in the holes I'd made. We hugged for a long time, a good piece of silence with each other.

"We took a big step tonight," she said. "We did."

Perhaps a little guilt settled over us then. Drained, tired, a little hung over, this had probably been the biggest event in our lives, except of course for that other when George saved me, or I couldn't have enjoyed this one. Some day I might tell Delores.

"I feel closer to you than ever before," Delores said, and passed me a cigarette.

On the way home, I think we were both wondering if we'd made a mistake, committed a sin. We talked around it.

"Why was it that you decided on tonight?" I asked.

"A few things." She laughed a little. "I've been so horny lately I can't think straight."

"You got that right."

"And you said one night, I've got this body full of all these desires, why waste them. Everybody talks about free love, not that I'd give it to anyone but you, but all the same why not share it with you. Love and sex go together. Right?"

"You're right." We were only a few miles from her house. I didn't think she was talking about love the way our parents would, and I wasn't sure if I knew what love meant.

"Anything else?"

"No." She took the cigarette from my fingers and placed her hand on my leg.

"Maybe one thing. After going as far as we'd gone this summer, I knew I could never wait to have sex until I was married. I mean I'm only fifteen." She laughed. "And still I don't know if it was the right thing to do." She squeezed my leg.

I stopped the car in her driveway and we kissed.

Finally, she said goodnight, and on the way home I remembered that second night with her when my lips had been so sore. I laughed and shifted around on the seat, aches in other places, too, not that I was complaining. Stupidly, laughingly, happily, I stopped at the big rock next to the river, climbed onto it and sang at the top of my lungs, "Strangers in the Night," in my best Dean Martin imitation, one of my mother's favorites. And thought it odd, with all the rock and roll tunes I liked, this song's words stayed with me. "Little did we know."

# CHAPTER 9

Through the month of August, any guilt Delores and I felt didn't interfere, at least not that we told each other, with our desires.

I picked up Delores in the afternoons before I went to work, and we went to the beach where I'd spent so many days with George. Exhausted, we'd nap in each other's arms, and I'd awake to gaze at her soft, tanned face, and sometimes stare across the river at the bleached white cribbing logs, then downstream where George had pulled me out. That darkness lingered, uncontrollable.

I wasn't sure if we were in love, or just fascinated with sex, or maybe infatuated with how we could make each other feel, and we found new, better ways almost every day. To a degree, I certainly had found one perfect fit, physically.

When I saw George the next weekend after that first time Delores and I made love, I think he knew before I told him. He laughed and patted me on the back, as if offering condolences, but he didn't ask a lot of stupid questions. The next night we rode around drinking beers and discussing women in general.

"You gotta watch out, Sam, or you'll be gettin' married instead of headin' for college."

"No way. You won't tell anyone?"

"Hey. Me? Of course everyone will know; no woman can keep a secret. She'll tell her best friend, and she'll tell her best friend."

"Delores does like to talk. Sometimes she flaps her jaws and it reminds me of a flock of geese going over. And she dislikes the whippoorwills almost as much as you."

I didn't mind so much kidding around with George about it. Hell, maybe I was like a woman; I had to tell someone. And it brought us closer than we had been in a long time.

For the next two weeks George had to work overtime on some big phone company project a long ways from home. The next time home he picked me up after work and headed the mustang for the back roads.

It was a dark, overcast night with a full moon occasionally showing through breaks in the clouds. We walked around a field, drinking, passing a joint back and forth. Then we sat in a soft grassy spot, the six pack between us.

"Life sure does get complicated at times," I said.

"I learned my lesson a long time ago," George replied.

I couldn't figure out what he meant, then it came to me. He must be talking about his father running off with that tramp. Staring at George's distinct profile against the moonlit sky, I imagined how hurt he must be, and all these years I'd never recognized it, not all of it.

"You can't change what your father did."

"Don't call him that. He's a cocksucker! That's what he is. Every time I come home and see what a weeny my little brother is; Christ he's still hanging onto Mom's skirts, and he's eleven."

"You'll say I'm wrong, George, but I'll say it anyways." I took a gulp of beer. "Life started to complicate that day you saved me from drowning. Maybe more for both of us than you admit."

"Long before that for me." He took a long toke on the joint, then passed it to me.

We didn't say anything for a few minutes, and I could barely make out his outline, even though he wasn't three feet from me, the moon behind a mass of clouds now.

Then, "You ever think maybe I shouldn't have saved you?"

I heard the bottle top tap lightly against his teeth, then the slow gurgle of beer.

"No, why would you think that?"

"You might some day." He tapped my shoulder. "Remember, Sam, memories can't change the facts."

"What?" I didn't understand at all what he meant.

"I think you wish it had never happened because you owe me," he said. "You think you're alive because of me saving you."

"Maybe that is true. I live with it. What about you?" I swallowed a big gulp of beer. "What about the way you live?"

Then George told me about the long hours on the road by himself. He talked more than I could ever remember him talking before, about what he was doing with his life: driving, working, living in motels, drinking, smoking dope, spending almost every night in a bar.

"I thought you liked it. If you don't, do something else." I reached for another beer.

"I've got to make a living, and that car won't pay for itself. I gotta eat, too. You'll know some day."

"I will." I thought of all the fun I had with Delores, and that I liked work, and playing soccer, and college ahead.

We talked slowly about these things for a while, almost as if discussing other peoples' problems. As I listened, I tried to make the connection between what his father had done to him and how it affected him now, and the worst of it was that he was afraid to make a commitment because of the possible results: marriage, children, running away, and then the pain and anger and sadness. And in a very strange sort of way I think he thought he'd been forced into a commitment to me because he saved my life. When I'd always seen it the other way around.

The problem was I didn't know how to tell him how much what had happened that day hurt me, too, because I so much wanted things to go on without that day ever happening. George was right about that.

A little later George said, "I like to remember those summers, too, Sam."

Something in the way he said it reminded me of how I'd felt struggling in the water that day, and I was still certain that if alone, I would have died. I wished I could think of a way to help him and kicked myself for not knowing he was unhappy before now. By then we'd finished the six-pack. George stood up and led the way back to the car, and no matter how hard I thought I couldn't come up with a way to make him happy. Like he said, memories don't change facts.

On the way back to town I remembered something from last fall's English class, a small miracle in itself. I told George about Thoreau, and asked him if he'd ever heard the statement, "Simplify. Simplify. Simplify."

George smirked and said he wished it could be that easy, stopped at a Y in the road, shifted to first and gave that car all it had through every gear. The force pushed my body against the seat, and once he'd hit fourth gear, George let up on the gas, and in the glow of the dash lights he smiled. "I may have an idea."

"What's that?"

"You wouldn't like it." George pushed the gas pedal to the floor, the four-barrel carburetor pulled in air and gas with a vacuum sucking sound, and before you could take a breath we were doing a hundred, and then I knew, and it took my breath even further away.

"Hold it!"

George hit the brakes like a deer had crossed in front of us. "What?" he yelled, and we sat, the motor idling a low rumble. I turned in the bucket seat. "Are you thinking about joining the army? Tell me no."

"Why not? How'd you guess?"

"What an asshole thing to do."

"No. It's an alternative." He shifted into first, and drove ahead slowly, shifting at low speeds.

I couldn't believe it, then it made sense that he'd talked so much out in the field. I shook my head. I said, "It isn't an alternative. Being a logger, electrician, Christ sell the car and go to college, there are any number of other possibilities." I decided to see if Dad would take George on as a helper.

"Maybe." And that's all George said for the rest of the way back to town, and as I kept listing possibilities he shook his head to each one and fought the wheel through curves at almost a hundred.

He pulled up beside my car at the gas station and I was exhausted. "It's surprising you and Delores have time for making love, if she talks like you say." He smoothed his mustache, then pushed my shoulder.

"Go to hell, George. You're jealous." I opened the door and he laughed.

"Maybe you're right, Sam." I looked back over my shoulder, as he said, more to himself than me, "Maybe I am."

# CHAPTER 10

The next morning, I got up earlier than usual and had coffee on the porch with my father. It was hot and humid.

"Have much work ahead?" I asked him.

"Enough." He rattled the Sunday paper. "Why?" He stared over the top edge of the paper, and that scar over his left eye he'd received in the Battle of the Bulge stood out, almost framed above the paper's edge.

"I think George might want a job."

"Lose his?"

"No."

"I couldn't guarantee him work all winter. It's too tough to predict, especially with the way this war is going. One day they say it might be over, and the next not."

"It's just an idea." Until George decided one way or another, I didn't want to tell Dad about his going in the army. "George hates all the traveling and living in motels," I said.

"Well, I sure can't pay him as much as he's making now. Tell him to come see me. I always liked George. Too bad he never had a father."

"Thanks, Dad."

The phone rang. Mom answered it and called me. It was Delores. "Hi," she said. "What cha' doin'?"

"Talking to Dad. How was your company?"

"Boring." She paused. "How about a picnic this afternoon?"

"Okay. It's so hot let's go to the river. I'll pick you up at one."

"I'll be ready."

I was, and knew she would be. "'Good, good, good vibrations,'" I whistled on my way out to the car.

"Where you going?" Mom asked.

"To see George, then on a picnic with Delores."

"Don't you ever stay home?" She stood on the front steps, in shorts and one of Dad's old tank top t-shirts.

"Naw. This place is too classy for me."

She glanced down at her clothes and tried to hide a smile. "You behave. I'm not so sure all this time with Delores is a good thing."

I stood behind the open door of the Corvair. "It's fine, Mom. Honest."

George's car wasn't at his Mom's apartment, so I drove around behind the bar and there was his Mustang. He was inside drinking coffee.

"What time you going back today?" I asked, trying to take in the place. People under eighteen weren't usually allowed inside, but it didn't make much difference on a Sunday morning before noon when they started serving booze.

"Around two. Long drive. Eight hours." He didn't look at me, like he was upset about talking so much the night before.

"I talked to Dad just now about you working for him."

"It won't work. I told you last time."

"You could get a cheaper car."

"No." He swallowed coffee, then leaned across the table. "I'm seeing a recruiter this week. Most everybody thinks this war is almost over. After my hitch, I'll go to college just like you plan to. Hell, maybe we'll get a place together. Forest ranger-ing sounds pretty good." He half-assed saluted me.

"No!" The thought of him in those pictures of death on television almost blinded me with anger. "You'll never come back!"

Calmly he sat back in his chair and said, "Don't you worry about me, Sam. Look at all the guys in town that have gone, come back, are having fun going to college. Only one didn't come back." Even though he tried to hide it, I could see that bothered him.

"You are really serious, aren't you?" I wanted to jump up and run away, and the anxiety started.

"If you're sitting where I am, it's the intelligent thing to do. Christ, Sam, listen to the news. By the time they sign me up and get me trained it will probably all be over."

"Probably isn't a sure thing." Visions of mortars and gooks with machine guns, helicopters, and blood all over seemed to explode in front of my eyes, all obscuring George's face not three feet away.

"I don't think so. Now is the time." He went to the bar for another cup and brought one back for me. Only three other people were in the place, way down at the other end of the room.

I sipped the coffee. "Wow," I said. "What's in it?"

"Irish whiskey."

"Shit." I sipped more. It tasted terrible.

"Have you been thinking about this for a long time?"

"Couple of months," he said. He stood up, walked to the pool table for a stick and rubbed its tip with blue chalk.

"Have you told your mother?" I tipped my chair back on two legs.

"She understands."

"C'mon, you're the head of the family."

"She understands, Sam. Don't push it." He brought the cue and chalk over and sat down.

"All right. All right," I said.

I could see that I didn't have any say over his decision, and that hurt, but then I reminded myself that it had always been this way.

"You know what I think," I said.

George smiled. "I knew you would tell me just what you thought long before I mentioned it last night."

So he was trying to lead me into it.

"Up yours, George." I raised my cup and took a gulp of the whiskey laced coffee.

He laughed.

"You worry more than an old hen."

"Take some time to think about it. I see people die every night on the tube."

"I have thought about it." He held up his hands, then pointed the cue stick at my heart. "You worry about getting into college instead of married. That's plenty to keep you busy without worrying about me."

"I guess. Never did get anywhere trying to argue with a stone."

"It's almost noon, you'd better go before they kick you out. See you next weekend."

I stood at the door for a second, raised my hand in a salute, and thought, then saw him coming home in a bodybag and my guts went to mush, for a second, then tightened into a mass of twisted steel rods.

I drove around town, then on the back roads until it was time to pick up Delores. I did my best thinking on my rock by the river or driving.

Everything was on the verge of dying, the leaves on the trees above dusty and brown at the edges from the dry summer, and the grass in the fields seemed more brown than usual. I wanted to cry because I had no say in George's decision. We were almost on opposite sides. Earlier in the spring at Kent state, four students had been gunned down by the National Guard. Even though I'd never protested, I certainly wasn't in favor of all those soldiers dying every day. I didn't know what I wanted to do; I did wish that war would stay out of my life.

I stopped the car on a one-lane bridge over a small stream and listened to the smooth gurgles as it passed over the round stones. Delores and me, we had a good time, but I had to admit that maybe some of the infatuation, if that's what it was, had worn off in the last three months, and lately after sex we didn't talk much, just rested, smoked cigarettes, and drank. We'll talk about that today, I decided. Maybe we'd reached some sort of dead end, and had to grow more, talk about more serious things. She sure liked to talk.

"George. George." I whispered his name. Carrying a rifle in the jungle. Too hard to imagine. He hadn't grown much since he was a freshman in high school, maybe five-ten, though he'd filled out some. It sounded stupid, but I kept thinking college loans were cheaper than life. Deeper down, I faced it: if George signed up so should I. That's why my guts had turned to mush back at the bar when I thought of him in a bodybag. I should go and stay with him. The thought scared the hell out of me, and the cowardly part of me relaxed because I wouldn't turn eighteen until the spring of next year, 1971. Then guilt settled down and in like an anvil weight. If he went and I didn't, and something happened to him I might have prevented, then I'd lost my chance to pay him back the life I owed him. And it would also be a loss of the chance to be close again like those summers down by the river. That suddenly seemed so impossibly distant.

After telling George last night to simplify, all I could do was complicate. I stared over the edge of the bridge down into the brook and three words tumbled over themselves: Love, Death, Fear, until they all seemed to mean the same thing, like the words of a song that will not leave you alone. The one repeating word: Fear.

Delores was happy and bubbly as she slammed the car door, scooted over as close to me as she could and gave me a kiss.

"Hi ya," she said. "Nice day, huh."

I turned around to back out of the driveway.

"Brought turkey sandwiches, chips, pickles, the works," she said.

"That's good."

"What have you been drinking, Sam?"

I couldn't think what she meant, then remembered.

"Irish whiskey."

"So early?"

"In coffee. I stopped by the Bistro to talk to George. He put whiskey in the coffee."

"Oh. How's George?"

"All right." I turned down the road that led to the birch grove.

"What's wrong?"

I thought she meant why weren't we going to the river behind my parents' house, then knew she realized something wasn't right.

"George is thinking of enlisting."

"Is he nuts?"

I glanced at her, her eyes wide, the whites so big with surprise.

"That doesn't make much sense, does it?" she said.

"No. I wouldn't say so." I parked in the usual spot near the brook, and when I'd turned the car off, it was totally silent except for the ticking of the motor.

We got out, and I stood next to Delores, staring down at the small trough of the brook's path.

"What happened, Sam? The bottles of wine we left the other day are out of the water."

All that was left was a small, almost motionless pool. Delores placed the bottles in this water and it barely covered the labels. Then I thought maybe beavers were working upstream. I told Delores, and she looked sad, like someone had taken away her favorite toy. I almost wanted to take her back home and spend the day by myself, maybe hike up the brook to see if there were any beavers.

Delores spread out our blanket, and I sat next to her. "School starts soon," she said, and flicked the insides of her fingernails against each other. Then out of the blue talked about that pony. And I understood its death still bothered her after a few years. She seemed different, more complex. After all, death to a young child is a serious thing. We stayed quiet for a few minutes.

"Worried about George?" she asked.

"He saved my life once."

"He did? How?"

"From drowning." I reached for her hand. "I know he'll be killed if he goes over there," I said, then wished I could take it back.

"Did you try and convince him not to go?"

"Of course. Do you think I told him it was a good idea? Jesus." I rolled away and stared at the pool of water. "I'm sorry, Delores. I never told anyone. George made me promise the day it happened. He didn't want people to think I owed him."

I rolled onto my back and Delores hugged me, and for the first time ever I didn't feel a thing. My mind, even my body seemed far away like an echo caught between two distant valleys.

Then I rolled over on my belly and for a long time rested my head on my forearms and Delores rubbed my back.

I wanted to change things I could not. Control. I wanted to control what and why people did things in order to create safety in my own life. For the first time I realized the impossibility of that. Did that mean I had grown up? What about the other stuff? My stomach answered with a twisting motion against the soft pad of birch leaves, and it seemed I couldn't breathe normally.

Delores rested her head on my back, and locks of her brown silky hair tickled the skin high up on my arm. I thought of all the times when I was young that I'd sat down with Mom and told her some bad thing I'd done, like going farther up the road than allowed on my bicycle or saying a bad word. She'd always listened, said not to do it again, and told me how glad she was I came and told her. The situation with Delores was beyond telling.

I slid toward the brook until I could reach one of the wine bottles, opened it and chugged till I couldn't hold any more, then I looked at her and said, "Thirsty." I handed her the bottle, and as she tipped it up, I stared at the tiny cupid's bow of her upper lip as it stretched around the bottle mouth, then down at the rest of her.

"You're all upset, Sam. Please talk to me." She gripped my right hand in both of hers.

"Nothing's right," I said. "You always hear that these years in high school are the best."

"Did I do something wrong?"

I smiled at her, squeezed both her hands in mine. "Maybe born two years too late."

"You wish we'd never made love."

"No, I wish there wasn't a war for George to go to." And Delores almost shouted that I had to promise not to go.

She said, "Sometimes I think we should have waited. Other girls I've talked to say they feel the same way."

"Really? What do they say?"

She pulled her hands from mine. "I don't know. I guess part of it is the idea that something that feels so good can't be right, and of course what parents say is always hanging over you."

I reached for the other bottle, and she took it from me before I could drink, then she said, "Some of the girls talk about free love and say we've been held down by our parents for too long. You know, because of religion and what their parents told them." She handed me the bottle and the label slid off, the side of the bottle sticky with glue where I gripped it. "I never thought guys felt any guilt about it. Do guys talk about it?"

"Not to admit guilt, that's for sure." I swallowed a big gulp, then lit a cigarette, suddenly sad the brook had almost dried up, wanting to go upstream and investigate, feeling obligated to stay here.

"I can't help but want you, Delores."

She smiled, and we laughed a little.

She said, "We are both scared I'll get pregnant. That has a lot to do with how you feel."

"What would happen?"

She whispered, "I'd get rid of it. We just have to be careful. We always are."

"Yes. That's true." I pulled her to me and held her close, feeling so responsible for what we both did. I finished the bottle of wine, then found another one, half full, under the seat of the car, our favorite, Strawberry Hill. Piss warm.

I stared up the brook and wished I could damn up all this guilt and forget it existed. Then I looked over at Delores and wanted to make love to her, be so close that she might keep me there forever, unremovable.

I tipped the bottle up and remembered, even thought I could smell that nasty old dandelion wine, and that caused me to think of George, and riding bicycles, and swimming, and that rock fight we'd had the day I chipped his tooth, and from that to small deadly pieces of lead flying all around him. It all led up to an uncontrollable crazy grip I could not control.

# CHAPTER 11

I worked from noon till five the next day, Saturday, and washed the windows sparkling clean. Between that and pumping gas, I was busy all day. Delores called in the middle of the afternoon, and she was excited about the last party before school began. Over the summer, she'd made up a lot of stories about the movies we supposedly went to at least twice a week. She even bought movie magazines to substantiate the lies and left them in the car.

I picked her up at eight, and by nine the party was definitely the biggest of the summer. A two-kegger. George didn't arrive until after nine, and I walked over to his car before he got out.

"Where the hell you been? You're missin' a great party."

He slapped the steering wheel. "Arguing. For Christ's sake. Arguing with my mother."

"What about?" As if I didn't know.

George said, mimicking a whine, "She doesn't want her oldest son, her big hope, going off getting killed, especially in something she doesn't consider a good cause."

"You didn't tell her before?"

"Get off my case, Sam." He opened the car door. "I told her the same things I told you, and today I told her I was going. She'll get over it." He kicked the ground, spit, then wiped spittle from his mustache, and I handed him my cup of beer. "You need it." He chugged it.

Two stereos blared in the hollow, echoes garbling all the instruments and voices. One played The Stones, and the other The Moody Blues.

"You've never seen anyone so mad, Sam. Steamin'. She just couldn't believe I'd sign up without talking to her." He slammed the car door so hard the glass rattled. "I'm twenty for Christ's sake."

"Can't change it. You know I wish you could."

"Not now." He walked over to the keg and filled his cup, and by the time I'd filled a new one for me, he'd wandered off; then I saw him talking to one of the Viet Nam vets, Leo.

Delores was standing by the Corvair talking about school with a couple of other girls, Emily and Denise. I reached into the car and took a cigarette from the pack on the dash. They all looked so young, their bodies so newly developed, almost as if it had happened in a few days. I took a deep drag on the cigarette and knew I'd regret it during wind sprints on Monday.

Bill, whose brother had been killed in Viet Nam, was drunker than hell by ten o'clock. I tried to have a conversation with him, ask him how he felt about graduation. He slurred his words all together and leaned against me, then rolled off my shoulder and almost fell down.

"Whoa there, Bill. The night's early."

"Fuck it. Fuck it!" He pointed at me with the top of his cup. "I can't wait to get out of this town. You wait. You'll see some day." He wandered off in the direction of the keg.

I didn't know what he meant and figured he didn't either. Delores yelled my name and waved her empty beer cup in the air. She was soaking the stuff up pretty good, too. What the hell. Summer's over. I handed her the beer and she gave me a big wet kiss, and her two friends walked off.

"You okay, sweetheart?" Delores asked.

"Sure."

"Oh, you," she said. "You don't understand anything." She walked off into the woods.

"Where you headed?"

She waved a wad of toilet paper in the air.

Now what. Everybody is either drunk or pissed off. One hell of a party. I chugged my beer and went for another, then followed the smell of pot over to where Leo and George stood. The joint eventually came to me, and I took in as much as I could hold, listening to their conversation about the cheap and powerful drugs in Nam. Then Leo told George he wouldn't believe the whores either. George listened close, and I passed the joint to Bob, who'd just come up. He played forward on the soccer team and was another one of the guys with long hair coach wanted off the team. He held the small joint in his outstretched hand, "Here's to ya coach," he said, and laughed.

Just as the joint reached me again, this time on a roach clip, a girl screamed, and we all turned toward the fire. Bill had either fallen or jumped into the fire, and as I watched he rolled over twice and flapped his right arm against the ground like a wounded partridge. A girl leaned down and threw a beer on his arm and shoulder, then he lay still. Everyone crowded around, nothing but the two stereos loud in the night.

Then Bill stood up. "Don't worry. Don't worry." He took a beer out of the nearest person's hand and chugged it, foam sliding down his chin.

"See. All better."

Everyone stared at him. Leo, the Nam Vet led Bill to the fire and looked at the burns. "He'll be all right," he said after a minute. The party went on.

Delores came over and put her arms around me. "Howdy," I said.

"Some party," she said.

I looked down at her face, and in the fire light the whites of her eyes reminded me of the inside of a freshly cracked egg shell. "Want to take a walk?" I asked.

"Sure," she said. "Meet you at the car in a minute. I'll get a couple extra beers."

Only one tape player was on now, playing Led Zeppelin.

I leaned against the car.

When Delores came up she said, "Sorry I was bitchy before. You know."

"Oh. Okay."

As I reached for my cigarettes another car drove in and parked not far from us. It was Lois. She'd come alone, and when she walked by toward the fire she smiled and said, "Hello."

"She looks different," Delores said.

"What do you mean?"

"Jesus, Sam. Did she ever dress like a hippie before?"

"No. I guess not." Then talking before thinking, "She was in Cape Cod all summer."

"How do you know?"

"She stopped for gas the other day."

"That better be all she stopped for."

"Oh, c'mon." I grabbed our blanket from the back seat.

"Let's walk," I said. "I hope Bill is okay."

"He's not quite right, is he?" she asked.

"Would you be if your brother was killed in the war?"

"You think George will die, don't you?"

"I don't know, Delores." I stopped and took a big gulp of beer. We were on the edge of the woods.

Delores walked several steps forward, then turned to face me. "I hate to tell you this, Sam." She kicked at a tuft of grass. "I'm two weeks late."

"No way. You've been acting like you had it, or at least were getting it.

"I didn't want you to know, so I acted like I did, and now I've told you. Oh, how I've prayed."

"Have you ever been this late before?" She shook her head.

"Damn." I stepped toward her and hugged her tight. Options ticked in my head like the receipt tape at work: marriage, abortion, running away. I wanted to cry myself, for the wrong reasons: self-pitying ones. The future disintegrating.

"It's horrible, Sam. My parents will die," she said, moving her face far enough from me so she could talk. "We're good Catholics."

I touched her under the chin and she stared up at me, the look on her face exactly like that of a little girl in trouble.

"Whatever happens, Delores, we'll go through it together."

We walked a little farther, the music's echoes distorted and soft. The bass guitar sounded like war drums. Three great months that end with this, I thought.

"Sam, tell me what we'll do."

"Okay. Listen." I placed a hand on each of her shoulders. "We wait one more week and hope you get it. If not, I'll go to my family doctor and ask if he can do a test and find out for sure, and not have to tell anyone else the results. When we know if it's for sure we'll decide what to do. Okay? Sound okay to you?"

She nodded, black mascara streaks under her eyes making her look like a raccoon.

"I feel so bad. It's all my fault."

"It isn't. It isn't. You know that." She picked up our beers from beside the path, and after she handed me mine, touched her cup against it and said, "Our love." And we drank. I wasn't sure to what. Our love child, I thought, and wanted to cry when I saw us married and living in town, me working for my father, college a distant wish.

We sat on a fallen log. No music came from the hollow for several minutes, as if the party had ended, but through the dense leaves and cedar branches we could hear muffled shouts and laughter, then a song we knew—from then on it would be ours. McCartney crooned the words to "Yesterday." The words echoed out to us so clear, and the music a half step behind. We cried, and at times our sobs and indrawn breaths matched as we held onto each other and rocked back and forth on that fallen log.

When the song ended I said, "We could be wrong."

"Maybe. I don't think so. Women know."

"You really think you are?"

"Yes. But, oh, no. I might be wrong. I want to be wrong. Sam, my father will go out of his mind."

"Marriage is an option."

Her eyes opened wider and wider as it sunk in. She'd obviously placed abortion as the only possibility.

"Do you know what that means? I'd have to quit school. Before I even start my sophomore year. Could I go back afterwards? Everyone would know." She waved her arms. "We can't do this to ourselves."

"All I said was that it's an option." I tried to figure out when it might have happened. I was always so careful, but nothing was a sure thing.

"C'mon." Delores gripped my hand. "We'll get through this together." We started toward the fire, her lower lip clenched tight between her teeth again, and I couldn't help it, I wanted to run away, and wished I'd never talked to her that day in the library. It wasn't worth it. That wasn't true.

The song ended, the last line, "I believe in yesterday," and the anxiety attacked me with a vengeance.

# CHAPTER 12

The first days of school and soccer practices were almost torture after a long summer of drinking and smoking cigarettes and pot. Delores was miserable, and her parents still stuck to their rule of her staying home on week nights. Worry. Worry. Worry.

Most nights on the way home, I stopped by the river and sat on top of my rock. The river changed from day to day. Now, in early fall, yellow leaves, twigs, and pollen floated on the surface. The high-water marks of spring on the far bank were two, maybe three feet below its level now. What is and is not normal? For the first time since years ago in Sunday school I seriously, very seriously, said a prayer to God, then stared at the bottom where tiny bits of green clung to the rocks; current tugged them straight out. I reached my hand into the cool water and slapped some against my face, then walked across the road and drove home, trying to act normal so Mom and Dad wouldn't know a thing was wrong.

After supper, I called Delores.

"How was soccer practice?" she asked.

"Lousy. I can't concentrate."

"Wait. I'll go in the other room."

I could hear the television as she passed from the living room to her parents' bedroom—the only place no one could hear what she said. "Still nothing, Sam. I'm so scared."

"So am I. I want to tell you something. It's my fault," I said.

"No. Don't say that. We're in this together."

"I wish Monday would come," Delores said. Then, "I gotta' go. Dad's waiting for a call. I love you."

"Me too," I said, and hung up the phone, thinking if I could get out of this, I'd never have anything to do with girls again. No pleasure was worth this mess. Then a pain in my gut almost doubled me over. Too much, the words repeated themselves like a flashing tilt sign on a pinball machine. I heard one of my parents coming and placed my hand on the receiver like I'd just hung up. Mom.

"How's Delores?" she asked.

"Fine."

"We haven't seen her in a while. Why don't you ask her to dinner this weekend?"

"I'll see."

Mom placed a hand on my shoulder. "She's a very young girl, Sam, and you'll be gone after this year. I remember how impressionable I was at her age."

"Okay, Mom."

I watched the end of the news with Dad, and during a commercial he asked when the first soccer game was. I didn't even know.

"Sixty-two dead," Walter Cronkite said, almost as if a number like that was expected. By Christmas, George could be included in that daily number. I wanted to ask Dad about his war, but figured that, as in the past, he'd avoid the questions. Mom had said Dad had some rough times in France, and he'd tell me about it when he thought appropriate. Could he still think I was too young?

Well, I had to tell them sometime. "George enlisted."

Dad leaned forward in his chair. Mom came in from the kitchen. "Did you say he enlisted? What does his mother think?" Mom asked.

"She's not happy," I said. Then I remembered I still hadn't told Delores.

Walter Cronkite said, "And that's the way it is," and then the screen went to white fuzz. Mom leaned against the doorway into the kitchen, Dad still sat forward in his chair, and I sat, my hands folded in front of me, all of us arranged like some sort of middle-American still life. I imagined a title: War Death Love. Dad for war, me for death, and Mom for love. A commercial came on, loud, and I stood up and moved past Mom, a daze surrounding me like cobwebs had the last time I'd been down to the tree house. Outside, in the dim evening light, I really did wish my life would end, had ended that day so long ago as I flopped and rolled underneath summer warm water against the smooth round river rocks.

The next afternoon Delores led me by the arm to her locker. She said, and pointed, "You know that girl over there?" It was a seventh or eighth grader I knew by sight only.

"Not really," I said.

"She had an abortion last spring, Sam. She's thirteen now."

"Like I said last night. Must happen more than we think."

"And I know a junior and another girl in my class that have had them."

"How did you find all this out?"

She stared at me for a second like I was dumb. "I asked around. We'll never keep it quiet." She leaned against her locker, kind of all sunk in. Then, "Walk me to class. It may sound awful, but now I don't feel so alone." She stopped in front of her classroom. "Call me tonight."

"I have to work right after practice. You call me."

"Seven?"

"Right." I headed for my last class of the day, history, glad something had happened to make her feel better, and me, too. It should be easy to find out where to go for an abortion, and her or my parents would never have to know. How much would it cost?

At work, Billy asked me about Steve, the guy that worked Sundays.

"What's up, Billy?"

He turned away and peered under the hood of an old Chevy. "Till was short Monday. Second time it happened."

"Not good," I said.

"You're damn right it's not good!"

Billy's temper was known all over town, he was either a pussy cat, or a real sonofabitch if you crossed him. "I'm going to check on the bathrooms," I said.

He grunted.

The bathrooms were clean, but I went back for the mop just to have something to do.

When Billy fired somebody, they were branded; no one questioned whether he'd made a mistake. It was always the employee's fault. I remembered a long time ago when I'd first started filling the soda machine. I was thirteen and a guy, either drunk or on drugs, had come into the station and used the phone. He started cursing and yelling at someone on the other end, and Billy came over, took the phone away from him, slammed it down and told him to get out. Well, the guy left but stood on the sidewalk, said Billy couldn't stop him from standing on public property. Billy nailed him with a left hook that would have stopped a train. The guy fell backwards into the dirt next to the sidewalk, and Billy went inside and back to work. A little while later, the guy got up and left.

I thought, "What would Billy say if he knew I got a fifteen-year-old girl pregnant?"

Billy finished work on the Chevy, cleaned up and got ready to leave. "See you, Sam," he said. "You're a good worker. Don't ever let me down."

"No, Billy, I won't."

# CHAPTER 13

"You sick or something?" the coach asked me at practice the next day. "You can't move any faster? First game is next week, Sam. C'mon. We need you at center halfback this year."

"I'm ready coach. We'll kill 'em."

"Atta boy." He opened another pack of the pink Canada Mints he was always chewing, sometimes spitting them out when he yelled.

I ran off down the field. "Yes siree," I thought. This should be my star year in soccer, and basketball, too. It all depended on one little test.

The coach blew his whistle and we lined up for wind sprints, and by the time they were over I was drunk again, or something close.

I called Delores after supper and her father answered the phone. He said she'd gone to a friend's to study, then asked how the soccer team looked.

"Fine," I said. "We'll do all right."

"Good to hear. See you later, and you keep takin' good care of my girl."

"Oh, I will. Bye."

I sat in the hall and stared at the phone, thinking of how long it had taken Delores' father and me to like each other. That might soon be over. It must be hard for fathers, especially with a good-looking girl like Delores. They knew what guys thought about.

I figured I was close enough to eighteen, so I took a beer out of the refrigerator and went in the living room to watch the news. At the commercial Dad looked over and saw what I was drinking.

"You eighteen?"

"C'mon, Dad. Next week."

"Don't give me that, and what about soccer?"

Mom chimed in, "You've been out awfully late. You shouldn't be out so late with such a young girl."

"She has to be home at midnight weekends and can't even go out week nights. What the hell is going on with you guys?"

"Don't talk back," Dad said. He slapped his magazine against the chair arm.

"Jesus, I'll be in college next year. Who will watchdog me then?"

"You're still here," Dad said. "I think you need a little more self-discipline. I stuck my head in the Corvair the other day and it smelled like a brewery. Too much of anything is not good."

The evening news started, and Cronkite said only twenty-four dead today, the peace talks stalled again.

The phone rang. Delores calling from Emily's.

"You told Emily."

"Can you pick me up here?" she stuttered.

"I guess so, if my parents are finished bitching. What's going on?"

"Just come get me. It's seven and I told Mom I'd be home by nine."

I stood in the doorway. "Delores needs a ride home from Emily's house. I won't be long."

Dad waved his magazine, and I expected Mom to say I should be nice to her, but nothing. They had been hard to figure out, or maybe they sensed what was going on somehow.

The small stream beside where we made love had more water in it, and brightly colored leaves, too. I was glad because I wanted things to stay the same. While I spread out the blanket Delores took another one from the trunk.

She pulled the blanket up over us and hugged me tight, and the solution, the only fair and just one came to me. I'll marry her if she's pregnant; we'll just make the best of it. Even if I'm not sure I love her.

I stared up at the stars and decided working with Dad would be difficult, but probably not too bad if I followed his orders. It all seemed so noble, but I kept it to myself. Selfishly, I wanted to hold on to my good intentions, enjoy my resolve to do the right thing. Yet, deep down I wanted to reserve the right to change my mind.

I dropped Delores off a block from her house at five to nine. Before she kissed me goodnight she said, "I don't think I am, Sam. Maybe something else is wrong."

"Good. If you are, will you marry me?"

She stared and stared at me, then said, "Thank you. Let's wait and see."

Mom and Dad seemed pleased when I walked in the door ten minutes later. I wanted to tell them everything. I'd just asked a fifteen-year-old to marry me.

An hour later I got out of bed, dressed, rolled the Corvair down the hill, tires whispering on the pavement.

I parked down the street from Bistro and listened to the muffled noise from inside. Next week at this time I'd already have been eighteen for a day, and know whether I'd be a father, and two days from then might be the last time I'd ever see George. In a way, spread out evenly like that, it was a terribly organized spider web, and I was the fly, still alive, waiting for the spider's sting. Anxiety city.

I heard George's laugh, even above the loud juke box playing a Dolly Parton ballad. Maybe one-night stands were the best way. I thought, The Dolly way. What in hell is George doing home on Wednesday?

I walked across the parking lot to the bar, and opened the door, put my head inside and yelled, "George!"

He came to the door.

"Why are you home? Can I talk to you for a minute?" Not sure I could or should share my problem.

"Sure." He came outside, and we walked toward the gas station.

"Next week this time I'll be buyin' drinks for you. No more work, ol' buddy."

"You didn't tell me."

"Sam, I just came home tonight. No sense in wasting my vacation days. Yah Hoo!"

I decided. If he'd be home all week I couldn't keep it to myself. "Listen," I said. "I got a problem. Big."

We'd gone around the corner and it was quieter; my voice sounded too loud. Did I really want to bother him; he had his own life to think about.

"Give it up," he said, and I half think he was expecting another lecture about the war.

"Delores might be pregnant. I'll know on Tuesday or Wednesday."

"Oh, boy." He took several steps up the street, then came back, said, "Let me think," then walked away again. "In a way you are a lucky sonofabitch. You know that?"

"Why? I haven't been feeling lucky."

"If you were eighteen and her parents decided to press it, your ass would be in jail, that is unless you could blame it on someone else?" He raised his eyebrows.

"Not hardly."

"How many people know?"

"Not many."

"Any more than you two and it may as well be in the newspaper." Then I remembered the people Delores had talked to about abortions, and figured he was right.

"Jesus, I hope she isn't. Wait here. I'll be right back."

"What?" He'd already disappeared around the corner. I lit a cigarette, careful to hide it in case someone went by that might squeal. Then I thought of the shape I'd be in for the game on Tuesday. Our first home game in my senior year and look at the mess I'd created.

George came back. "Follow me," he said.

"What? I don't need any more mysteries."

"C'mon." He walked across the street past the gas station and into the vacant lot.

"We can talk here," he said. "I went for this." He took a pint of Four Roses whiskey from his hip pocket, then we sat down on a flat rock that had sheared off the low cliff behind us.

George took a big drink, then passed it to me. "So, let's see. Let's really see. You're the one that always wants to talk. Let me try this time."

I thought he was wound up about something else. Probably the army and war. He watched me drink, then take a big lung full of smoke.

"Now you have two things to worry about. You think I might get killed in a war, and your girlfriend might be preggo."

"That's it," I said. I took another swallow, the whiskey hot in my belly, my key to understanding, or not. "That sure is it."

"Tell me this. Can you do a damn thing about either of them except deal with the consequences if the worst happens? I know you always see the worst happening. Hand over the whiskey."

"Delores and I could run away, you could decide to head for Canada."

"I wish you could hear yourself. Today on the way home I realized that if I do get killed you might end up like Bill when he lost his brother. You and I are like brothers."

"I know." I couldn't believe how nice it was to hear him say that, and warmth without whiskey spread out.

"Well, after next week, if they don't give me a leave before heading over, we may not see each other for a long time."

All that I'd been trying to balance seemed to fall apart, and I rested my forearms on my knees and my head on them. I thought of how George and I had drifted apart when he first moved away, and for quite a few years we weren't like brothers. Now he said we were, but he was going away in a week, and then what?

"Are you losing it?" he said. "Maybe this is more than you can take. It's not wrong to admit that."

"C'mon. I'll know about Delores next week, and we'll decide then."

"I'll be here."

"You always are when I'm in the biggest trouble."

"Tell me. What's the plan if she's pregnant?"

"You don't want to know. You'll disagree as much as I disagree with you enlisting." I took a drink, swallowed and tipped the bottle neck away to say, "Marriage," then drank again.

"No." He stood up, took the bottle out of my hand and the top rapped against my teeth, and a second later I spit out a sliver of glass. George slapped the half empty bottle against his thigh. "No way. And you said I was ruining my life."

"Did you listen to me? And be careful, you knocked a piece of glass off the bottle top."

"Fuck it." He swallowed the remaining three or four shots then heaved the bottle at the face of the cliff.

"It's what Delores wants, too," I lied.

"She's fifteen. I can't believe you'd think of marrying her when it's so easy to get an abortion." He walked up and down in the dead grass in front of me, stirring up the smell of fall.

We went all through it. What I'd do for a living, where we'd go, how she'd finish school. At one point he said, "People in our parents' time had to do what you're talking about. It's almost unheard of now."

"I can't see making her have an abortion if she doesn't want one. She's scared to death of the knife."

"Talk reason to her. Tell her plain that your lives will be shitty. She'll have to drop out of school and stay home. Christ, you've got to graduate." George stomped his foot on the ground. "You got her to have sex, and that took a while, use your line of bullshit on her now."

"It won't work. We both decided when to have sex, her mostly. I'm telling you she's in love and to her everything will be okay by that fact alone."

"Tell her she can't know what love is at that age."

"Now, you be realistic," I said, and wished we had something more to drink.

"I gotta think," he said. "And you been tellin' me I'm fucking up my life."

"I think you are. I didn't decide to get Delores pregnant. You did decide to sign that paper."

"You didn't have to have sex with her."

"Like you wouldn't have."

"All right. All right. It's over and done, and you don't even know that she is."

"True."

George stopped pacing and stood in front of me. He said to me, just like an older brother, I thought, "You go home and get some sleep. Can we get together tomorrow?"

"Yeah. I don't have to work. Bob is paying back some time he owes me, and Delores has to do something with her mother."

I stood and almost fell down.

"Whoa, there. Guess I'll drive you home."

"No. My legs went to sleep. Feet feel like they're froze." Even though I was drunk, I'd been fine till I stood.

We walked across the street. In front of the bar, George said, "I'll call you in the morning."

"Thanks." I couldn't form any of my thoughts into words.

He walked toward the smoke-filled loud bar, and I glanced at him as he stepped inside. A girl hugged him, and she waved at me over his shoulder: Lois. Then she whispered something in George's ear, as the door closed.

# CHAPTER 14

After I left George, I stopped on the straight stretch by the river. I was very drunk. On my rock beside the river, I sat and wondered at weird things, like how clean my eyes felt, how numb my fingers, and how blank most of my brain. I tried to remember all George and I had talked about, and wished we'd talked about drowning. I stared into the black current, illuminated here and there by a star's reflection. The sky was mostly cloudy, a few bright stars in black patches of sky. I got sick into the river and everything seemed to hurt, except my head, and even though I wanted to curse the booze and the sickness, I welcomed the relief they brought.

I staggered across the road, drove home, and passed out on my bed.

"Sam, get up. Billy is on the phone."

"What?"

"Billy is on the phone."

I walked through the living room, the kitchen, and picked up the phone. "Hello."

"Sam. Bob called in sick. Can you help me out?"

"Sure. Give me half an hour, okay?"

"You got it. Thanks."

Mom stood in the door way. "You slept in your clothes," she said. "It's after eleven."

"I gotta take a shower."

"You're drinking too much. Is something wrong?"

"No, Mom. Just havin' fun. Maybe it got out of hand." It always made her happy when I admitted she was right. "Where's Dad?"

"He had some work to do, I guess."

After a shower, shave and into clean work clothes, then after Mom's fresh coffee, an English muffin, and almost a quart of orange juice, I had a buzz again—a little numb.

On the way to work, I remembered seeing George with Lois and tried to remember if he'd said anything about her. Might be a good thing.

Billy told me Bob had the flu and thanked me for coming in. It was five after twelve, and after Billy left I walked around the station yard, the pavement freshly sealed in the last couple of weeks, shiny smooth and black. The breeze pushed grains of sand and leaves out into the road, swirling, polishing. I wiped up a pool of transmission oil near the pumps, then walked inside, a little sick, trying to remember all that George and I had said. Dull, like a bottle top, I couldn't remember much, except that I'd told him about Delores and he thought marriage a stupid idea.

For a Saturday it was busy and stayed that way for almost two hours.

Delores called. "Why are you working? Why didn't you call?"

"Bob's sick. I figured you'd call the house and Mom would tell you."

"I did."

"Why are you mad, then?"

"I have to go with my parents to Lenox to spend the night with relatives. They're making me go!"

"Calm down."

"So we won't see each other today."

"You call me if anything happens," I said. "Okay? You know what I mean."

"Yes. I gotta go. I love you."

I picked up around the garage, swept, and took out some old tires. I filled the soda machine, thinking we'd move it inside soon.

George drove in. "Big head today?" he said.

I started to fill his tank with high test. "Not so bad now."

"You never said anything about working today."

"Didn't know till this morning. Bob's sick." I came up beside his window. "George, I know we talked quite a bit last night." I kicked the pump island with my heel. "Some of it I don't remember."

"Want me to fill you in?"

"Yeah." I topped off his tank, and he parked off to the side, the blue car shining from a fresh washing.

"Car looks nice," I said. "Want a soda?"

"Sure."

I took the key ring off the cash register and got him a Coke and me a Mountain Dew.

"You remember the part about love and marriage?"

"A little."

"Boy oh boy. What a mess this could be." He tilted up the bottle and white fizz rose to the top as he regulated the amount with his tongue. Then, "Do you know how important a decision you may have to make in three days?"

"I remember your saying something about our decision to get married, and how it would affect us." He started to say something. "No. Let me finish. What say did I have in you going to war? Little to none. That's what."

"We talked about it. I had to decide. My life is not yours."

"Right. Maybe. You know how I feel about me and Delores. I think it's my responsibility to marry her. I'm part of it."

"All right. We're both stubborn." He drained his Coke and placed it in the wooden case.

"We each want the other to agree, and if that doesn't happen, then what?"

"I think you're crazy to go fight when you don't have to. You think I'm crazy to get married if I don't have to. Guess that's it."

"No. We're too stubborn to admit there is even tiniest possibility the other might be right."

"Well?"

Neither of us said much for maybe thirty seconds; both of us walked around the garage, stared at anything but the other, and I think something important hinged on that short span of time.

"We might get one thing straight," he said.

"Go ahead." I leaned against the wall and accidentally hit the valve to the hydraulic lift, a hiss of air escaped, and George jumped.

"Sorry."

He went over to the soda machine and took another soda. From there, maybe twenty feet away, he said, "Ever since we were kids and I dragged you out of the river our lives changed." He walked toward me.

I guess I'd always thought it was my life that had changed and started to say so.

"Listen," he said. "For a long time, I thought it was because I moved away so soon after it happened. It isn't true, is it, Sam?"

"No." I scuffed at the red paint on the floor. "Much more than that. I owe you a life, and if you go to Viet Nam I might never repay it. You don't have to go. If you'd been drafted I couldn't do anything about your going. Why can't you see that?"

"I figured something like this." He pointed his finger and shook it only inches from my face. "You are a stupid sonofabitch. Best friend, or not, that's what you are. You must have an electronic score board in your head with a number beside each person you know. That's bullshit!"

He stepped away.

"Maybe it is, and maybe it isn't," I said.

George walked up next to me, and I looked down and saw his fist clenched. He raised it shoulder high, then down against the air lever that controlled the lift. We heard the air power surge and the shining steel column rose in the air. "I should put your head under that thing and squash it flat."

"Yours too."

The lift reached its maximum height and he released the lever, flopped it the other way; the loud hiss of escaping air filled the garage.

I thought, "He's been holding this stuff in for years. It's bothered him all this time, too." I bent at the waist, leaned toward him. "You are just as bad as me," I said. "All this stuff about saving my life didn't just pop into your head today."

"No. No, it didn't." He hollered above the noise. "Would it have done any good? Could we have found a way to even the score?"

"No."

"Will you ever see how stupid it is? It could have been me, and you know that."

The hiss died to a whisper and the lift settled onto the floor.

"What it comes down to," he said, "is that you think you can be responsible for what other people do. Like because I saved you, you owe me, and because Delores is pregnant you must do what she wants."

"I probably could talk her out of it if I really wanted too, and yes, I would like to have the fucking opportunity to do something for you. Not much of a chance of that when you're off in the jungle."

"Why can't I live my life the way I want?"

"Who's stopping you?"

George paced up and down the garage like before. The bell rang, and I went to wait on a customer. When I finished, George was sitting on a stack of new tires, his ass sunk low, forearms resting on the top tire's sides. I put the money in the cash register, and stayed there, my hands running over the numbered keys.

A minute or two later George said, while I was staring out the door, listening to the electric clock whine above and behind me, "Did we accomplish anything today? Any good?"

"Yes. I do remember, now, that you said something last night about us and brothers. Did you mean it or were you as drunk as me?"

"I did."

I went into the garage as he was shoving himself up out of the tires. "Christ," he said. "Give me a hand." I did, and he stood up, a tire stuck around his butt. He duck walked a couple steps, then knocked it off and we laughed. Then he slapped me on the back and we walked out by the cash register.

"No one can ever take those years away from us, can they Sam?"

"No. They can't. Or this day either."

He took a step outside the door, turned, stood at attention, and saluted. "Gotta practice," he said.

I whipped my hand to my forehead, middle finger only extended.

George laughed and walked over to his car.

In the car, motor running, George yelled, "This growing up is a pain in the ass." He gave it the gas and burned rubber, then slowly drove to the stop sign, then across the intersection.

A few cars came in shortly after he left, and a portion of me was healed like a nasty cut exposed to the air after a few days bandaged.

"My brother," I whispered, and some of the anxiety lessened.

# CHAPTER 15

On Monday morning at the school pay phone I dialed our family doctor's number and his secretary answered. I told her I wanted to talk to the doctor. She said to tell her the problem, and I almost hung up. What other choice did I have? So I told her, and as soon as I mentioned that my fifteen-year-old girlfriend might be pregnant, she said, "Sam, hold on."

In less than a minute I heard Dr. Swarthman's soothing, professional voice. "Listen, Sam. How long since her last period?"

"Almost six weeks."

"Okay. I know you are worried, but it simply may be that she miscounted. Tell her we need a urine sample today."

"Thank you, Doctor." I spoke to the wall so passing students couldn't hear, glad no needle was involved for the test.

"Goodbye, Sam. Come over at noon."

What must he think of me? I walked to the training room and found a small glass bottle, then found Delores and told her what she had to do.

A few minutes later she came back and handed me the hot little jar, which I shoved into my pocket.

Neither of us said a word after I told her I'd see the doctor at noon. She walked with me to my locker, and when I turned, expecting to see tears in the eyes of the girl I might be spending the rest of my life with, all she said was, "You didn't notice." And when I looked down at her skirt, I thought she meant she was getting fatter, no need for the test.

"I wore your favorite skirt," she said. "My lucky one."

"Oh. Good." I stared at the blue skirt with the tiny threads of purple and tried to remember if it was tighter than before. "Let's hope it brings us luck today."

"Yes." We hugged, leaning against the lockers. A teacher walked by and frowned at me, and I wanted to punch the sonofabitch. Rules. Delores might have to drop out in a month or so because she was showing. It all went through my head. Fifteen, pregnant, married, living in town, working with my father, the future mapped like a straight road in the desert. A baby crying.

The bell rang. "I'll be late," she said, and we let go of each other.

As she walked away I knew that she believed she wouldn't mind if the test was positive, and maybe even a part of her wanted to be pregnant. Then I decided, and the decision caused me to stop dead in the middle of the hall because I knew I meant it. If she's not pregnant, within the next month I am going to break up with her.

Dr. Swarthman guided me ahead of him into his inner office. I placed the bottle on his desk and he nodded, acknowledging its receipt.

"Sam," he said, and leaned back in his chair, rubbing his eyes with the back of his hands.

"I appreciate your help, Dr. Swarthman. It can all be done anonymous, can't it?"

"Yes. Certainly." He placed his hands on the desk and leaned towards me. "What are your plans if she is pregnant?"

"I'll tell my parents first, then hers. We'll get married."

He sat forward in his chair, sat on its edge almost. "You said she's fifteen?"

"Yes."

He raised his eyebrows. "She's almost still a child. Young for sex. Young for marriage." He said these last two things as much to himself as to me.

"I wish it hadn't happened. You don't know how much."

"For both your sakes, I hope the test is negative." He touched the bottle with the back of his hand. "I'll know by tomorrow at this time. Stop in again."

We shook hands and I walked the two blocks back to school. In one of the yards a few houses down on a side street, a For Rent sign was up in front of a trailer. Probably even too expensive for my budget. Three people to support.

On the next block, in between the houses, I could see the soccer field. My last day of sports, school, any kind of school. No college.

Tomorrow the first soccer game of the season. It all seemed so opposite. So terribly, terribly opposite. And I felt the searing stab of anxiety in my gut. Lately a more physical dilemma.

I met Delores, as we'd agreed, in the vacant lot next to school and told her when we'd know. She hugged the book she'd been reading.

On our way back inside, Bob came up and thanked me for working for him on Saturday. "No problem. I can use the extra bucks." Delores gripped my arm.

"Any chance you can work tonight?"

"You sick again?"

"No. Parents twenty-fifth anniversary and we're going to dinner in Albany. I screwed up and forgot."

"Okay."

"Thanks. I owe ya," he said, walking away.

"You're working a lot of hours lately," Delores said.

"Like I said, we may need the money." I glanced at her stomach.

I sat in history class, staring at the blackboard, worn gray in places from so many erasings.

Coach gave us an easy practice, then sat us all down in the bleachers for a pep talk.

"Tomorrow is important," he said. "It can set the pace for the rest of the season. Win or lose, it will show me the areas we have to work on." He paced in front of us. "No matter what, teamwork is important." He raised his voice. "Work together like you did today. Hustle." He smacked one fist into another. "Hustle!"

I wanted to win, wanted my senior year to the be the best ever in sports. The crowds cheering me and the team after a good play, a good feeling all over. And in a few months, basketball in the small gym, the noise so much louder, more intense.

Coach finished, telling us to get a good night's sleep. We all yelled and tumbled off the bleachers. Paul, Emily's boyfriend, came up beside me and asked out of the side of his mouth, as we trotted along with the team, "Any luck?"

We dropped back from the rest. "No. You better be keeping this quiet."

"I haven't said anything."

"If I hear you did, you'll wish you didn't." I ran ahead back into the rest of the team and yelled louder than anybody else as we entered the locker room.

I worked. Mopped the floors twice, cleaned the bathrooms, washed some of the garage door windows; all the time thinking, thinking. What would I say to her parents? Would her father hit me? I'd welcome it.

I was pretty sure my father would agree we should get married and I go to work with him. Sweet and simple. Mom would cry for Delores' sake. No mess could be worse.

George stopped by at eight, hair wet and slicked back, clean blue jeans and a powder blue mohair sweater.

When he stepped by me onto my wet floors I could smell Brut cologne, maybe half a bottle's worth. I said, "Going to the prom or something?"

"Got a date." He put a dime and a nickel into the soda machine.

"Anybody I know?"

"Sure. She's in your class. Lois."

"You were with her the other night at the Bistro."

"Just talking."

"Oh. That what you call it?"

He shoved the neck of the Coke bottle up into the opener and levered the cap off.

"You bet. You okay?"

"After tomorrow, I'll answer that."

George turned at the door and we stared at each other for a couple seconds before he said, "All those things we said Saturday are important. I never talked with anyone so serious before. I'm not shittin' you, Sam."

I stared down at the cement floor. "Best friends again."

"That's right!" He took a step toward the door, then turned. "Fuck this sentimental shit." He shuffled over the pavement to his car. "Yee Haw!" he yelled into the cool night air, then started the car and took off.

I mopped the floor one more time and wondered if that's who he'd been with last night.

Delores called at ten to nine as I was closing up. "Why didn't you call?"

"Delores, you can call me."

"I'm a mess," she said. "I don't want to argue."

"Especially about who should call who." I shut off the lights in the garage and stood in the dark talking, lights from passing cars like search lights through the windows.

"Dad has to make a call," she said.

"See you in the morning. Try and rest. Say a prayer for us."

"I have been."

I hung up and leaned against the wall and wondered what she asked for in her prayers, and I thought of a big freight train, me and George on it, bums, running away, like in a book my father had shown me when I was a kid. He'd called it the depression times and said it was one of the worst times our country had ever gone through. The words to "Yesterday" came along, almost in front of me, the words like a ten-foot ribbon riding a light breeze. "Now it looks as though they're here to stay. Oh, yesterday came suddenly." I wasn't even sure that's how the words went, or much else.

# CHAPTER 16

At breakfast, Mom asked what time the game started.

"Four, Mom."

"I'll come pick you up," Dad said. "Be ready."

"Yes, sir," she said, and I couldn't tell how much she was kidding.

"You guys gonna win?" Dad asked.

"No sweat." I looked at the clock and stood up, ready to leave.

"Ask Delores to come sit with us for a while," Mom said.

"I will."

The last thing I heard as I closed the door behind me: "She's such a nice girl and I'll ask her what she thinks Sam wants for his birthday."

The sky was a hard blue and reflected all the colors on the ground; I kicked a windblown pile of yellow birch leaves, then sat in the car. While it warmed up I started to pray; and even that didn't seem right, I so rarely did it. I remembered all those years of Sunday school, fooling around, not paying attention. If I had, maybe it would be different. Delores had gone to Catholic classes and she still said yes. Or had I forced her?

I backed the car out of the driveway, and decided whether I was to blame or not, if Delores was pregnant, the blame would be on me by most of the people that heard about it.

At school, Delores met me in the parking lot.

I put my arm around her. "Only a few more hours," I said.

She looked at me, and a stab went through me. I gripped her side tighter to me. "You can make it. Please try."

"Sam, I had a terrible dream."

"Tell me."

"We ran away, and when the baby was born it had two heads." I rubbed her back. "One of the heads was yours, Sam, and the other George's. I'm so scared."

"Oh God. What have I done?" I whispered and didn't think Delores heard me. "I'm so sorry." I pushed her shoulders away. "Remember, you might not even be pregnant."

"The dream was so real. I wish I was drunk," she said. "I wish we were alone and drunk and at our spot. If the sun was shining like now, I could lay back and rest and listen to our brook."

"We'll do that again."

"It will never be the same. Never."

"C'mon. We'll be late." I laced my fingers through hers as she slid her books off the car roof, then we walked into school as the last bell sounded. Late.

I stood in front of the doctor's desk and waited for the answer.

"The hospital just called with the results an hour ago and I asked them to do it again. They just called."

"It's positive," I said.

"Yes, Sam. I'm afraid so." Dr. Swarthman stood in front of me, a little shorter, a slight smell of spice cologne drifted my way. Then I caught a whiff of alcohol coming from the adjacent examining room. It almost seemed like I was going under, like so many years ago when Dr. Swarthman had used ether so he could remove my tonsils. "Count backwards," he'd said, then nothing.

"Yesterday," I heard the doctor say, "you said you plan to marry her."

"Yes, sir."

"You know her parents will have to sign."

I nodded. He sat and swiveled back and forth, then leaned forward, his hair black, peppered with gray. He stared at me. "Sit," he said, then, "I'm in the business of saving lives, Sam. You could have a bright future." He emphasized the word 'could', I thought.

I let out a big breath. "Might have had, probably."

"Both you and this girl are beginning your lives." He placed his hand on my knee and gripped his own with the other. "Not an auspicious beginning, and life is short, often much too short for success."

I thought of George. "I agree, Doctor. It's what Delores wants. She's terrified of an abortion, the knife, the cutting. It's my fault; she is so young."

"Tell her there is no cutting involved. It is certainly an uncomfortable process, don't misunderstand me. And you must realize, Sam," and he gripped my knee tighter, "after a certain number of weeks, there is no going back. No doctor will perform an abortion for you."

"I thought so," I said. He stood up and so did I. I thanked him for keeping all this quiet for us.

"I brought you and most of the other kids your age into the world. Unfortunately, sometimes things like this happen. I think it's a good idea you've decided to tell your parents."

"That remains to be seen."

He walked me to the door. "Let me know if I can help in any way." We shook hands and it was obvious, though he couldn't come right out and say it, that he was in favor of abortion.

All the way back to school I had to control an urge to run. I could see myself telling her parents, then mine, and the truth sank into me the way I'd sunk in the river that day. I looked up from the sidewalk and saw Delores walking toward me. I wanted to run away, maybe into the dense forest of the Adirondacks, until I was lost and alone with the animals.

I didn't have to say a word.

We walked back to the car, her head against my arm. People we passed looked at us. I circled my arms around her waist and lifted her onto the car hood. The first thing she said, "Hello, husband," and the second, "I'll be a good wife," then she placed her right hand on her stomach, "and mother."

I hugged her tight, almost pulling her off the car, and I'll admit I wanted to squeeze that second life out of her. The trap had sprung, and I imagined the beating her father would give me; I hoped he had a gun.

She pushed me away. "Now that we know, we have lots of plans to make."

"Why aren't you crying?"

"It won't do any good."

"Did it before?"

"No. Except it made me feel better. It wouldn't make me feel better now."

"Oh. We better go. I'll come over to your house after the game and tell your parents, then go home and tell mine."

"All right."

She walked with a lighter step than I'd seen in some time.

I made her promise not to tell Emily or anyone else.

The afternoon classes were a series of ifs, ands and buts, with intervals between classes with Delores so weird I couldn't hope to understand them. She actually seemed happy.

In the locker room Paul brought his spikes over and sat next to me. "Well, is she or isn't she?"

I stared at him and smiled. "No, by Jesus, as a matter of fact, she isn't." We slapped hands.

"All right!" he hollered.

Then we finished tying our spikes and trotted out into the early fall sunshine.

I could see Delores over at my parents' car as I warmed up. They all waved, then Delores leaned closer to my mother and said something. They were on the other side of a chain link fence, probably seventy-five feet away. Mom hollered, "Win!" and shook her fist in the air. I trotted over to the fence and Delores met me there. Dad winked as Delores kissed me through the chains link fence, cold metal against our cheeks.

I imagined her stomach as big as the rest of her, everything so out of proportion.

Less than half a minute into the game the ball came to me halfway to their goal from the mid stripe and I dribbled around one man, then dubbed the damn thing trying to cross it to my left wing. The ball rolled ten feet away and almost stopped. Me and a player on the other team headed for it from opposite directions. Like a trigger pulled, I was mad, angry at the way all that was going on affected my game. Both of us got to the ball at the same time, and I drove my foot into and through the ball and kept right on going into and through the other guy. I could hear the crowd cheer, then the sharp referee whistle close by. I turned. The guy was on the ground, both hands clutching his ankle. "Fuck 'em," I thought. It was fair play, the whistle for the injury.

Two of his teammates lifted and helped him walk to the side. My team members yelled encouragement to me as I lined up for the free kick. I gave it a good boot and it sailed two feet over the goal.

"Toe down!" coach yelled.

The ball sailed back and forth up the field, and I cursed the booze and cigarettes, but Coach didn't take me out.

By half time we'd scored one goal, the left inside had placed a quick short kick in the upper right-hand corner. At the beginning of the second half, I thought I was stoned. The clouds above seemed to hang like white balloons and the ball drifted unnaturally against the sky and hills.

Coach noticed and took me out. He pulled me off to one side away from the other players. "C'mon Sam. The team is flat and they need a leader. Are you okay or in la la land?"

"Fine, Coach. Just need a breather."

"Have a drink, then go back in."

Shortly after I went back in, the other team scored, not directly because of anything I'd done. We huddled up in back of the center line and I said, all their sweaty faces turned toward me, "If we can't beat these assholes, we'll never win the league." I stuck my closed fist into the circle and they all grabbed it and yelled, "GO!"

I stood at the bottom of the half circle in my center half back position and nodded at the right inside, Jeff, to kick it back to me. The whistle blew, he kicked it back, and I lofted a nice one to the right wing. We all ran down the field. I was having fun.

After several long runs up and down the field, my lungs ached, starved for oxygen, and the other players looked like tiny figurines, tennis ball size. This time I took myself out of the game. As I passed by the coach he said, "Tell me when you're ready."

I asked the timer how much was left.

"Six," she said.

Standing still, my legs started to cramp, and I walked up and down the sideline, everything weird.

With four minutes to go, I went back in and played hard. I drove one hard toward the net from fifty feet and it came back to me off a defenseman's shin. I nailed it again and it hit the cross bar, coming back again, and I couldn't quite believe it. For a split second, I heard the crowd, then the center forward leaped in front of his man and headed it past the goalie.

Cheers echoed off the school buildings.

We lined up defensively for the kick off and it came to me clear: enjoy this, Delores is pregnant, no one will cheer when they find out.

The other team never came close to scoring and, when the timer shot her pistol, the fans cheered and blew their horns.

We yelled and jumped all the way to the locker room.

Coach called me into his office after I'd showered and dressed. He closed the door behind us. "Sam, the center halfback has to be in the best condition of anybody on the team." He pointed one stubby, calloused finger at me. "You're not, and I suspect things I can't prove."

I stared around at the office walls, full of his old trophies, certificates and diplomas.

"You're a senior, and the others, especially the first-year guys, look to you as an example and for leadership. Do you understand me?" He rubbed his fist through his crewcut hair.

"Yes," I said. "I'll work harder."

He smiled. "Damn right. I'll run you ragged until you're in the shape I think you should be in."

I turned and started out of the office.

"Good game," he said.

I turned toward him again.

"Might not have won without you."

In the car, I decided to go home and tell my parents first.

"Good game," Dad said when I walked in the door.

"Listen, we gotta talk about something." I leaned against the sink. Mom turned from the stove where she was frying bacon and slicing tomatoes. Dad looked up from his paper.

"Delores is pregnant."

Silence. The smell of pork filled the room. As if he hadn't heard me, Dad slowly turned another page of the paper.

"No." Mom held the knife mid-air.

"You'll have more responsibility than you bargained for," Dad said, and threw the paper on the floor, its pages separating, slip-sliding, floating.

I watched Mom push the bacon around, a tear fell and sputtered in the hot grease, popping. She whispered, as I thought she would, "A fifteen-year-old girl. What will her parents do?"

I touched Mom's shoulder and she twitched, as if afraid.

"I'm going to their house right now."

"Guess you'll be getting married," Dad said.

Definitely not a question.

"I'll ask them to sign a consent form."

"You'll need money."

"Can I work with you after graduation?"

He slammed his fist on the table and one of the dinner plates jumped off and smashed against the floor. "Graduation hell!" He kicked the paper across the floor. "You drag your ass to the principal's office tomorrow and quit school. You're responsible for a woman and her child." He looked at Mom as if waiting for her to argue. "You think you're going to breeze through school drinking and playing sports while your girlfriend sits someplace pregnant? Oh, no. You don't need any more learning to drive nails with me every day, and you'll earn your goddamn pay."

"All right, Dad." I turned to go. At the door I said, "I didn't want this to happen." I turned the door knob. Mom took a step toward me. "I'm sure you didn't," she said. "No one wants these sorts of things to happen. Please, Sam. You must do what Delores' family wants."

"I plan to," I said, opened the door, wanting to, yet afraid to, look at my father, then walked out and closed the door behind me. As I backed out of the driveway, I wished I had enough balls to go somewhere else and keep on going until no one could find me.

On the way down the hill past George's old house, I sang the song "Yesterday" and I wanted to stop by the river, but I knew it was mean to keep Delores waiting any longer. I told her I'd go to her house first. I also figured the sooner I told her parents, the sooner I could go out and get drunk. George and me, we'd really tie one on, I thought. My troubles were certainly here to stay. I turned into the driveway, parked and through the window, I could see her family eating supper. So normal. Her mother passed Delores a basket of dark bread, her father forked a piece of chicken into his mouth, and I went in to tell them their daughter was pregnant.

I knocked light; they all looked up. Her father waved me in.

"Hi," I said.

"Hello. You're one hell of a soccer player, Sam," her father said. "Couldn't have won without you."

"Oh, I don't know. It's teamwork."

I couldn't look at Delores.

"Have something to eat with us?" her mom asked.

"No." I held up my hand. "I just finished. Thanks."

"Help yourself to a drink," her Dad said. "Big birthday on Thursday, Delores tells us."

"Yeah." I walked over to the sink, thinking thank God I'm not a year older or you'd be calling the cops in a few minutes. My hand shook terribly as I tried to raise a glass of water to my lips. Should I wait till they finished their supper?

"Now do you think you'll win the league?" Mr. Prairie asked, as he had the other day. He still had on his coat and tie from working at the bank.

"Good chance."

For the first time since I'd arrived, Delores said something. "Sam and I have something to tell you."

"Good news, I hope," her Mom said. She looked at me. "Well?"

"Well, uh . . . Delores and I want to get married."

Mr. and Mrs. Prairie looks at each other and smiled, as if to say what foolish things kids want to do.

He said, "We all know you're both too young for that."

I stood up straight as I could and said, "We have to. It's all my fault. Delores is pregnant."

Her father chewed one more time, and I didn't know if he'd swallow or spit. He dropped his fork and knife to the table, then stared at his wife.

Delores started to stand, and her father pointed one finger at her, like you would a dog, to stay. She stayed, stiff.

Then her father turned toward me, pointing the same finger. "You get out of here right now."

I took a step toward the door. "We want to get married. At least hear us out."

"Get out!" He reached behind him for the door knob, twisted it viciously, and yanked the door open. I stared at the serrated knife on the table. He said, "If I move out of this chair you might not ever be able to leave." He said each word slowly and distinctly.

Mrs. Prairie got up and walked around to his other side, between him and Delores, and I slow stepped behind his chair, hating to leave Delores.

She started to get up again.

"Young lady," he said.

"I love him," she pleaded.

"Get your ass to your room! Right now!"

I took a quick look at Delores, pushed open the screen door and ran out to my car. "Holy shit," I said over and over again.

My hands shook as I lit a cigarette; the smoke choked me, and I'd never wanted a drink so badly. Whiskey, beer, wine. Anything. I drove past George's house. His car wasn't there so I headed for Spott's Landing for a beer. A case, I decided. A whole fucking case!

# CHAPTER 17

This was bad. What did it mean? Maybe Delores' father just had to get over his first reaction. Poor Delores. They'll really give her hell.

Or would they?

Maybe they'd blame it all on me. They'll have to let us get married. Delores always said what good Catholics they were.

Then I started thinking about myself. No senior year. Working with Dad. Starting tomorrow, I'd work at the gas station, too. Maybe and maybe not, depending on what Billy thought of the situation. Years stretched out flat, and I imagined a life like some of the fifty year old men I saw at the gas station regularly. Work, eat, sleep. Yell at the kids; fight with the wife. Some day my kid will think the same of me. And the bite of anxiety, the worst ever, crammed in my gut.

I bought a case of ice cold Budweiser and drove back to town, mostly on dirt roads, drinking, throwing the empties over the roof at signs, rarely missing. After the first six-pack, I drank more slowly. Music by The Doors, some of it hard and fast, some so sad it almost took my breath away.

What would her parents do? I ticked off the alternatives: let us get married, take Delores to have an abortion, what else? Then one I hadn't thought of —they could ship her off to relatives, or someplace where she could have the kid, then put it up for adoption. My kid. I convinced myself that's what they would do. No abortion for a good Catholic. No marriage for a girl so young.

I pressed down the accelerator and headed for town. I wanted to talk to George. Maybe he'd disagree or have other ideas I'd missed. Besides, I didn't want to drink alone. Beer bottle collapsed, fell to the ground as I hit a curve sign.

George's car was in the driveway. I tooted the horn and he came out. I could see his little brother, Albert, not so little now, at an upstairs window. George bent down, sat back on his heels. "A mess, right?"

Did my face say that much?

"I'm sorry, Sam."

He walked around and opened the passenger door, saw the beer and said, "Park this bucket. I'll drive."

George backed the Mustang around the Corvair and out of the driveway. He wound the Mustang up in every gear, then let off at ninety miles an hour in fourth. Somehow that helped. The pressure against my chest eased, and I concentrated on the corners ahead. Then George left the main highway and turned down a road that passed the abandoned quarry. The road had been resurfaced that summer and the wide tires gripped, then slid as he shifted from fourth to third to second in the real tight curves, the speedometer never falling lower than fifty. On a straight stretch, he pushed the car up to a hundred and twenty, the motor flat out and screaming—at top end it was as if we'd reached another dimension. I wanted to open the door and hop out. At the almost ninety-degree corner at the end of the stretch, George drove slow, normal.

"I didn't think it would go that fast," I said.

"Believe it," he said, and patted the dash affectionately. "Hand me a beer and tell me all about it."

He took a path barely wide enough for the car, posted signs on most of the trees. Then just out of sight from the road he turned into an open spot that faced the quarry toward the Hudson River. It was almost dark.

"I've never been here," I said.

"Me either, until the other night. Some relative of Lois's owns this land."

He drank, gave me a sideways glance and I started with the doctor at noontime and ended with the final words of her father.

When I finished he said, "You've got about as much chance getting out of this as you would having a wish come true." He took another drink.

I drank more beer, surprised he'd said that, but really, what difference did it make what anybody said? The sun's last rays reflected in the side mirror, and a few minutes later, the horizon dull orange. I looked ahead and saw the first star, almost dangling on a thread over the quarry. I didn't know what to wish, except of course, that Delores not be pregnant.

I said it, staring at the star. "Abortion."

And instead of George answering, the immediate repetitious song of a whippoorwill sounded as the word left my mouth, then George rolled down his window and answered back out over the quarry, "Whippoorwill, whippoorwill, whippoorwill."

The bird answered his call once, then flew across in front of the car and out toward the Hudson.

"Remember when I used to scare them off at the tree house?" George said.

"Yeah. You always complained about the noise."

He turned in his seat toward me, rested his left hand on the pistol grip shifting lever. "Maybe look at it this way. If she has an abortion now, you could stay together until you finish high school and college and then, if you want, you could get married and have kids."

"Maybe. I'd be afraid to have sex with her. With my luck she'd be pregnant again next month."

"Sam, you could find something to worry about having the best time of your life. What good does it do?" He twitched the shifter for emphasis and it went out of gear; the car rolled toward the quarry edge.

I pressed both feet hard against the sloped floor.

George scrambled for a few seconds, his left leg caught under the wheel, then he hit the brake pedal. The edge was still twenty feet away.

It made me laugh.

"That would solve everything," I said. George started the car and backed away at least fifty feet.

"Right." He set the emergency brake. "I'd expect that from you."

We took long drinks, finished our beers, then reached for another.

"This helps," I said.

"You can't stay drunk all the time."

"No. I suppose not." I got out of the car and threw an empty out over the rim of the quarry. It took a long time before I heard the vaguest tinkling of glass, then I walked up closer to the edge. And I knew I was too damn selfish to ever jump. Poor Delores, I couldn't imagine the hell they'd put her through.

"Want me to give you a little shove?" George asked, coming up beside me, grabbing my sides.

"I'd be dead."

"Sometimes you're a real asshole. I suppose you think if I hadn't saved you, you wouldn't be in this mess?"

Something moved down in the quarry, and we strained our eyes staring into the grey-black light, eerie shadows on the milky walls. "Probably a bird," George said.

"Or bats."

I told him about my idea of Delores' parents sending her away to have the baby, then putting it up for adoption.

"Possible," he said, and an owl hooted way on the other side. "Ever think her whole family might just move away?"

"Jesus, no. They'd never do that."

"You can't be sure, Sam."

"I'd never see her again."

"Think about it," George said. "If this gets around, no matter what happens, and it probably will, think about what it will do to Delores and her family's reputation."

"I hadn't really thought about that. Shit. Maybe I'd better go home. They might have called Mom and Dad."

"You sure?"

"No. Let's go anyway."

George drove slowly where before we'd gone over a hundred. I said, "I'm wishing for the death of something I helped create, so I can go on with life the way I want. It's not right."

"You're thinking about yourself too much, that's my opinion. What about Delores? Is it really the best thing for her to have a child? She has a life ahead of her, too. You can think up a hundred reasons for having the kid, but it always goes back to having an abortion is the best thing for you both, and all your parents, too." He flicked each side of his mustache, then smoothed the whole thing.

I opened us a beer and lit a cigarette.

"The drinking isn't going to make this go away."

"You're going away. In five days."

"Yes."

Who would I talk to then? Another gap opened like a missing front tooth.

"Sometimes it's almost as if all this is happening to someone else. Even at the soccer game today it was like another person playing. Up and down the field, then coach telling me afterwards that we might not have won without me."

"You played a good game."

"I didn't see you."

"I sat with Lois in her car."

"No kidding. That's more than a one nighter."

George gulped more beer. "She's nice. We have fun together."

"Is it serious?"

"That'd be difficult, don't you think?"

"Yeah. I guess so."

"See, that's something good that happened today," he said.

"Better take me home."

"Fast or slow?"

"Pedal to the metal!" and before I'd finished he'd swung the shifter into second, gave it the gas, and the four-barrel sucked extra gas, then in third we were doing eighty. The last five miles to town passed in a guard rail blur, George fighting the corners, staring over the wheel, like I imagined a fighter pilot would streaking over the jungle.

He stopped next to the Corvair.

"Well, good luck. I'll do anything I can to help."

"Thanks, George. Tell Lois I said hello."

"Will do. You working tomorrow night?"

"If I'm alive."

"See you then."

Mom and Dad were both still up and, in the living room watching television just as if everything was normal. I walked in and Dad lowered his recliner a position.

"Dammit, will you ever listen?" He gripped the arms until his knuckles were white.

I started to say something.

"Sit down," he said, then let the silence hang.

Mom finally said, "Mr. Prairie called."

I looked at her and saw she'd wound the hem of her flowered nightshirt into a ball. Dad held up his hand. "If he could I think he'd throw you in jail. He's already called a lawyer and decided against trying that. Mostly because it would ruin Delores' life."

"What is going to happen?" I lit a cigarette.

"Not what I wanted. Not what your mother and I think is the right thing to do."

A little weight lifted from my chest, and I gazed at a painting of a bowl of fruit some long dead aunt had given us.

"As soon as possible she will have an abortion," Dad said, and leaned back, staring at the ceiling.

I wanted a beer, a shot of whiskey.

Then Dad looked at me again. "You like that, don't you? Well, goddammit, you aren't getting off that easily. No, not that easy. You do anything against Delores' parents' wishes I'll throw you out of this house with nothing so quick you'll be sick."

"What?" I looked at Mom. "What's he talking about?"

Mom stared at her lap. "Such a mess," she said. "You are not to ever go out with Delores again. Ever. They realize they can't stop you from talking to each other at school. Nothing more." She stood and took a couple of steps toward me, her nightshirt up above her knees. "They're having a judge issue a protection order in the morning. You can be sent to jail if you break it."

"No kidding," Dad said. He sat on the very edge of his chair. "Is that perfectly clear? Absolutely?"

"Yes." It sunk in deep, as if a solid steel beam had slowly eased onto my chest. Yet, too, a portion of lightness and relief contradicted that: no marriage, no work with Dad. Still ahead, my senior year, then college. I started to stand.

"Stay sitting!" Dad yelled. "I don't know what you're thinking, but I don't like the look on your face. Maybe this will wipe it off."

He walked out into the kitchen and I heard him open the front door, then shut it behind him.

"Mom. What?"

"He's taking the car away from you."

"No! No! Dad!"

He came back a minute later, keys jingling in his hand. In his chair again, he removed the ignition and trunk key, then threw the rest at me. "That's that," he said, and I could tell he was pleased he had his way, at least in this respect.

"For how long?"

He snorted. "Until you buy your own goddamn car, that's how long. You don't seem to understand what you've done to our family, to say nothing of Delores'."

"Sam, she's only fifteen," Mom said. "How many times did I ask you to be nice to her. I can't imagine what such a horrible experience will do to her. Your father said he could hear her screaming while he talked to Mr. Prairie."

Dad shook his head.

"I want to see her," I whispered.

"Her father will not allow it," Dad said. "If you're caught with her off school grounds, he'll have you sent to jail. And something else. In two days, you'll be eighteen. Get it in your head how serious this is!"

I'd never seen him so mad. He yelled, "Right now! Tonight! As angry as I am, I don't want you in jail."

"All right," I said. "Please stop yelling. I'm so mixed up. I thought they'd let us get married just like you did. I was willing to do that. They're supposed to be good Catholics, now they can't wait to get her an abortion. Delores does not want an abortion. Doesn't that count for anything?"

Mom said, "Not at her age. No." She paused. "Perhaps it's hard for you to understand, but at fifteen she's too young to know what she's deciding. Abortion or marriage to her are like you and George playing down in your tree fort.

"Then it's all my fault."

"That's certainly what her parents believe," Dad said.

"Is that what you guys think?"

Dad looked at Mom, then said, "Not all, Sam. I don't want to discuss it any further." He went out to the refrigerator for a beer, and as he walked past my chair handed me one. I held the cold can tight and thought, the first beer my father hands me is now. I slowly began to crush in the sides of the can.

After several swallows, he said. "You are our only son. This hurts us terribly." He tipped up the can for a long time. Then, "I don't know if you think you are in love or not, but I can tell you the Prairies are dead serious about sending you to jail."

"Please tell us you'll do as they say," Mom said.

"It's such a hard thing to do. We've been so close for such a long time."

"Oh God," Mom said. "You don't have a choice." She clenched her hands into fists. "You must see that if we sit here all night!" She was screaming. "I don't want my son in jail."

"Okay. Okay." I raised my hands in the air. "Then hear my side. She and I did this together. Now she has to go through probably one of the worst experiences she'll ever have without me. That's not fair."

"That's the way it has to be," Dad said. "Your mother and I have already agreed for you. Don't make us go back on our word."

"Can't you imagine what this is doing to me?" I stared at the reflection of Dad's red shirt in the window behind him and for the first time considered suicide.

"Of course," Mom said. "But you must realize that what you feel isn't as important as what you must do."

That seemed to make more sense than anything else we'd said. I had to let go. "All right," I said. "I'd like to think about it."

Dad checked his watch. "It's after eleven." He came over and stood, looking down at me, beer in one hand cigarette in the other. "Take the time you need, tonight. You'd better, for your own sake as well as everyone else's, come to the right conclusion. Stay away from her."

"I hear you, Dad."

After he was in the bedroom I turned to Mom. "I'm sorry to put you through this." Dried tear streaks stained her cheeks. She told me everything she had before, again, and added that Delores' parents had given up an important part of their religion for Delores.

I slowly butted my cigarette out, then stood up.

"Another thing to consider," she said. "They may manage to turn Delores against you. It may not happen. But they may make her life hell until she blames you for all that is about to happen, has happened."

"I'm going for a walk," I said. "I love you, Mom."

She followed me out into the kitchen and we hugged for a long time, then she walked toward the bedroom, and I knew the weight she carried was much more than mine. What a thing to do to your mother and father.

# CHAPTER 18

Delores didn't come to school the next day, Wednesday, and the day was a blur of my own and others' questions. Several of her girlfriends came up to me during the day and wanted to know where she was, asked if she was sick. I almost panicked, convinced they knew, were testing me. "Must be sick," I'd said. Two of them gave me a real funny look, girls in her class, and they did seem young. What had I done? Then I decided maybe Emily had figured out what was going on and told her friends. After soccer practice, by the time I got to work, I was exhausted, and the next day we had a tough away game.

Mom brought my supper, and I didn't like watching her drive away in the Corvair. What in the hell was I supposed to tell people about that? Riding a stupid bicycle. A senior, and eighteen tomorrow. I threw the whole supper, everything, plate, silverware, and food into the steel trash can.

George stopped by a little after six-thirty. I didn't feel like telling him all that had happened when I got home.

"Where's your car? Break down?"

At least I could tell him the truth. Between customers, I told him all that went on with my parents, and that Delores' parents had decided on abortion and a protection order against me ever seeing her off school grounds.

"That's heavy shit," he said, picking at his teeth with a match book corner. "Like I said before, though, if you'd have been eighteen you might be in jail right this minute."

"I want to talk to her," I said. "She didn't come to school today. For all I know she had it today."

"I doubt that."

"It's killing me George. It really is. I think I'm becoming another person. And you'll be gone soon. And who will I talk to then?"

He leaned against the wall and smoothed the edges of his mustache. "They haven't left you many choices. If I were you I'd do as they say and feel damn lucky. Look forward, you're letting the past fuck up your whole view of things." He pointed at me with the wet frayed corners of the match book. "Again."

"I know you're right. I know."

"Listen, Sam, I'm taking Lois out. What's the big plan for your birthday tomorrow night?"

"Drunk. Served at a bar for the first time."

"I'll pick you up after supper. Seven?"

"I'll be ready."

The next day we lost the game four to two, and the short ride home was quiet. When I stepped off the bus in back of our school, coach pulled me aside. He said, "If you want to stay a member of this team, you stay out of the bars. You got that?"

"Yes."

I went in, changed, and outside yanked the front tire of my bike out of the rack, and just as I was about to push off, coach pulled up alongside in his station wagon, "Happy Birthday," he called, then drove off.

The sonofabitch, I thought. He was like that, though, always coming at you from all sides. He was the only coach I'd ever known since elementary school; he'd always been tough but fair.

After playing most of the game I was tired and stopped by the river to rest and have a cigarette. In the almost six months Delores and I had gone together, I couldn't remember not speaking to her for a single day. Now almost two had passed. I couldn't think of a way to get in touch.

So, it was my birthday. I picked up a stone and threw it into the river. It must have happened today. The second day she hadn't come to school.

How long could it take to get an appointment? She probably wouldn't come to school tomorrow either, and then I'd have to wait till Monday, and by then George would be gone. Did Delores hate me yet, like my mother said might happen?

I stood up on top of my rounded rock and screamed at the top of my lungs, and the sound amplified and reverberated back and forth across the river, and my lungs were hot and felt as if the linings had been torn. I pedaled home slowly, the bike much too small for my long legs.

Dad wished me a happy birthday when I came in the door and handed me a beer. Mom gave me a hug and a kiss, then served up one of my favorite suppers, hot dogs and fresh bread-and-butter sweet corn. Everything subdued, as it should be.

"Going to the bars tonight?" Dad asked.

"Coach said he'd kick me off the team if I did."

"Stay here with us," Mom said.

"I probably would if these weren't George's last few days home."

The phone rang. The time Delores usually called.

It was George. "Happy birthday."

"Thanks. Come and get me, would ya?"

"Be right there."

In the kitchen Mom handed me a present. "Who was that?"

I could see she, too, hoped it was Delores. "George." I tore the paper from the box, everything so awkward. Inside a Cross pen and pencil set, and a bottle of champagne.

"Thank you," I said to them both. "Guess I really ruined this birthday."

Dad didn't say anything; he picked up the last ear of corn.

I stood with one hand on the kitchen door knob, champagne in the other. "What do you want me to do, Dad? I'm sorry about what happened. I wish I could change her parents' decision. Christ! For all I know she had the abortion today."

"Calm down, Sam." He sat like a stone, stared out at the road like I wasn't even his son any more. "Try and not get into any more trouble. You've hurt us enough."

I walked down the road, hardly realizing I still held the bottle of champagne.

On the flats, George pulled up beside me. "Oh, boy, champagne. Is it cold?"

"Piss warm." I popped the cork and a third of the bottle spilled on the road. I drank, choked a little, passed it to George.

"Get in," he said. "Which bar? Bistro?"

"Forget it," I said, and slammed the door. I told him what coach had said.

"Shit," George said. Then, "I know what. We'll go to Albany. I heard the guys in Bistro talking about a topless bar off the main street. Called Shimmy's."

"You feel like drivin' that far?"

"Shit yes."

"Let's go, then."

He handed me the champagne and took off down the road, fast.

I hurt like I'd been kicked all over. So little sleep, too much worry, and the game today had been tough.

"You and Lois have a good time last night?"

"She's a little screwy, but yeah, fun. We argued some about the war and she tells me I'm a fool for going. I think we understand each other, though. You guys win today?"

"Nope. It doesn't matter." I chucked the bottle and the rest of the piss warm champagne at a sign and missed by two feet. George laughed.

We stopped in the next town and I went in and bought a cold six-pack of Budweiser. The guy behind the counter, a real redneck, proofed me, and I threw my license on the counter.

"Happy birthday, Sam," he said, and took my twenty-dollar bill.

"Thanks," I said.

I handed George a beer and he passed a big fat joint. "From Lois," he said.

"Alright." I took a deep drag as George drove out of the town.

A few minutes later I was stoned. It felt like I'd fall over in my seat if I didn't hang on in the curves, and the white dashes or yellow stripes seemed to stretch forever.

"Hey, George," I held my hands out toward the windshield. "I'm an astronaut. Weightless."

"Good pot, huh?"

He pushed in a Doors tape and music blasted out of the four speakers. Morrison chanted, "Variety is the spice of life, yeah. That's what the judge is gonna tell my wife." George and I sang along, the sun setting behind us.

No. I thought it was her father's decision to kill what Delores and I had accidentally created. He'd decided not to let me see her. Let him live with it, too.

Morrison kept singing, and I knew my attempts to pass the guilt to Delores' father didn't totally work either. I'd started the whole thing; he'd been forced into it. Sex with a fifteen-year-old virgin. The soft irresistible touch of her, the small cries from her half-closed mouth, and those beautiful hazel eyes, so wide open as she came closer and closer to orgasm, then that totally sparkling look as she writhed and gripped me with amazing strength.

"Hey, Sam. Are you stoned or stupid?" George had turned the music way down and I hadn't even noticed.

"Both. Good weed."

The moon came up over the horizon and I wanted oblivion. The death, or impending death would not leave me alone. In Delores, in George right next to me going to war, in myself escaped from drowning with his help. Was life waiting for death, or death some presence in each of us waiting for life to end? Both life and death surprised me—sometimes like a child peeking around a corner unexpectedly, then like a tractor trailer coming head on. I knew how to cure that. More beer. Like Morrison sang, "We is all stoned, immaculate."

"Too bad your old man took your wheels."

"I thought I was done with that bicycle years ago."

George whistled a couple bars of Happy Birthday.

"Don't be a wise ass," I said.

He patted the dash. "This is a good car. Be paid for too, in a couple more months."

"Be all ready when you come home." If you come home, I thought.

"Take damn good care of it. Happy Birthday, Sam."

"What? What did you say?"

"I mean don't smash the fucking thing up."

"No. No way."

"No shit. "

I sat back against the seat. Me driving this car. This beautiful car, not much over two years old. Mine to have for two years.

George said, "You gotta pay the insurance. It isn't cheap on this high-performance stuff."

"I can do that."

"I'll turn it over to you tomorrow at motor vehicle. I get to drive it till Sunday, if that's okay with you."

"Do you really want to do this?"

"Yes. I know you'll take good care of it."

"I will." Into the night air I yelled a long Yahoo, and punched George on the shoulder. Hot shit and hominy grits. My grandfather used to say that some times.

I rubbed my hand along the seat edge, then touched the shifter with the back of my hand, listened to the purr of the motor. "I'll take very good care of it. I promise."

"One thing I'd ask. Leave it parked when you're drunk."

"Okay."

We came into an orange glow on the horizon, and George found the topless bar, right where one of the veterans said.

Tits jigglin' and ass shaking. That's all I saw when we walked in the door. They didn't even proof us. We drank shots of Seagram's and chased them with glasses of beer, mesmerized. George insisted he pay for everything and it was expensive. Buck a beer and two bucks a shot. But the scenery was nice.

I didn't even look at anything but the dancer till she walked off the stage. The place was crowded, mostly with guys older than us. A few of the guys kept yelling at the dancer. Two bouncers kept a close watch.

"Will ya look at that," George said.

After an hour I decided I didn't like seeing something I couldn't have, and I told George that. "She must be pushing thirty."

"Naw," George said and pushed my shoulder. "She's just got a lot of miles on her."

After we finished our drink I didn't feel that great, and the smell of stale beer, cigarette smoke and the heat started to get to me. "I've seen enough," I said.

"Okay. It's your birthday."

The smell outside was different, but worse: Albany. Diesel fuel and raw sewage rose up from the street, and I felt dirty, and couldn't walk straight.

"What a mess, George."

"And you are drunk."

"Yup, and I'd like to stay that way for a long, long time."

I leaned against the car and thought I'd be sick, then it passed. "Let's get out of this stinking, fucking city," I said, the words swirling and slurred.

George drove slow over the pot-hole-covered streets. A clock on a bank read eleven-thirty.

"Half hour left," I said. "Aren't you drunk?"

"Some."

"We drank a lot of whiskey."

"Not really. Four or five shots."

"You should have let me buy some." I leaned my head on the back of the seat out into the wind from the open window.

"I won't need money for the next two months."

"Oh, that's right." I was where I wanted to be: not much registering. Thoughts murky, no stress, drifting. No Delores. No George. A feeling like when someone takes away a child's favorite toy. Mad until something else comes along. Just like a little kid. I smiled and waved my hand out the side of the car, letting the wind take it up and down.

When I next looked out the window we were only four or five miles from town. George took his hand from my forearm, and I wasn't sure if he'd shaken it to wake me up or had been holding his hand there. What a great guy. Letting me have his car.

"You awake?"

"Sure."

"Do you remember?"

"What?"

"You talked in your sleep. For a while I thought you were awake."

I sat up. "No. What did I talk about?"

"I always knew you were a hippie." George laughed.

"C'mon. Tell me." I lit a cigarette.

"First you said something about peace, then mumbled something I couldn't hear. Then 'I love everybody'."

"You're bullshitting."

"No, I'm not."

I settled back in the seat, feeling better, except for the terrible taste m my mouth.

"It will get you in trouble. Lois and I have talked about this free love and flower power stuff. It's dangerous. It's something to shoot for, not something that happens very often."

"I don't think so. If people want it, it will happen."

"You should think more." He stared at me, a strange glow from the dash lights around him. Serious. "You give all your love freely yet expect something in return. That's what you do, Sam. Free love means you give and expect nothing in return."

"Maybe."

"You get burned and can't deal with it." George slowed down. "You better think about it."

"Like what's happened with Delores, and my having no say?"

"Worse."

"Such as?"

"You know what I mean. You've already considered what your life will be like if I come home in a body bag."

"Like Bill ever since his brother was killed."

"Yes. It's almost like you're preparing for the worst. If you ask me that's stupid."

"I guess you're right." I drew hard on my cigarette. We were coming into town. Like George said: I thought he was heading for death, Delores and I were responsible for another, and I was working to create my own. I couldn't think of a shittier set of circumstances as George headed for the dirt roads on the other side of town.

# CHAPTER 19

The next morning, first thing at school, coach called me into his office and kicked me off the team.

On our way back into town after sitting at the top of the heap for a while, I'd convinced George we should stop at the Bistro for a night cap. One of the six or eight people in there must have ratted. My last season of soccer down the tubes.

As I left the office, I said, "Thanks, Coach. Now I can really put time into drinking."

"Hold it, mister." He stood up and pointed his forefinger at me. "You listen. I didn't say you couldn't play basketball. You start hanging around in bars and that'll be gone, too."

"Who cares?" I walked out of his office and down the long, empty corridor.

As I'd guessed, Delores wasn't in school. I wanted to talk to her so badly it hurt. Didn't her parents understand the unfairness of their decision?

At noon, George picked me up and we transferred the registration, then went to the local insurance office.

Then he said, "Drive."

I took it through all the gears, slow. The car was tightly built; everything fit precisely.

"You sure you want to do this? It could be covered up at your house, no extra miles when you get home."

"I'm sure. Just don't drive it when you're all fucked up."

"Okay."

"One other thing." He slapped my shoulder. "You've probably already thought about it. If I don't come home, I want you to sell the car and give the money to Mom."

"You'll come home. Remember you told me to think positive."

"Whatever." He slipped his feet out of his sneakers and rested his heels on the dashboard. He didn't look happy.

"Wishing you hadn't signed up?"

"Who wouldn't? On the news last night over a hundred killed and more missing in action."

"God, I'd hate to be a prisoner."

"Fuck 'em," George said. "I'll show the little bastards just what tough is, dammit."

"You say that now." I wanted to stop talking about it. What happened to just having a desk job, like he told me when he first signed up? Then I thought he might want to talk about all this instead of my troubles for a change. I won't even hear the sound of his voice in another two days.

"Don't you have to go back to school?"

"No. Not today."

"Why?"

"Delores isn't there and coach kicked me off the team this morning."

"For what?"

"Someone squealed that I stopped at the Bistro last night."

"I tried to tell ya."

"Fuck it, George."

"Bet that will piss your old man off."

"Shit, I hadn't thought of that." I grabbed hold of the pistol grip shifting lever and squeezed until my hand ached.

"So, what will we do this afternoon?"

"You tell me," I said, and shifted into third, gradually pushing the motor speed up to seventy, then easing into fourth, almost unable to believe the distance still left under the gas pedal.

"Let's get some beer and ride up into the Adirondacks," George said. "Maybe some of the trees are changing. I don't like that I'll miss fall."

"Sounds good. One thing first. I'd like to ride by Delores' house and see what cars are in the yard. Not knowing sucks. Abortions go bad sometimes."

"No offense, Sam. I'd say they're all bad."

"You know what I mean." I turned down her road.

"You know, Sam, sometimes I think hanging around you, I'm starting to think like you. All this talk about death and we're so young."

Delores' house was around the next corner. Both of her parents' cars were in the driveway, the curtains on the living room windows were shut. She must be home. I took a deep breath, then drove toward the back roads that led to the highway heading north.

After a while I said, "I wish I knew why death bothers me so much."

"C'mon," George said. "You know damn well you've always believed I saved you from it that day down by the river."

"Yes." And for a few seconds I think we were both back at that hot, blue sky day.

Then George had moved a few weeks later and we'd grown apart. Now we were close again, and like playing Cowboys and Indians in the woods around the tree house. Instead of my saying I wanted to get in a girl's pants, I'd gotten one pregnant. And I think if I'd known all this that day, I'd have fought him off as he grabbed my hair and gripped me under his arm until he would have had to let go of me in order to save himself.

"Lost in space?"

"Remembering."

"Delores?"

"No. Me and you. The river. Tree house."

Then I decided I wanted to see Delores' and my spot, share it with George before he left. I took the next right, then another.

"This won't get us to the mountains," George said.

"I know." I turned into the narrow road that led to the birch grove and brook; a warmth and contentment came over me.

"Holy shit," George said, and laughed. I looked to where he pointed. In the little cedar trees behind the big rock next to the brook, at least a dozen rubbers were hanging like Christmas ornaments from the branches.

"What's this, Sam?"

I had to laugh, too. It had been a long time since Delores and I had come here in the daylight and I'd always tossed the used rubbers over my head, not thinking they'd land in those trees.

"Jesus Christ, Sam." George was out of breath from laughing so hard. He got out of the car and walked over to the brook. I followed.

"Enough, George."

"This is a nice spot," he said. "I like how you've decorated the place." He smirked, then the laughter came again, and I stared around, then pointed to the spots on the ground where I'd dug up the earth with my toes.

"Like a gopher," George said.

"All right. All right."

We both took a drink from the brook, then leaned against the rock.

As we drove away from the birch grove, I stared in the rearview mirror, all those rubbers hanging stationary like some kind of oddly shaped fruit.

While George was inside a small store, I remembered I had to work that night. Christ, that's all I needed was to miss work. It was one-thirty.

A few miles down the road, after a couple of beers, we could see the Adirondacks in the distance. Delores seemed to fade away like the green color from some of the leaves. Not particularly something I wanted, and yet for the first time I started to accept the way things had to be, the way her parents wanted.

I started to tell George, but suddenly he pointed to the side of the road, and I saw the raised white tail of a deer.

"Big sonofabitch," George said.

"All I saw was ass."

"Trust me."

Ten miles later we were in the western high peaks. The colors up high were like mists of orange and red and yellow, overlapping in places, and always the bright green of the fir trees as borders.

"We can't go much further. I have to work at five."

We turned around in the town of Blue Mountain Lake. I spun the tires in the gravel at the side of the road, then left a few feet of rubber on the pavement.

"Have fun. If these tires are bald when I come home, you're buying new ones."

The rest of the way home we listened to music and watched the scenery, and I think both of us were trying to remember this day as something special, something good to save for the future. I wanted to believe he would come home.

# CHAPTER 20

George took me home and said he had a date with Lois.

"Jesus, that's almost every night this week," I said.

He shifted into first, and as the car started forward, he gave a big thumbs up out the driver's side.

Something told me more was going on with Lois than he would say. Then Mom came out.

"Hello, George. We'll miss you."

George shut off the car. "Thanks."

"Come in for a minute."

"Mom, I have to go to work."

"C'mon, George."

George followed me inside, and Mom took a cake from the bread box and cut off a sizable piece.

"I can't eat that much," George said.

"Of course not. This is for after your supper with your mom and brother, and I suppose Sam has told you of his troubles?"

"Yes, Ma'am."

She turned to me. "Delores' mother called two hours ago and said it was all over; everything had gone fine." She paused and looked at George, then at me again. "Something terrible could have happened to that girl."

"I think it did." A weird sinking kind of relief went through me, and I imagined the loss Delores must feel, and I wanted to know what else she thought.

Mom handed George the tin foil wrapped cake. "He'll miss you the most."

"He'll get along. Thank you."

"Bye, George."

Mom patted my back, then turned as something boiled over on the stove, potatoes. It was twenty-to-five and I got dressed for work. The last thing I wanted to do was hop on that bicycle.

In the kitchen I said, "Sorry to put you through all this, Mom."

"I know," she said. "I'm sure you didn't do it on purpose."

"No. I didn't. And one more thing." She turned, expecting bad news. "I love you, Mom."

I glided down the hill, no hands, but chickened out near the bottom. George's old house slipped by as if in a dream.

Work was slow for a Friday, and right after I closed up I went over to Bistro, feeling quite important, not much different than when I'd played a good game. I took a stool in the corner and ordered a mug of beer. Imagining an opening game whistle, I took a big swallow of foam and cold beer. Several people came up and wished me a belated birthday and bought me a beer. The bartender lined up upside down shot glasses to keep track of the free ones.

It seemed like old home week, or a welcome into a new club. I watched a couple guys play pool, then put my quarters up. I liked the mostly country tunes from the juke box, though I'd never listened to many before. I'd made a number of friends, it seemed, in a short time. Instant friendship, I thought: add beer and a comfortable place to sit.

I'd considered asking the bartender who he thought could have squealed about the night before, but decided it was over and done with.

The drunker I got the better I felt, and told myself I was quite a good drinker, could keep up with the best of them. I watched other people in various states of drunkenness, laughing, arguing, every once in a while some good natured pushing and shoving. See, I said to myself, Delores and I would never have worked out; it'd be three whole years before she could even come in here.

At one o'clock George and Lois came in, and I could barely keep my eyes open. We talked for a few minutes, then they played a game of pinball. Not long after George and Lois arrived, Bill came in, drunk and dirty like he'd been rolling in mud and grease. Very drunk.

He walked over to George. "You're a fool to go," he said, barely able to stand. Everybody in the bar was listening. George kept pushing the flipper buttons, jiggling the machine a little. "Take a hike, Bill," he said.

"Fuck you," Bill said. "Don't you tell me what to do." A little drool ran down Bill's chin as he swayed back and forth. "Listen to me, George. I'll help you across the Canadian border."

"Right." George waved his hand like you would at an irritating fly.

I took a step toward them and offered to buy Bill a drink.

"Somebody's got to fight the politicians' wars," Bill said. "My brother died for them fuckers."

"Look what it's doing to you," I said, and I knew all the people around us were listening.

The bartender came over. "Two mugs," I said.

"You got that right," the bartender said, and laughed. "You behave Bill, or I'll put you out on your ass."

"You'd never do it if I was sober."

"Fat chance of that." He took my dollar and walked to the cash register.

Bill leaned close to my ear and his terrible smell hit me. "Maybe we should kidnap George. If he doesn't report on his day, they'll put him in the stockade." He gripped my shoulder. "Huh. Whaddaya think, Sammy?"

"Sure, Bill. You grab him and I'll open the door." God, he was in rougher shape than I'd understood from what George had said.

Bill chugged down his beer, a good part of it running down his chin. "I give up," he said, after he'd finished the beer.

I looked over to the pinball machine. George and Lois were talking. She lightly touched his wrist. The place was fairly calm.

I walked back to the bar and waved across the pool table to George. He bent and said something to Lois.

"Gotta go," I said, and pushed the outside door open. I stood in the fresh cool air, a scent of fallen leaves in the air. I felt much better, especially after I'd puked all over the side of the building, then I rolled over into the tall grass. When I came to, George was beside me, and for a second I thought we were on a camp out in our tree house. "Huh," I said.

"C'mon, get in the car."

He woke me up again at home, and all I remember was Lois saying, "Happy Birthday, Sam," and George laughing as I opened the car door and staggered toward the house.

# CHAPTER 21

I woke up at eleven, the sun bright, leaves outside my window a brilliant orange. Must have been a hard frost, I thought, lying there. Everything hurt.

After a shower and Alka Seltzer, I could at least open my eyes all the way, but I still felt like a freshly showered drunk.

"Morning, Mom. " I shook the coffee pot, its grainy sound reminded me of a propane bottle. I took a bottle of Coke from the fridge and sat at the kitchen table.

"Work today, Sam?"

"Yeah." I lit one of her cigarettes.

"Sam, what about soccer?"

"What about it?"

"Smoking. And don't get smart with me after the week we've had."

"Soccer is over for me."

"What? Why?" She came over from the sink and sat across from me. "Tell me."

"It doesn't matter, Mom. Compared to this thing with Delores it doesn't mean a thing."

"You're ruining your life. Next it will be your job."

"Oh, no. Billy and I get along great." Then I remembered I'd left my bicycle at the garage yesterday after work. "I need a ride to work," I said.

She shook her head, then walked into the bedroom to get ready. What if she gave up on me?

She stopped the Corvair in front of the station. "Sam, I wish you'd promise me no more trouble." She gripped my arm.

"I promise to try."

"You're drinking too much."

"I'll slow down. What do you expect when a guy turns eighteen?"

"I don't know. One day I think you're turning into one of those hippies, and the next you act like you might sign up with George."

"Neither, Mom. I want to go to college."

"That's what we want."

I sat back in the seat. "You don't know how bad I feel about Delores, Mom. Drinking helps me forget. And George leaves tomorrow." Drinking helps anxiety, I almost said.

"I know," she said. "Booze isn't the answer for any problem. Sam, I've never told you about your Uncle Ed. You remember him?"

"Yeah. Sort of." I probably hadn't seen him in ten years.

"He has an awful problem with alcohol and mental illness, and that's why seeing you drink so much worries me so."

"He go to jail or something?"

"No. He's been divorced, lost his job, spent time at an asylum." She sniffled and dug in her purse for a tissue. "He's my brother"

Billy walked up to the car. "Everything okay?"

"Sure." I got out and slammed the door, then turned and waved.

Inside, Billy said, "Hiya, Sam."

"Hi."

"Happy belated eighteen."

"Thanks. How did you know?"

"Bob told me when he came to work this morning. He also said that he's working tomorrow."

"That's right. I'm taking George to the train station in Albany."

"You got kicked off the team." He stepped closer to me, wiping his greasy hands on a clean rag.

"Bob tell you that, too?"

"No. News travels fast. Especially bad news."

"I got caught and I'm paying the price."

"Okay. I'll tell you another thing. You ever come to work drunk or get caught drinking on this property, kiss your job goodbye." He pointed his finger in my face. "You understand?"

"Yes." A customer rang the air bell and I went outside. Jesus, I didn't like to see him mad.

When the customer had left, Billy said, "You're a damn good worker. Don't ruin your good name."

"Okay."

"I'm telling you this for your own good."

"All right. I've had about all I can stand this week." I leaned against the wall and wanted him to go away.

He placed his hand on my shoulder and for some reason I was sure he was about to fire me; that he was waiting for me to say something to give him a reason. He gripped my shoulder, and I seriously considered popping him one if he fired me.

"Calm down, Sam. Is something else wrong?"

"No. How would you like to get kicked off the team your senior year?"

He left a few minutes later, and I sat on the stool behind the cash register, running my fingers across all the keys.

Quite a few customers came in for the next hour, most of them from out of town heading north for the fall colors.

At around two I was eating a Mounds bar and drinking a Coke when the phone rang. I couldn't believe it. Delores.

"Hi, Sam."

"How are you?"

"I guess I'm okay."

"I wanted to be with you through this. Was it really bad?"

"I think you know it had to be," she said. "I can't talk long. My parents are out working in the yard."

A short pause. Then she said, "You got kicked off the team."

"Who told you?"

"A girl in my class, and George is leaving tomorrow."

"Yeah."

"I think about our spot, Sam. I'd like to be there with you right now."

"Me, too. Are you coming to school on Monday?"

She whispered, "Here comes Dad."

Then, "Yes, Emily, I'm over the flu and I'll see you in school Monday."

"I'm glad you're okay," I said, and heard her father say something in the background.

"Bye, Em," Delores said, and hung up.

I traced the joints between cinder blocks on the painted wall and understood a little better how I felt about her. So cute, fun to be with; she'd given me her virginity, but love? No, I didn't think so. Love only existed in story books. After talking with George the other day, now I'd decided free love meant sex, little else. Some fun. I started to wash the big plate glass windows. The fall pollen and road dust lay thick on the outside glass, and I changed the water often. If nothing else, I had to keep this job, if only to pay for insurance and put gas in George's car. George's car. What will the old man say about that? Let him bitch.

Something else. I had to start looking for a college. Might as well start Monday after school. I finished the inside windows and decided Monday would be a good day to keep busy all day.

Billy drove up to the pumps and I walked out. "Fill her up," he said.

"Yes, sir." I started filling the tank, then cleaned his windshield. Something was up. He rarely stopped at the station, though he often drove past. I waited.

"Three-fifty," I said.

He handed me a five. "Windows look good."

"What's up, Billy?"

He leaned out of the car window. "Talked to coach a little while ago." He paused.

"What?"

"You're suspended all next week. Screw up once more and you're not only finished with soccer, but basketball, too. How's that?"

"You're bullshitting me."

He shook his head.

"You're not. No kidding." He was serious. "How come you have so much pull?"

"Don't forget I was on the school board for years. Let's just say I called in a favor." Then he pointed at me in exactly the way he had before.

"The favor you now owe me is to keep your nose clean." He motioned over his shoulder toward Bistro. "Stay out! You get that?"

"Yes, sir."

He smiled. "Good." He started his truck and I looked at the five in my hand. "Your change."

"Keep it. Buy your girl a hamburger." He waved and drove off down the road.

I leaned against the pumps, the sharp smell of gasoline in my nose. Back on the team. That must've been some favor Coach owed Billy. A part of me felt like I'd been holding my breath ever since he'd told me I couldn't play the day before, and now I'd let out all the air.

Hell, I said to myself, basketball season is over by February, I'll just sneak around like I did before I was eighteen. I looked towards the bar and remembered all those instant friendships; they'd still be there.

A little later, around four, George stopped for gas and his mom was with him.

She said, "We're gonna miss him, Sammy."

"You bet." I went to the back of the car and started to fill the tank. Through the back window I saw George shrug his shoulders. He looked small behind the wheel, the bright chrome shifting lever in his hand, as he listened to his mother. Much too young to kill somebody, even a communist.

I walked to her side, and she rolled down the window "He'll come home. I made him promise."

"I'm praying, and I'll pray every day." I tapped the hood. "He'll come back to make sure I take good care of his car."

"You'll come visit me, won't you, Sammy?" she asked. "Once in a while?"

"Sure. If you make tuna fish sandwiches and cherry Kool-Aid like we used to have all the time."

"Of course." She brightened up a bit.

George paid me for the gas, and when I brought back the change I asked what was up for his last night in town.

He looked at his mother, then at me. "I'm taking Ma out to dinner, then I told Lois I'd see her later."

"She's a very nice girl," his mom said.

"Yes," I said. "What time you picking me up in the morning?"

"Eleven."

"Okay. I forgot to tell you, I'm only suspended for a week. Billy fixed it with coach."

"Great." He slapped the side of the shifter, then pushed it into first.

I punched his shoulder. "Take off." I smiled as he gave it the gas, then tooted his horn and really gave her the gas and burned rubber up the street. I could see his mother yelling at him. Some things, like mothers, never change, and I guessed that was a pretty good thing.

I checked the windows for places I'd missed and wondered that it had turned out to be a half-decent day, and who'd have thought that a week ago. Delores seemed okay, I was back on the team, and even though I didn't want George to go, it just wasn't my choice.

# CHAPTER 22

Mom brought supper at five, two hamburgers and fried potatoes with lots of onions.

"Probably one of the last barbecues this year," she said, handing me the food.

I told her I was back on the team.

"Don't kid me, Sam."

"I'm not. Honest." I held the supper plate in my left hand and placed my right over my heart. "Billy fixed it with coach so I'm only suspended for a week."

"Then you stay out of that bar! You understand? "

"Yes. Let's not tell Dad about soccer. He doesn't have to know."

"I guess not." She smiled and put the Corvair into drive.

"Maybe your father will let you have the car back soon."

"Don't need it. George loaned me his until he comes back."

"Oh." She took her foot off the brake and rolled out into the road and toward home.

After supper and two Mountain Dews everything seemed better, except George leaving. I thought I should feel worse about Delores; all I felt was relief.

George. I looked out the sparkling clean windows into the setting sun. I imagined him in some muddy, snake-infested jungle. All those years we'd played Cowboys and Indians or War and now the real thing. I couldn't do a damn thing about it, except sit around and hope, maybe pray and I hadn't done much of that since Sunday school. Fight the fucking anxiety.

Lois drove up to the pumps.

"You don't look so good, Sam. What do you think about his leaving?"

"I can't do anything to stop it."

She gripped the steering wheel tight until her knuckles turned deep red. "I wish I could."

She let go of the wheel and crossed her forearms across her chest. "George and I talk about you. He wants me to keep track of you after he leaves."

"Is that all?"

"Listen," she said. "When George and I started going out, we agreed we were friends having sex, and it hasn't gone further. We like it that way."

I bent down and gripped the car's window edge with both hands. "That all sounds very nice, Lois. We'll see. I don't think either of you believe that."

"C'mon. Finish the gas. I gotta go."

"Okay." I topped off her tank. "Five even," I said.

As she drove off it occurred to me that I probably wouldn't see her until after George was gone. I tried to whistle through my teeth and no sound came out except for one like air escaping from a leaky tire.

The next day, George came to my house an hour early. I was still in the shower. He stuck his head in through the shower curtain and scared the shit out of me. "Hey!" he yelled. "Drag ass. This boy's got a date with Uncle Sam."

I gave him the finger, and then wiped shampoo from my eyes. "Yeah, to have all your hair cut off, learn to march, and run miles. Oh, boy, am I jealous."

"Why so early?"

"In case something happens. Never know. Flat tire. Whatever."

"I won't be long."

When I came out of the bathroom and was getting dressed in my room, I could hear Dad questioning George about the sense of leaving his car with me.

"Not good for it to sit around," George said.

"Maybe." Then I couldn't make out what was said. I came out to the kitchen.

"So, you're going to have a car again."

"I guess."

"I wouldn't if I was you, George."

"Let's go," I said.

Dad shook George's hand. "You're welcome to work with me when you come home."

"Thanks. I'll see what happens."

Mom gave him a hug and said she'd write. When we were at the door, Mom almost yelled, "Keep your head down."

We all looked at her.

"Isn't that a good idea?" she said.

We all laughed, and George said, "Thanks. I'll try to."

George went out the door first, and when I turned and reached to close the door, there stood Mom. She'd had to say goodbye to Dad a long time ago, and it probably never changed.

I followed George to the car. Maybe our last two hours together. Maybe. Then: the death of a child, not so long ago.

George drove, and for a while we listened to The Doors, then he asked me to find a Beatle's tape, The White Album. He pushed the tape in and found the channel he wanted. "That's it. Yeah."

I listened. So long ago, when The Beatles first hit came out, we'd argued about if they'd stay popular. I didn't think so and told him The Rolling Stones would beat them out. George turned up the stereo and yelled above the music. "I want you to listen to this song when you get in one of your stupid moods that nothing is any good." 'Revolution' came out of the speakers and George sang—yelled might be a better description—along with them. The guard rails flashed past and McCartney sang, "It's gonna be all right. We all wanna change the world." And I thought, it isn't and you're full of shit.

After the song, I pulled out the tape and read the other selections, then shoved it back in and said, "I should have brought my Stones' tapes."

"No. The Beatles and The Doors today."

"Jesus, I wish you weren't going."

"Don't start." He turned the music down. "Sometimes, between friends, you don't have to say what you're thinking. This is one of those times."

"We did that too much when we were little," I said. "Maybe."

"Is it hard not having a father on a day like this?"

"No. It's like he never existed."

"I'm glad it doesn't bother you. Boy have I screwed up with this abortion thing. My parents don't trust me."

"You better win it back."

"It'd be easier if you were around."

"So would a lot of other things."

The road weaved through a small gorge and George drove fast around the corners, constantly shifting. We came out onto a flat straight section and he pushed the car to over a hundred.

After he slowed down I said, "How did you leave things with Lois?"

He stretched back in his seat. "I dunno."

"That's a good answer."

"All right. We like each other, but we have different opinions." He waved his right hand in the air. "She's for this free love, peace is the answer to everything. And here I am going overseas to shoot holes in people."

"You like," I said, "more than you'll admit."

He glanced from the road to me, then did it again. "Yes, and I'll tell you something else, too. I'm hanging on to her like you did Delores when she was pregnant." He stopped, and I could tell he didn't know how to explain it. "But different," he said. "It's need, Sam. If her parents allowed it, you'd have stayed with Delores as long as she needed you. I want Lois to stay with me, write me, because I need her. Do you see what I mean?" He twisted the end of his mustache.

"A little." I'd never seen him so nervous and tense about a girl.

"Maybe it's this simple: I want to love her, but I don't, and I hang on to her so I'll have something good to remember while I'm over there."

"Did you talk to her about this? What's she think?"

"She'd like us to have more time together. She feels like you and my mother about my enlisting."

"Are you sure it's what you want?"

"I don't know. Half of me hopes they'll find a reason to kick me out, the other half wishes I'd joined the Marines. What a fucking mess!"

It was worse than I imagined. I'd thought he was so sure. All I could think of to say was, "Can't go back."

"No. So many things over and done and we can't go back."

We tried to talk more about it—our lives—and it came down to the same thing: keep going. Carry the mistakes and the fun, and the sufferings we caused or shared. I folded my hands in my lap and stared straight ahead at Albany's ugly skyline.

We stopped at a bar before going into the city and had hot dogs and beer, nothing much more to say. I thought, as we sat in that smelly bar: two best friends, and I owe him a life.

At the train station, I tried to tell George how I wanted him to come home so I could pay him back, and it pissed him off so much I thought he'd hit me. I stood quietly under the high domed ceiling and his voice seemed to echo so all could hear him bitch me out. "This owing me a life shit is garbage. If you do nothing else until I come back I want you to think and think and keep thinking." He pounded his fist on his thigh. "Until you understand that the only thing that matters is we're friends. There is no such thing as one owing the other anything. It's stupid!"

People walking by stared at us, then walked a little quicker.

"All right. I know."

"Like shit! You don't."

He paused and stared at me until I looked him in the eyes. He whispered, "I worry about you, Sam. Who's gonna kick your ass into gear every time you stall now that I'm leaving?"

I couldn't keep looking at him and stared at the granite floor. "I'll be fine. We'll write. You can give me hell in your letters."

He shook his head back and forth, and I'd never seen him so unsure. "I will," he said.

They called his train, and I wanted to say something important, something that would last till he came home.

At the train door we shook hands, gripping tight, then I reached and he did too, and we hugged awkwardly, then he dropped his suitcase and for a brief second picked me off the ground.

"Please come back," I said, grunted really, all my air gone.

"You take care," he said, then he was gone.

I left the station quickly, a shadow across my eyes like the thin white curtains in my mother's bedroom.

On the way home, a hollow creeping darkness entered me like dye spreading in a glass of water. I stopped at the same place we'd eaten lunch and drank boiler makers till the darkness eased, and I knew it was death, knowing I'd think of George's possible death, Delores' and my baby's death every day, and I didn't know how I could stand it. A thought of suicide became a real possibility to end the pain and shame.

# CHAPTER 23

The next day in school, Delores was even a little more matter of fact about the abortion and the fact that we hadn't seen each other for five days.

"Delores," I said, "I thought you wanted to get married and have the baby."

"Now that it's gone everything is different." She touched a button on my shirt. "I'll miss you very much, Sam. I don't want to stop seeing you." She grabbed my hand.

"We'll figure a way." More confusion, fear. I felt I was losing myself, a part of my soul.

"Dad's not kidding. He'll have you put in jail."

"You really think so? He'd be telling the whole town what happened." I looked around the busy hall, people going every which way; the bell was about to ring. Delores reached for my other hand and placed something in it. My senior ring.

"I don't want it to end, Delores."

"It has to," she said, and looked up at me as the bell rang.

"If we don't, it will tear us apart." She turned away, then reached into her locker and took out a small gift-wrapped box. "Happy Birthday." She handed it to me, then kissed me on the lips. "I love you," she said.

She walked down the hall, and I remembered everything we'd shared. I walked to my next class and stared out the window for a few minutes, then opened the box. Inside, nested in tissue, a perfectly round stone seemed to stare up at me. "An agate" were the words printed on a small slip of paper, "from the mineral celestine." An almost delicate chalk blue, and striped white, yet also translucent. I held the inch-across ball in my palm, squeezed it. Where had she found such a thing? I barely let go of it for the rest of that day.

And in the days that followed, Delores hardly acknowledged my presence and wouldn't even talk about the past, our past. Mom had been right: Delores blamed the whole rotten situation on me. How could she do that to me, someone she must have said 'I love you' to a hundred times? Unless her love never existed.

Two weeks after George left I learned a new word in English class. Extrapolate—to infer that which is not known from that which is known." I immediately understood the word to identify how I imagined where George was each day and what he might be doing. Christ, he'd been gone two weeks and only one lousy post card. I wrote him every other day, and Lois told me she'd sent letters a couple times each week.

The day I learned that word we had a home soccer game against our rivals from Spencetown. In the stands during warm-ups, I saw Delores with another guy, holding hands. I had a hard time breathing for a few seconds. Delores and I had talked less this last week; once she said her father reminded her often that he'd throw me in jail if we tried to get together. I couldn't figure out if she was scared or couldn't make up her mind what she wanted. I could now.

"That's not fair," I'd said to her earlier in the week, when she wouldn't agree to stay after school and talk to me outside.

She turned from her locker and slammed the door. "You didn't go through what I did." I'd never seen such a look on her face. That baby smooth skin all red and scrunched. Anger. Fury.

"I'm going to do what my parents want. Don't tell me what to do." Then her voice softened, "Let's just live the best way we can without trouble. No more trouble."

She certainly is moving on, I thought, and kicked a ball coming at me as hard as I could. The game started. I ran over the first guy that got near me and was called for a penalty. Minutes later I ran over the top of one of their fullbacks, passed off to our center and he scored. The fans cheered, and I was much better, a part of something.

We won the game by a goal, that first one. Afterwards, I drove George's Mustang home slowly and stopped by the river. Always the river, I thought. Always here. Its water higher on the banks in the spring after hard rains, then low in the hot summer. Always moving downstream.

I smoked a cigarette and sat on top of the rounded rock. A small whirlpool sucked around the front edges of the stone and corrected my thought of a moment before. Only eventually does all the water go downstream, perhaps to its own kind of freshwater death, as it mixes in with the briny ocean.

I was slowly breaking up inside. More and more my thoughts scared me, ones of death: even at Kent State in May soldiers had killed students. 1970 and students in National Guard uniforms are killing students. What the hell was going on?

I spat into the water: death so certain, the time and place a mystery, usually. A light breeze blew across the water, sailing bright red and orange leaves across the current. Dead after a year's growth. A chill vibrated through me. George marching, firing a gun, plodding in the jungle, creeping through the slime on his belly, firing at sounds, at rifle flashes up ahead, constantly looking out for his buddies, they for him. Me here. Booby traps, mines, beds of sharpened bamboo stakes.

Could she really have another boyfriend? So often I'd kissed her tears away, then shared their saltiness with her as we kissed and held each other.

Firm memories. Fuck extrapolation, a fancy term for imaginary possibilities. I wanted George to come home, having saved the lives of others, medals and ribbons all over the front of his uniform. I stared into the clear flowing water. You are stupid, I told myself. You only imagine the worst. Always torture for no good reason. It had to stop. Why couldn't I stop? Another piece of me, a small bit of my soul gone.

I stood on the rock and spat upwind and its spray wet my face like a warm slap. The small whirlpool looked far away as it sucked in a leaf with a power like the current that had pressed me under so many years ago. Death pulled. It constricted like a heavy wet rope drying on a hot sunny day.

At home, Mom congratulated me on our win. Dad hadn't been able to come; he was working out of town, building a two-car garage.

When Dad came home, I asked him what basic training had been like for him as he washed up for dinner.

"The usual, I guess." He looked over my head at the wall clock. "Lots of yelling, not much sleep. Especially the first weeks." He dried his hands on a towel.

After dinner, I followed him into the living room to watch the news. Cronkite said sixty had died today.

"You make a lot of quick friends in basic. Everyone seems the same, mostly, and it's drummed into you that everyone has to look out for the others."

I listened to hear where Mom was before asking, "Did you kill any Germans, Dad?"

He glanced at me, then back at the TV, then out the window. "No. I'm not sure."

During the commercial he talked about the towns in France where his company stopped and told about sharing some old brandy with a farmer. I wanted to hear the blood and guts stuff.

"You have to do what the brass says. Even when you don't see any reason for it." He stopped and pointed at me. "You tell George that the next time you write."

"Okay." I went into my bedroom and started a letter, telling George all about the game and how things were with Delores. I told him about her holding hands with another guy and how much that pissed me off, then told him what Dad said. Then I wrote how I was really feeling, something I hadn't done in any of the other letters I'd written in the fifteen days he'd been gone. How the days seemed too long to consider, each almost chopped off into a huge piece of immovable time since he'd left. And I really gave him hell for not writing more often. I asked several times if there was any chance he'd come home before going overseas. Then I told him a stupid knock knock joke I'd heard the other day. It went: Knock knock. Who's there? Ah go. Ah go who? Ah go fuck yourself. It didn't seem as funny on paper, but it had made me laugh when one of the guys on the soccer team told me a few days ago.

I wanted him to think I was all right and trying to do my best. I wasn't. Something was wrong. I was stale, old and crumbling, like one of Mom's cakes in the bread box. Crumbling back into the original flour.

It seemed I continually tried to push more confusion away each day and tried to convince myself that if I could act like everything was okay, it would be, but confusion and blackness crowded my brain.

I sealed the letter, licked a stamp, then stared out the window in front of the desk. We'd played soldiers in this small room when we were kids, one of us hiding under the bed shooting marbles at vast numbers of plastic soldiers, machine gun sound effects sputtering, while the other sat on top of the bed lobbing tin foil bombs into the scatter of soldiers and marbles.

On other days outside we played cowboys and Indians. I could still hear the sounds echoing from our rubber-headed drums.

Something snapped. I war-whooped out of the room, my palm flapping over my mouth, and I imagined George doing the same, half a step behind me, motioning to head outdoors. Dad sat straight up in his chair and started to smile, then that froze on his face. George's whoop seemed closer and I yelled, "cowboys, there!" and pulled an imaginary arrow from the quiver at my back, fitted it to the bow and fired the arrow and my fist straight through one of the living room windows and had started to climb out when Dad gripped my elbows and yanked me back into the room. I'd seen the two-story drop.

Mom started to scream.

I held up my arm for them to see, shards of glass protruding in five or six places, blood dripping to the carpet. "Go get the bastards, George! I'm wounded."

A fly crawling across my nose woke me up. I was alone in a hospital room. I could hear a television playing nearby, and I couldn't stop the tears. Over and over I said in a whisper, "Keep telling yourself you'll be okay, and you will be okay." I didn't think much time had passed; I assumed I was at the local hospital. The bandages on my arm startlingly white as I tried to move my fingers. They worked okay.

A nurse came into the room. She took my blood pressure, temperature, pulse. I wanted to say that wasn't what was wrong. She looked at me and I said, "Stay away from me you little bitch," I wasn't quite sure why. She walked out, and another nurse came back with a needle. She pushed it into my arm. A few minutes later I sank into a gray-black blanket of haze.

Dark when I woke up, thirsty enough to drink the brook dry. Piss on a whippoorwill.

Mom's voice in the corridor.

"How's my son?" she asked someone I couldn't see.

"He's asleep." A different nurse from before.

"What happened to him?"

"We're not sure. You can talk to the doctor in the morning. Go in and see if he's awake if you like."

Mom came into the room.

"Oh, Sam," she said, and held my hand, hers so warm and smooth, then I thought of Delores' hand, and I wanted her there.

"Does your arm hurt?"

"No."

"What's wrong?"

"I'm scared, Mom. I think I'm losing my mind."

"Don't say that."

Then she stared at me as if to find some indication of whether I had or not.

"Where am I?'

"Scinton," she said, a big hospital twenty minutes from home. I shook my head no.

"They stitched up your arm in the hospital at home, then . . . well, you weren't yourself, and so they brought you here."

"What? Why?" I was starting to understand. I just didn't want it to be true. "Where?"

Mom stared at the floor and said, "This is the psychiatric wing."

I stared at the tiny holes in the tiles on the ceiling and wondered what type of a machine could punch all those holes in such a random order. Then I thought, Order, out of order. Tilt.

"Where's Dad?"

"He stayed downstairs."

"Why?"

"He doesn't understand, Sam. You would have been out the window if he hadn't grabbed you. You could have died, broken your neck. What were you thinking?"

"Oh." I didn't want to remember.

Now I understood the camera up in the corner, a little red light on its top, and locks on the windows. I could remember thinking about playing cowboys and Indians, and like a flash of lightning it all came back, so real. Something lingered on the edges of my mind, something dark and mean, cold yet silky and safe, a part of real meaning.

"Mom?"

"What? What?" She stepped closer to the bed, leaned her thigh against the mattress.

"It almost happened again."

"Don't let it. Please don't let it."

Her voice moved the danger and fear away like the river at home, and I imagined certain stretches of river gliding by, always moving. Depth, clarity, motion. All these weird thoughts must be from that shot they gave me, and I looked over at Mom and it was like looking at her through the bottom of a Coke bottle.

She touched my cheek, rubbed my forehead.

"How are we?" A nurse, a different one.

I stared.

"Visiting hours are long over, Mrs. Caster. He should rest."

"What time is it, Mom?"

The nurse said, "Almost eleven."

"Your father will want to go home," Mom said.

"Will you come tomorrow?"

"Of course."

"When? I don't want to be alone."

The nurse said. "You should be up and around in the morning."

"When, Mom?"

"In the morning," she said, and kissed my forehead. "I love you."

"I love you, too."

She left, and I watched while the nurse took my blood pressure.

"Do you feel like talking?" she asked.

I almost said I felt like dying. Good God. Eighteen, and in a mental institution.

"I'm thirsty," I said.

"Be right back."

A few minutes later she returned with a large plastic glass of ice water and I drank half, quick, like in the morning after a good drunk.

"Do you know why you're here?" the nurse asked. She sat down on the foot of the bed.

"Yes. I suppose. What do I have to do to get out?"

"Well, that's a sign of improvement already."

"Right." I wanted to tell her to go to hell, to let me go, to give me another shot. George. Delores. A sense of terrible loss weighed me down. A pain in my head. What could I do?

I stared at her, a nurse, or whatever she was: might be a shrink for all I knew. She stood up, became stern and serious. "I know what you said to the other nurse that came in, and that's unacceptable behavior. I think you might want to throw that cup at me. Don't."

"And why not?" It hadn't entered my mind.

"Do you remember fighting the restraints on the way here in the ambulance and the first hour you were here?"

"What? What the fuck are you talking about? Restraints?"

"Okay." She held up both hands.

It came back, like my memory was on some sort of weird time lapse and certain words or gestures triggered it. When Mom said the word "Indians" I remembered, and now this hands-up gesture by the nurse helped me remember the trip here. They'd tied me to the stretcher with thick straps and placed me in the ambulance and they wouldn't let me go no matter how loud I yelled. Oh, shit. My mind seemed cracked in so many places, like the shell on a rolled hard-boiled egg. I concentrated on the healthy thoughts, so few, the bright places and tried to push away the anger and fear and blackness. A heaviness too hard to conquer. I wanted to be whole again, regain the missing parts of my soul.

"I'm not feeling so good," I said, and handed her the glass. She visibly relaxed and it hurt that she was afraid to be in the same room with me.

"We want to help you," she said.

"What's your name?"

She touched her chest. "Oh, I'm sorry. Forgot my name plate. It's Sarah."

"Can I have another shot, Sarah?" I said it soft, like melted honey on toast. I needed it to hide the fear.

"I'll check."

She came back and inserted the needle; the medicine burned.

She sat on the bed again, and really for the first time, I looked at her: reddish hair, a little gray at the temples, freckles high on cheeks that seemed old and stretched, faded. Maybe in her later forties, comfortable looking.

She almost whispered, "Why did you break the window?"

I stared at my bandaged arm. "I don't know. It was like something took over from something else, and I was firing at real cowboys as if the window wasn't there."

"Can you tell me some more?"

I told her George was my best friend and I'd remembered when we played cowboys and Indians. It all came back, and the medicine held it at a far enough distance so that I wasn't living it again, but close. I looked out the window, then at Sarah. "I started our war whoop," and started to bring my open palm up to my mouth, then let it fall back. "The memory wasn't a memory any more. George was behind me, I think we were surrounded, yet I remember Dad sitting in his chair in front of the television. Death comes out of the television every night."

Sarah patted my ankle. I kept going. "I war danced, and out the window saw cowboys coming for us, called to George, fitted the arrow to my bow string. Some of the cowboys were running away but a few were still coming at us. George was right behind me, but he didn't tell me what to do. I wanted to protect him. I was very scared, disconnected."

I glanced at Sarah, then out the window into the black night. "Now it sounds so fucking stupid."

Only a small part of the here and now was in my grasp, the rest a memory from when George and I were kids, played all day, almost every day.

"Sam."

I stared at Sarah and thought for a second that she was an Indian with red hair.

"When I shot the arrow, I must've put my hand through the window, and the cowboys began to run for it, and I yelled for George to hurry or they'd get away, and then Dad grabbed me."

"It's good that you can remember." Sarah squeezed my ankle, her hand warm through the sheet.

What will George think? Me in a nuthouse. And Delores. Her parents would say it was more proof that I was no good, and worse, she might agree.

"Tired," I said.

She stood up.

"Home." I mumbled, "Please, home."

Sarah rested her palm against my forehead and that is last thing I remembered.

# CHAPTER 24

The next morning when I woke up, and before I opened my eyes, for a few seconds it was like I was under water, and that was horrible and scary, yet fascinating. Bright shafts of sunshine down through the water created shadows on the large clean river rocks around me where I was pressured by the current against a huge submerged tree trunk.

I held my breath and opened my eyes. A dream?

The drugs.

Against the windows sheets of rain slid down the glass; oddly translucent green, red, yellow, and orange leaves trembled in the wind on the limbs a few feet from the windows. My arm hurt as if I'd been swimming upstream against a strong current for hours.

Outside in the corridor, the stink of food and plates clattering against one another. I don't want George to ever know, I thought, and knew the impossibility of that wish. How long ago had I wished that Delores not be pregnant, as I sat in George's car staring into the rear-view mirror? Two weeks, no, a month. Time all mixed like puke on a plate.

A nurse came in, the one I'd called a bitch. She told me I should get up for breakfast.

"No." Why did I dislike her so much?

She walked out.

Bitchy witchy, I thought, and could sense some of the drug affecting my brain. A calming, almost tingling sensation at my nerve ends. No, that didn't quite describe it. More. I needed more. The bitchy one and another nurse came in. The other one handed me a cup with two pink football-shaped pills inside. I looked at her name plate: Pam. Then the bitch's: Alice.

Pam said, "The doctor will see you soon."

"Will he let me go home?"

Alice frowned. "Give us a little time to help you understand what brought this on."

Pam held my wrist and her lips moved very slightly, counting.

"Will you get dressed?" Alice asked, eyebrows raised high. I expected to hear the tap of her foot.

"Why?" I wanted to bait her into saying something inappropriate.

"Why not?"

"Get lost."

They left, and I turned to stare out the window. Later I walked into the bathroom, holding my arm across my chest. After a minute the arm was like an anvil and throbbed like hell if I lowered it below my heart.

Out in the hall, a woman screamed like a baby for a few seconds as I reached for my pants hanging in an open closet. Cigarettes. I lit one and sat on the toilet leaning against the cold moisture-speckled flush mechanism. A few days rest and I'd be fine. A minor setback from too damn much worrying.

A knock on the door. "Sam." Alice the bitch. The cigarette hissed out in the toilet. I opened the door.

"No smoking in the room or in there either."

"And you are an asshole." I pursed my lips to spit in her face. She stepped back and I smiled.

She held out my shirt. "Dr. Thorpe is waiting."

I saluted with my left hand.

"I'll wait outside."

"Fine."

I expected some crewcut guy in his forties, I'm not sure why. Maybe a German with a glint in his gray eyes, then remembered extrapolate, and the little I'd heard about Freud and psychology.

Dr. Thorpee was around thirty, hair black, long enough to touch the edge of his corduroy sport coat, his face smooth and a little oily looking.

"Sit down, Sam," he said after we shook hands. "I hear you're already asking to go home."

"Naturally."

"Do you drink much?"

"Who told you that?"

"You did just turn eighteen. Listen, honesty will help us out here."

"Maybe a little too much." I stared around the windowless office, several small prints on beige walls, boring, nothing personal about it.

"Why do you think last night's episode occurred?"

So, I'll tell him, I thought. Mom probably has already. "In the last two, almost three weeks my girlfriend had an abortion and my best friend left for basic training."

Dr. Thorpe leaned back. "Certainly, a good amount of stress from those two problems." He folded his hands across his chest.

"No shit," I said. Then, "Sorry."

His eyebrows raised, then he said, "I'm going to order some more tests. And please watch your language around the nurses."

"When can I go home?"

"You need a rest. We should talk about what's going on with you. You don't want to put your hands through any more windows, or worse."

"No."

"Please cooperate."

"That one nurse, Alice, she is a bitch. I mean isn't a part of her job to be friendly."

"Yes. I'll talk to her if you agree to act more appropriately."

"What is this, elementary school?" I didn't give a fuck what he thought, and almost added, 'And you can kiss my ass.'

"You are a very angry young man," he said.

"I just might have a few good reasons to be a very angry young man," I said and stood up, scowling at him. I wanted to go outside, be home by the river, and part of me wanted to walk over to the wall and pound my head against it. It seemed like such a long time since I'd had things the way I wanted them. George to stay, me and Delores to be together.

"It's like I'm in prison, punished because I didn't handle a couple of problems just right."

"It's for your own good."

"Can I go outside?"

"Later. Someone will go with you."

"Afraid I'll run away?" I gripped the back of the chair. My arm hurt.

"When I get to know you better, you can go out alone."

I wanted to mimic his smooth, liquid-sounding voice. I wanted a drink. I wanted to see George. If he was here he'd kick my ass in the right direction.

"Can I go?"

"Yes. They'll take you for the tests soon."

I went back to my room and had started for the bathroom with a cigarette in my hand when a guy came in with what looked like a tool tray in his hand. He wanted blood.

I sat on the bed.

"How are you today?"

"Guess," I said, and held up my arm. "This and a bed in the nut wing. My life is complete."

He slid the needle under my skin and blood spurted into the glass tube, then another and another and another, and one more, a bigger one. Then with no more said, he left. Anger. Growly like a grizzly. I'd really screwed up. Snapped. Nervous breakdown. Loco. Nuts. All those things that happened to other people.

George so far away, going farther in six weeks. Delores holding hands with another guy, then my mind blipped like a messed up vertical hold on the TV and I saw that guy about to enter her, and through the blips I thought they were at our place in the birches.

Then a knock, a face in the door way. Lois?

"Sam, can I come in?"

I nodded.

She stood by the bed for a second, then rested her warm palms against my cheeks. "Please hold me," I said, and sat up a little, and she squeezed me tight, her breath and voice soft in my ear.

She said, "You'll be all right," her hands, each finger gripping my back.

"How did you know?" A new fear. "Everybody must know."

"No, Sam. No."

"How?"

"My uncle drove the ambulance. He thought it was for your arm, that you were in shock."

"Don't lie. I caused trouble at the town hospital."

"No one knows. I didn't know till I got here and asked for your room number."

"Ready for more tests?" A nurse and orderly came into the room.

"No."

"I'll wait. I'll go shopping. Sam don't get mad."

"How long will all this take?" I asked.

"Back for lunch."

"See you then." Lois kissed me on the cheek, and I remembered that musky, smoky smell of hers.

The nurse positioned my arm under an x-ray machine. "Does that hurt?"

"No. Absolutely exquisite."

Then I sat with a psychologist for an hour doing ink blot tests, and word games. It was humiliating.

Mom was in the room when I came back with the orderly. She said she'd talked to the doctor.

"What did he say? When can I leave?" I sat on the edge of the bed. My arm throbbed.

"He didn't say."

"Sonofabitch."

"Sam." She stepped closer. "He did say you have to behave . . . or . . ."

"What. What's worse than this?"

A nurse came in. More pills.

Mom stared at the waxy linoleum. "The state hospital."

"Oh, great. The big loony bin. I've heard of that place. Shit."

"Then cooperate. Get well so they'll let you come home. You've worried yourself sick about George and Delores. Neither of them wants that."

"I know."

Mom walked to the windows and stared up at the bright sunlight, everything outside looked clean and bright after the rain. Mom's wrinkles under her chin and under the one eye I could see seemed more creased than I remembered, and I knew I was to blame.

"Lunch," a nurse called from the corridor and I heard the shuffle of feet in the carpeted hallway. People of various ages walked by the door, most of them taking a quick glance inside. They all looked pretty normal, several a little skittish. I didn't want anything to do with them.

"Please try your best," Mom said.

"Where's Dad?"

"He can't face it. He just can't. He's so sorry."

"Ashamed. Something to add to all the rest."

"Go eat. I'll wait. No. I'll go with your father for a sandwich."

"Okay."

A cafeteria worker helped me find my tray on the large aluminum cart and he showed me a card to fill out for what I wanted the next day. The room where we ate was warm and sunny. All the windows faced a parking lot and I tried to find Dad's car. Then it seemed like everyone was looking at me, and the tray started to slip out of my sweaty left hand, then I saw the redness of the ravioli on the clean linoleum, and a broken plate, cup and glass. I stepped over the mess and walked out. The faces of those people. The tray had dropped in slow motion and I saw their eyes as they watched it. Emotionless. Vacant. Like fish eyes. Dead fish eyes. Only one of them had jumped at the loud crash.

In my room, I stared into the mirror, not a glass mirror, a piece of polished metal. My eyes were swollen, from crying, or drugs, I couldn't tell, and I lifted my hand to strike the metal, and the thought of the state hospital stopped me. If things were this bad here, what must that place be like?

"Damn," I whispered loudly, and heard a nurse come into my room, her shoes squishy on the floor.

"Are you all right, Sam?"

"I'm sorry. It slipped. My hand was all sweaty. Honest."

"Don't worry. I asked them to send another tray."

"I'm not really hungry."

"You better rest."

I faced her, I hadn't seen her before. "I think I almost blacked out. All those people, their faces so blank."

"Come along," she said.

I rested against the pillows, tried to get it together. A whirl. A blackness. Then all gray. Was it the pills or was I getting crazier and crazier all the time? No focus.

I stared at the leaves. George's and my favorite time, and me here and him in boot camp.

I slept.

Lois sat in a chair at the bottom of the bed. Mom in the chair next to the window.

"Hi," I said.

"Oh, good, you're awake," Lois said. "I was about to leave." She came over and stood by the bed.

I came more awake. Those last pills acted different. "How long did I sleep?"

"It's almost three," Lois said.

"People have been calling the main desk to see how you are," Mom said. "Coach, Joey, the principal even."

"Do they know where I am? What are they telling them?"

"Calm down," Mom said, and Lois placed her hand on my thigh. "They're saying you'll be here until your arm is better and you don't want visitors." Mom paused. "Your father told me to tell them that."

I reached for Lois's hand. "How'd you get in?"

"Sneaky," she said, and smiled.

"They'll all find out," I said. "I'll be treated different from now on."

"No. I don't think so," Lois said. "Not people that matter. Just get better. Your friends will stand by you."

And then she told me about a phone call from George. He'd wanted to know if I was all right, and she told him where I was.

Mom said, "She's right, Sam. Lois told me how close you and George and she have become this summer. Trust your friends."

"Then why did Dad say that no one should visit?"

Mom came over and stood next to Lois. "He wants to protect you. You're his only son and so many things have happened in the last month that he can't understand. He blames himself, too." Mom touched my forehead. Then turned to Lois. "Will you stay a little longer?"

"Yes."

"It was nice to meet you."

Mom said goodbye and that she'd come tomorrow. I waved, and she stepped out onto the carpeted corridor and noiselessly disappeared.

Lois and I stared at one another.

"I'll do anything I can to help," she said, and I knew she meant it.

# CHAPTER 25

Supper. Alice, the blond bitch, nicer today, and I tried too. She carried my tray to a table by the window and introduced me to Ronnie across from me.

"Hello," I said.

He nodded.

I checked the contents of my tray, then stared out at the parking lot.

What do you say to people who are nuts? I wondered.

"Arm hurt much?" Ronnie asked.

"No." I looked at him, really for the first time, early forties, I'd guess, short, little heavy, receding brown hair.

He glanced my way. "Good," he said, his smile a little crooked, and he seemed to talk more out of the right side of his mouth than the left.

I stabbed the pork chop on my plate and started to saw it with the knife in my left hand. Didn't work for shit. I tried the mashed potatoes, then a few French cut green beans. The talk around us was a muted hum, a distinct word now and then. I counted the people, twenty-three, and wanted to know why they were all there. I didn't want to tell why I was here. So far away from home. A mental wing seemed so foreign and isolated. Alarms on doors, cameras, locks on windows, and straitjackets. That triggered something, and I remembered why I was so angry at Alice. I'd been in a different part of the hospital when I first came, and she was there. She'd tightened the straps and held a towel over my mouth to quiet my screams. I remembered what she'd said, "Quiet, Mr. Caster, or they'll take you to a worse place," and I'd thought she meant jail, and I hadn't done anything against the law. Or had I? If I could have slapped that bitch, then I'd've knocked her so far, she'd never come back. What the fuck kind of help was that any way? And what else didn't I remember? Something.

I couldn't eat any more. I asked Ronnie, "Is there a place I can smoke?"

"Yup. Sure. Hang on, and I'll join you."

I left my tray on the table and followed him down the hall and into a room where there was a television, upholstered chairs and a couch.

I pulled out a crumpled pack of Marlboros from my pocket and Ronnie held a match for me.

"Thanks," I said. Inhale. Exhale. We watched the local news.

Several other patients came in and said hello. I nodded. A community of nuts, all instant friends because of our predicament, just like the bar at home.

Walter Cronkite with the war news. Over a hundred dead, the war escalating, he said, many more than a hundred wounded, a sick sensation, almost boiling, hot knifed through my chest and down into my stomach. A woman in back of us said, "Jesus help us all." The camera centered on a helicopter spiraling down, then the red ball of fire.

I was used to my parents' black and white television. This was totally different. The blood was very red, the green uniforms black with the soldiers' red blood. The camera focused on a reporter, sweat running down his face, obviously scared. He told how many had died in the helicopter crash, ten; he called the action a skirmish. Then back to Walter.

I took out another cigarette and Ronnie lit another match for me. George could be there for Thanksgiving or soon after. The hand holding the cigarette shook.

I wanted out.

I walked to the end of the hall and stopped at the double doors, red alarm box on the top, convex mirrors in each hallway corner above them. In the distorted mirror a nurse's face watching me.

I walked past the desk situated at the top right-hand corner of a T-shaped corridor.

"Please don't try to leave," Alice said.

"I remembered you holding a towel over my mouth, and I remember what you said." An orderly and another woman behind the desk looked at her, then me, waiting for me to say more. "It wasn't right."

I walked into a small room down the shorter hall next to the nurse's desk. In this room on a refrigerator, a printed sign, Patients Only. That's me. I opened the door. Rows of chocolate milk, juice, regular milk, and in the freezer ice cream bars, popsicles and sherbet. A woman walked up behind me.

"The blue ones are the best," she said. She pointed over my shoulder at a barely discernible blue color behind the white packaging.

"Okay." I took it.

She giggled, one hand covering her mouth, a thousand freckles on her forehead. She must be in her mid-twenties, I thought. I ate the blue popsicle and couldn't figure out what flavor it was supposed to be, then drank two cartons of chocolate milk.

My room seemed cool and deep like a huge aquarium; more rain, the drops winding their way down the window.

The pills must be wearing off; my nerves seemed on edge, restless, mind jumping from place to place. George. Delores. Me in a nut house. What will people think? Then around again. Questions without answers.

I'd never been shut in a place before and told I could not leave. It was almost as bad as those restraints they'd put on me in the ambulance. That's how they operate this place: authority and restraint. They call all the shots, used the state hospital as a threat.

Near the window, I walked in a baby step circle. Floor, wall, rainy window, wall, bed. Around and around in the tightest circle I could manage. Tiny steps around one square of linoleum.

A nurse came in and asked if she could help.

It was Alice. She had the tiniest bit of smile on her face and I decided she was glad I was nuts.

"What do you think, you fucking bitch!" The song "Help" by the Beatles roared into my head the lyrics pounding clearly.

Alice turned to go, then stopped.

I stared at her. "Listen," I said. "Will you admit what you said to me last night was wrong?"

149

"What did I say?"

"C'mon. Do you tell everyone they might be sent to jail if they don't behave?"

"I didn't say that."

"You sure hinted at it."

"I don't think so."

"You're lying to save yourself. You do your job about as well as a monkey wipes his ass."

She left, and I could tell she had more she'd like to say. Well, fuck her and her threats.

Sarah came in, the first time I'd seen her today. I could see Alice waiting off to one side of the door.

"Sam, what's the matter?"

I'd started my circle again, even tighter this time. "Keep her away from me. She lies."

"Sam, please." She handed me a cup with pills and poured a cup of water. "Lay down and relax," she said.

"She's a bitch."

"Relax." She rubbed my shoulder, then leaned closer. "Don't let things like that get out of proportion. It won't help you get better and go home, will it?"

"I guess not."

We talked for a few more minutes and the sound of her voice, soft and clean, her perfume sweet like violets, helped more than the pills. She had to leave, but said she'd be back soon. I listened to the murmur from the television down the hall, and the wind blowing the rain against the glass. Then the round of thoughts came back, and I wondered if I would have to take drugs forever to stop the Ferris wheel with George and Delores and death and drowning on it stop for good. By the time Sarah came back so had the calm from the drugs. I asked her to tell me about how they worked.

"For one thing, you are lucky they seem to work. Often we have to try a number of different types before one works well."

"They wear off pretty quick."

"Give the doctor time to adjust the dosage."

"I'm missing my last year of soccer and school. I should be applying for college now."

"All the more reason to cooperate and let the doctor and your therapist help you."

"Who's that? I haven't seen a therapist."

"You're talking to her." She smiled.

"Oh."

"We'll talk a little while each day. I work from three to eleven."

I stared at the dark window. Was this another deception?

"Sam, please look at me. I didn't tell you before because you seem to resent people you think have authority over you. I want to help you, so you can go home and do all those things you talked about before."

"It's sneaky," I said, but smiled.

"Between those pills and our talk, we'll have you home soon."

After Sarah left, the evening wore on with periods of hard rain against the window, the noise of slippers on the carpet outside, and that camera eye watching.

After a while, I gave the camera the finger, the anger seeping like a glass of spilled water soaking into wood. Time for more pills.

At nine o'clock Alice came in. "Truce?" she said. She twitched her neck and a long strand of her blond hair, just like that of Mary's in Peter, Paul and Mary, flipped over her shoulder.

"Okay. Fine."

"It's easier not to argue, isn't it?" she asked.

"Not always, not if you have a good reason."

"Well, let's try." She left.

I walked down to the smoking room. Faces staring at the television; they seemed as two-dimensional as the screen. I wanted to run away. Instead I walked up and down the hall past others walking up and down the halls. At the end, the convex mirror with far away faces. That reminded me of the Sergeant Pepper album and I decided that's one thing I really missed. Music. How did that song go? Something about 'a boat on a river, tangerine sky and looking glass eyes.' That was it: looking glass eyes. What was it The Beatles had meant?

The Doors. The Rolling Stones. The Beatles. I paced in rhythm to different tunes as the medicine veil shifted in different shades of nervousness and complacency. At the end of one corridor, a room on the right contained plants and two walls of glass. I hadn't noticed it before because the door was closed. I went in and sat down. A sign, No Smoking, please. I lit up and blew smoke all over the plants. A deep inhale, let it all go. You bastards. Keep me inside all the time. I blew smoke. I can be a bastard, too. A child is dead. Morrison yelled in one of his songs, "True sailing is dead." Jagger crooned all about Satisfaction. I couldn't say I hadn't had my share of that this last summer. Oh, Delores. I wanted to spit on the clean windows. Turn back the clock and change things. Who doesn't?

Later, I started a letter to George. I tried to explain the difficulties of the nuthouse. And included a little bit about the cowboys and Indians incident. But couldn't bring myself to say about my attempted leap. Maybe another time.

# CHAPTER 26

The next morning, I talked with Dr. Thorpe again, and it all seemed so general I barely paid attention. I guess I didn't think he cared much; it was a job to him.

He asked all about my drinking habits, and how that made me feel. I wanted to tell him that after I'd been drinking, I felt like I'd been drinking.

Jesus, ask a stupid question what do you expect? I told him it was for kicks, just like it was for the people I drank with. Then he asked about mood swings, and I said yes, I had them, didn't everybody?

He pointed out that everyone didn't try to jump out of windows. He had a point. Then Dr. Thorpe asked me how much the medication helped and I told him it did for short periods. "What am I taking?" I asked.

"A general class of drugs referred to as mood elevators." He reached and flicked his hair back from his collar as if it bothered him.

"They usually help with mild depression."

"Oh, so that's what's wrong with me."

"Not quite that simple, Sam." He leaned forward in his chair and steepled his fingers. "Due to the stress you've been trying to deal with, I'd say what you've experienced is a psychotic episode, and perhaps before that occurred you were suffering a depression. When you first came here, I prescribed Mellaril, a strong anti-psychotic drug, and now I'm lessening that and increasing the mood elevators. You also can have something else if you feel another episode coming on. Just ask for it at the desk." He sat back. "You do seem a little better today."

"I'd agree." I liked all this fancy medical talk. "When can I go home?"

"Perhaps the middle of next week." He raised a finger. "One caveat. Behave yourself." He nodded, more to himself than me, then on silent wheels pushed back from his desk.

I stood in the hall outside his door, leaned back against the textured beige wall paper and closed my eyes. A light touch on my shoulder.

Delores.

Oh, Jesus. Jail city. Tell me the whole town doesn't know. She gave me a hug and I thought, almost everything that happens makes me want to run away.

She held herself away from me and I saw the ivory soap whiteness of her eyes mixed with the hazel color sparkling with tiny stars of light. I could see nothing else. Yet they, too, seemed a little changed, perhaps more knowing since the abortion. The first time I'd hugged her since that day Doctor Swarthman told me the results of her test. I squeezed her close.

Then we stared some more, and I believed we each remembered the best times, then I managed a, "Hello." She was wearing striped jeans and a grey flannel shirt. Was she fatter than the last time I'd seen her? Trying to hide it?

"I had to come and see you, Sam. They insisted at the desk you weren't even here, until I told them I was your sister."

"Great. How did you know I'd be in this part of the hospital?"

"Lois." She gripped my arm. "Don't be mad. She cares about you."

I didn't want to argue. But here she stood by my side; something, another thing I wanted and couldn't have. Or did I?

"Well, don't worry, Delores. I've got so many people telling me what to do and, when to do it that I'll never screw up again."

She walked beside me toward my room. I waved my good arm in the air. "Hell, I've even got people to worry for me, and even cry for me."

I stopped in the door way of my room. "And you, Delores. You've got a boyfriend to hold your hand and do whatever else that you say is okay, and you say what we had is gone, a memory you've let your parents ruin."

I started down the hall.

"That's not true, Sam."

I could see the nurses listening, like this was another episode on a soap opera. I headed for the plant room.

She came up beside me. "That's not fair, Sam. Dad would put you in jail. Is that what you want?"

"Might even be better than here."

I walked into the plant room and she followed me and closed the door. My hand shook as I sat on the couch and lit a cigarette. I wanted her back. She'd never come back. Why was she here?

She leaned against the door.

"I'm in a nuthouse, Delores." Delores, only fifteen, yet already a woman. Oh, all those days this summer, and then she came over and sat tight against me and leaned her head on my shoulder. Maybe something good would happen if we could just sit like this for a long time, the best times might rise above all the shit. Dreaming.

I slowly relaxed.

"This is the first time we've been alone since it happened."

"Yes." I felt the nod of her head against my upper arm.

"I'm sorry you had to go through it without me." I couldn't help look at her stomach.

"I wish it could have been different, too," she said.

I dragged on the cigarette, then put it out in the nearest plant. When I moved back toward her, I almost continued into her arms. No. Why try for what you can't have, and I thought of all the things I shouldn't have done with her.

"I think you'll be all right," she said.

"Probably. Some day." I picked up her hand and examined the long nails, so clean, as if they'd never been dirty, a dim spot of a different color where she'd worn my senior ring. "Problem is," I said. "I have a feeling that when I'm okay other people will still treat me differently." I squeezed one of her fingernails till it was white, let go, and the pinkish color came back instantly. "People know. Don't lie about it, Delores. Not today."

"I guess." She wouldn't look at me. "It's a small town."

She ticked them off on her fingers, rasping each fingernail inside her thumbnail. "Lois, George, Emily and probably her boyfriend have a good idea, both our parents."

"I can't stand it."

"You will," she said. "Just like I do. Maybe in a different way."

"No."

"Listen to me." She shifted around on the couch, faced me. "I don't want to tell you this now, but it might help you. You don't know what it's like to be on a cold metal table at eight-thirty in the morning and have a life sucked out of you. Then be told you can't talk to anyone else about it."

I looked out a tall narrow window next to the door and saw an old woman staring in at us. She placed a finger to her lips, then walked away on her tiptoes.

Delores walked to the windows, touched the leaves on a hanging plant. "It's good we can be alone. I had to tell you."

"You were right. It helped. Is that why you came?"

"Yes."

A nurse opened the door and came in. "Lunch is here, Sam."

"Okay. Be right there."

"How did you get here, Delores?"

"My mom. I had an appointment. A follow-up."

"Huh?" Then I knew. "They did it here."

"Yes. The closest safe place."

"Are you okay?"

"Fine. A minor infection. Nothing. Really."

I whispered, "It happened here."

"Sam." She gripped my good arm. "I've got to go. Mom will start looking for me."

She kissed me, on the cheek. I stood, and she walked toward the door, then she stopped and got that stubborn look like she was mad. She came back. "A hug and a real kiss," she said.

And it was just like old times. Lips so soft and silky.

Then, again at the door she turned. "Do you mind if I ride up with Lois?"

"No. I'd like that." I'd barely finished saying that and she waved and was gone. Dazed by all that had happened in the last twenty minutes, I walked to the dining room and sat across from Ronnie. He'd brought in my tray for me.

"Thanks," I said, and the sight of the food made me sick.

After lunch I refused to answer the nurses' questions, I'm not sure why, and at four Sarah wanted to talk, and we went into the plant room, Solarium, a sign outside on the wall read. We sat in almost the same spots as Delores and I had, except not so close.

"You had a visitor I hear. What happened?" I shrugged my shoulders.

A breeze pushed whipped up brown leaves against the windows.

"Winter soon," Sarah said.

"George will probably die this winter," I said, and believed it, wanted to be ready for it, and thought of the preparations as building a strong stone wall.

"Were you trying to kill yourself the other day at home?"

"No." I smiled. "The cowboys. George and me, we usually played the Indians, the underdogs. We liked that cartoon, always watched it together Saturdays." I said a little louder, "Underdog."

"Are you sure?"

The drugs must have been increased too much, I thought, but that's okay. Everything through a gray veil again. All I had to do was remember. "About what?" I said, irritated that Sarah kept asking questions.

"You weren't trying to hurt yourself?"

"In a way. Trying to stop the confusion."

"What happened, then?"

"Too much of everything. I lit a cigarette and she didn't say I couldn't. "Do I have a say in who visits me?"

"Yes."

"Good. No one but Mom, Delores, Lois. They can tell the others to call."

"Okay."

I stared outside.

"You're avoiding me today. You haven't made eye contact once."

"I want out of here, and I don't think I'm getting better."

"Think of it this way. It didn't all happen that one night and you won't get better that quickly either."

"You seem more a therapist today, less a person."

"Different things for different times."

"Oh."

"When you begin to make more sense of all that's happened, you'll see more reasons for why things are the way they are. In a sense that's what it's all about."

"Does war make sense?"

"Perhaps not. Living with the outcomes of certain experiences we have no control over does make sense."

"George didn't have to enlist."

"No. Is that your fault?"

"He's gone."

"Should he have stayed for your sake?"

"This is bullshit." I dragged at the almost finished cigarette, then the taste of burnt fiberglass gagged me.

"I know I can't control what he chooses."

"That's a step forward."

"Can the emotions that come from love and friendship be controlled?"

"Sam." She reached across the space that separated us. "Yes, at least to the extent that those emotions don't push us to jump out of a window."

I smiled. "Those bad old cowboys," I said. "They got me."

"We all want to return to our early years sometimes. Do you think your life was simpler then, Sam?"

Before I thought about what I was saying I said, "Before George saved me it all did seem very simple."

She picked up on that like a miner finding gold, only she tried to be subdued about it. So I told her the whole story.

I hesitated several times and she urged me to go on, said it would be beneficial. Then I kept right on going and told her about Delores right up until, but not including, today. That was too fresh.

"We can move forward, Sam. It explains a good many things about what brought you to this place. I'll help you all I can."

"Is this how you operate? Be nice and kind, have another nurse that's a bitch, then I drop my guard and spill the beans."

"Not quite, Sam. You and Alice have a personality conflict, and I'd say it's a two-sided one." She winked and patted my arm.

"It doesn't stop one problem: being here now. No matter how much help I get, I'll still have to live with having been here. It may prove to not be worth the help. I'll have to fight both stigma and mental illness."

"Give it time. You'll see."

"When can I go outside?"

"I'll check."

"My reward for cooperating?"

"You're better," she said, then pushed herself up off the couch. She laughed a little, then walked off down the hall.

I tried to figure it all out. It seemed that Delores had lost something in the same place I was trying to find something. Answers. George made his decision. I must do the same.

I scribbled a note to George and lied about how I was doing. Scratched that out, and explained my try at leaping out the window.

# CHAPTER 27

Mom called after supper. She couldn't visit because Dad had taken the car to go fishing, and she said he was drinking too much. She was worried.

As I watched the evening news on this Thursday, in a nuthouse where I'd been since Monday night, I pledged to act normal so they would have to let me go, and I willed those uncontrollable parts to go away, then I mentally crossed my fingers. The dead count for the day was low, twenty-one.

An hour later, a woman started screaming some place down the hall, and a few minutes later they wheeled her by in a straitjacket; it was a middle-aged woman I'd barely noticed. She was cursing better than I could, and I thought: they can strap your body, but not your mind.

She was still screaming and moaning when they wheeled her out again, and I looked at the guy sitting next to me in the television room.

"State hospital," he said. "This is the third time something like this has happened with ol' Susie."

"That must be rough," I said.

"You screamed pretty good when they brought you in," he said.

I wanted to put that behind me, just hearing him say it caused a shrinking inside. Control-less.

"Name's Roy," he said. "Got a smoke?"

"Yeah." We lit up.

"I been to that hospital," he said, kind of puffed up about it, I thought, like he'd endured and overcome, or something.

"Sometimes," Roy went on, "these depressions hit you like a thick plate catching you full in the face flat ways. Really knocks you one."

I stood up and he followed me. "Want to see my room?" he asked.

"Sure." His was three or four down the hall from mine.

"You want to know what it's like?"

"Tell me." I was having a hard time paying attention.

"The buildings are old and the ceilings are high, I mean they're up there at least three stories. One of the attendants told me in old times they believed high ceilings like that would give the evil spirits that cause insanity a place to go."

I'd thought he was going to tell me about depression.

"First they take you to an admitting ward, and if after a certain time you don't get better, they send you to one of the back wards. Boy, you don't want to go there. I spent a winter in one of them. If you weren't crazy when you got there you would be soon." He rubbed his hand across his bald head, then squeezed his small nose.

"Don't talk about it if it bothers you," I said.

"No. It gives me perspective to remember. They say it's good to have perspective."

He blinked his eyes often, and I wondered if they called that astigmatism, or if it was from the drugs he was taking.

"I'll never go back," he said. I could tell he wasn't very sure about that.

"Do you think mental illness can be willed away?" I asked him.

"Partly. Maybe. Let me finish this."

He told me all about the months he'd spent at the state hospital: the shock treatments, loss of memory, moving around to different wards, each a signal of a further descent. He said once they locked him in dark room and he lost all track of time.

"How long ago we talking about, Roy?"

"Let's see. I'm forty-five. First time at state hospital was twenty years back. Of course, some things change. You'd be surprised how little though."

"When were you last there?"

He stared at the ceiling. "Three years I'd guess."

"Can't they permanently help you?" I couldn't imagine living like that. I'd find a hell of a lot higher window than my parents' two story one to jump out.

"I guess they can't, Sammy," Roy said, and lay back on the bed. "It comes and goes without rhyme or reason."

"I couldn't live like that."

"You'd be surprised." He squinted at me.

"Why's that?"

"Death is like a switch that doesn't work, at least for some people with depression. The tiniest spark of life will keep you going through the worst hells you can imagine. No matter how many times you try and hit the switch in all the ways you might imagine, it won't work."

I stared at him. He rolled over on his side facing away from me. "Pray that this is the first and last time for you."

"I will. Thanks." And the anxiety bit at me.

I chain smoked cigarettes in the solarium for about an hour, wishing for someone normal to talk to. It seemed like these other peoples' illnesses, all the people who had ever been here, permeated the air like a drenched sheet—a sheet that had been left in a dark wet place all wadded, and the center had rotted and stank with mildew. The outside whiteness only a memory, like youth and innocence. Delores' blood not far away, seeped into a linoleum floor, never clean enough to be gone. Only the appearance of antiseptic, that cutting smell.

Again. I pledged to control whatever it was that prevented me from living normal, to get out and stay out before the normalcy of being sick like the others here was routine. I imagined those high ceilings, and thought, what a strange temple for youth. Does time ever change or only revolve differently for each person? Some healthy, others sick, some honest, others corrupt. And some capable of love, so many not. Where did I fit?

No one came to visit that night, and I went to bed. I really did not know who I was, or if I could love, or if the sickness would worsen or improve. And it seemed as if I had nothing at all. No pill could help that.

More blood work the next morning, then finally, after five days if you counted the last few hours of Monday, I was allowed to go outside for half an hour, and all by myself. Down the back stairs and out into the bright sunshine and fresh air; it hit me in a wall of smell and color. Cool and clean, a slight twist of fall and late marigolds blooming nearby. I took a few steps across concrete to grass that seemed to squeeze up through my toes as if I was barefoot. Never in my life had I been cooped up for so long. I wanted to play soccer, kick the ball back and forth, practice throw-ins, following through and gently falling to the ground for extra distance.

I walked across the lawn, admiring everything, heading for the well-kept woods ahead. I couldn't wait to tell Sarah how much better I felt and knew if she gave the doctor a good report they'd let me go.

I actually enjoyed lunch as I sat with Roy and two other older women. I looked around the room and remembered the first day I had dropped my tray, and now my arm felt so much better. Roy started questioning me about why I was here and why I had problems with authority, and I almost got up and left. Then I thought about the nurse, Alice, my not paying attention to coach, my parents upset with me, and all that I'd built up in the morning came tumbling down.

I placed my tray on the big cart and asked for a pill at the desk.

"Why?" the nurse asked.

"I'm jumpy, nervous."

She checked a chart. "Okay." She shook one pill into a white paper cup and handed it to me; I swallowed it, dry, then crushed the cup, sure I'd just increased my stay.

An hour later Lois came, a McDonalds bag under her arm. I was a little dazed, sitting in a chair, staring out the window.

"Howdy," I said.

She smiled, winked, and I noticed again, how white and even her teeth were.

Thoughts floated through my head as if each one was in a tiny helium balloon, sometimes bumping into each other. Must be the new pill. Teeter totter thoughts. Glad Lois was here, pissed that I had to be.

She handed me a burger, then a bag of French fries, and put a Coke next to me on the floor, all the while chatting about school and other things in town.

"I'm sorry," I said, my mouth full of fries. "What did you say?"

Our eyes met and stayed. "Are you stoned or stupid," she said, and we laughed. Good, clean, sharp laughs, so out of place here.

"Both," I said. "New pill."

She stood in front of the window, fingering one of the locks.

"Something is on your mind. News about George?" I asked.

"No."

"Worried about cutting school?"

"Only half day today. Teachers conference."

"Thanks for spending it with me."

"Delores is downstairs." She came over and kneeled down next to the chair. "Do you want her to come up?"

"Seems like I'm always seeing or thinking about things I can't have."

"Your injuries are usually too big for the help available."

"Huh?" I repeated the sentence to myself.

"You're probably right," I said. Then, "You know if I'd gone through what Delores did I'd probably be in worse shape." I told her about the screaming woman they'd taken away the night before.

"You're stronger than you realize. You're better today." She stood and rested her hands on my shoulders. "What about Delores?"

"Will you come visit me in jail?"

Someone touched my arm. Delores. I reached my other arm across and gripped her hand, then closed my eyes again. So young, so pretty, and me the first. Not now. Not ever again.

"Right? " I said, as if I'd spoken those thoughts.

I could see in her eyes that she knew I was far away, half dreaming. She squeezed my hand. "It's me, Delores, Sam."

"I know. I wonder why you came back."

"I want to help. Please get better. I'm a part of this."

"No," I almost shouted. "You are not a part of my weakness. I told Lois what tough shape I'd be in if I'd had to go through what you did."

"You've probably put yourself through worse because of it. Do you want me to leave?"

"Left. Right. Wrong. Up. Down. Teeter. Totter. Don't mind me, Delores. They gave me a wicked strong pill a while back."

It's so hard to want things you can't have. I wanted to touch her like before. Laugh. Kiss. Caress. I wanted to prove to myself that I could please her. It wasn't right or fair.

"Sam, what are you thinking?"

I shook my head from side to side.

"C'mon." She leaned closer.

"Will your father ever loosen up?"

"I doubt it." She stepped away from the bed. "None of this should have happened. You should be playing soccer and I should be cheering for you."

"Is there a game today?"

"Yes."

The ball against my instep. Crisp passing. Running. Running. Here I am in a nuthouse with a girl who used to be my lover and isn't any more because I got her pregnant.

And I didn't want to look at Delores. In seconds those hazel eyes were staring into mine. We hugged in a clumsy way as she bent over me. My brain like a dumb weight. Then I felt the brush of her cool lips against my cheek, and I heard her soft footsteps leaving the room. Then I slept, dreamless.

When I woke up there was a letter from George. He explained about basic and one prick of a Sergeant who never let up, yelling at them to learn or be sent home in a bodybag.

# CHAPTER 28

At home the window looked the same as ever—maybe cleaner, a little smoother than the other windows facing the two-story drop. On the way home Mom had talked and talked. Dad or I answered in short sentences. The road, the movement, felt good underneath the seat. The trees and sky, the grass and rocks, everything dressed in the height of fall.

I went into the kitchen and handed Mom the prescription slips and asked if she would have them filled at the drug store.

After she left, I went into the living room to try to straighten things out between Dad and me.

"I'm better, Dad."

"I hope so. You really scared us."

"I don't think I'll ever know what happened. I guess I snapped like a fishing line caught against a sharp rock."

"Maybe."

"Dad, I lost my mind. You don't understand that at all, do you?"

He patted his knee, then scratched at the thick hair behind his ear.

"I guess I think you should have seen it coming and prevented it, like a bad cold turning into pneumonia."

"I wish." I stared out the window and wanted a pill: Thorazine. "I wish we could move away," I said.

"We can't, Sam. I don't know. First the thing, with Delores, and now this. What next? That's what I'd like to know."

I wanted to cry and hit him at the same time. I stared at him and he seemed older, was older, he'd lost weight, too. Then, for the first time it occurred to me: he did care as much as Mom; he just didn't know how to show it. What a mess I had made. One that couldn't ever be cleaned up. I had to do what Sarah said, what Delores was doing: go on and do the best I could.

"I'm glad we talked a little about it," I said.

"This had been very difficult for your mother, Sam. Don't let her down any more."

I went out and sat in George's car; it still smelled of the musk cologne he used so much. I squeezed the steering wheel with my left hand and the pistol grip shifting lever with the other; it didn't hurt hardly at all. I wanted a beer, and even though I was old enough, for the first time I realized I wasn't old enough. All those things coming needed all the clearness I could give them. All the people I'd see tomorrow in school: Joey, Lois, Delores, the coach, teachers. Oh, shit. I rested my head on the steering wheel. What about Billy? Maybe I should go see him now. I reached for the keys under the seat and started to put in the ignition key. Did it matter I might have inherited it? Just waiting for the trigger to strike? I remembered what Mom had said about her brother.

No. Not without the Thorazine. Then, did I really need that?

I couldn't say for sure, and sat back in the bucket seat, my mind a mix of thoughts and images. I calmed down a little, the thought of Lois clearest, and I wanted to know more about her and George. She acted like it was a brother sister sort of thing, with sex thrown in for fun. Then why hadn't she slept with anyone else since he'd left. Three weeks she'd said at her last visit.

Free love. What the hell is free love? I sat and thought about that for a long time, and finally decided nothing is free, and I didn't have that much to give away in the first place.

"Goddamn you, George," I whispered. I wanted to know more about our relationship, and didn't even know how to ask the questions, of myself, say nothing about him.

I'd blown the whole drowning thing way out of proportion, let it rule me like a fake gun held to my head, trying, waiting, to pay back a debt that never existed. Saving a life is instinctive, like placing a fallen bird back in the nest, even though the mother may reject it. That's what I'd done. I'd rejected George's help, and couldn't appreciate it, no, I had to wait for an opportunity that might never—in all likelihood—would never happen.

Mom drove into the driveway, and I waved, then started George's car. The oil pressure gauge moved sluggishly, then came up to normal.

Mom walked over to the car and handed me the bag of pills. "Want some lunch?" she asked.

"No. I'm going for a ride, then I'll stop and see Billy. I might even show up for soccer practice."

"Be careful of that arm."

"It's mostly healed. Thanks, Mom. And I mean that for everything."

My arm only tingled slightly as I shifted through the gears. The majority of the cuts hadn't needed stitches, and those that did had been removed Monday. I slowed down and stopped next to the river. What I really wanted to do was put everything behind me: lead a normal life.

Always the water. I stared out over the river and remembered an elementary school lesson, fourth grade maybe, about the moon's effect on water. It caused the tides to rise and fall all over the world, fifty feet in some places. And the moon is the sign for all mothers.

I climbed down to the rock and sat and listened and stared. The water helped my head in the same way it cleaned the sides of the rock. It smoothed and rounded. No more sharp edges, that's what I wanted, and also understood that desire as impossible. But as I stared into the clean water, the rocks two feet below magnified, I knew that I could change things for the better. How should I act, though? That was the question since everyone, almost, knew I'd been in a nut house. "Act normal, you asshole," I whispered, and kicked my heels into the side of the rock. The ones that treat you different don't matter.

I walked back up to the car and drove into town. At the gas station I parked next to Billy's truck and walked inside the garage. He had the hood up on a Ford and his head was buried way down in, toward the starter at the rear of the motor. I waited.

He came up out of the car and nodded, then started to offer his hand, then saw all the grease. He wiped most of it off. "How's the arm?"

"Pretty good."

"Everything else?"

"I'll be okay. Do I still have a job?"

"Dumb question. Want the same schedule?"

"Sounds good." The bell rang.

"Would you mind, Sam?"

"No. Course not."

It was a woman I didn't know. I put in five dollars worth of gas, the smell so familiar, sweet, yet it burned my nostrils a little. Normal. Just like always. I washed the windshield and took her money. A smile and a thank you, and off she went. I worked the lever on the cash register and placed the five in the till. Pace and schedule and one thing at a time. I walked over to the car to tell Billy I'd stay for a while.

"You okay, now?" he asked, his head down inside the car. He asked in a different voice, like he didn't want to face me with the question.

"In what way?" I decided I wouldn't give in to him or anybody if they treated me different. But I'd also decided, with Sarah's help, that I wouldn't blow things out of proportion either.

Billy came halfway out of the car, his hand still on the socket wrench, loosening a bolt. "Uh, Jesus, Sam. I don't know."

"You do. Say what's your mind."

"Is it true what they say about that place?"

"Depends on what they say."

"People screamin', straitjackets, everybody on drugs."

"Some of them."

"You weren't there that long," Billy said, and started to lean back into the car.

"What's that mean?" I said.

"That's good, isn't it?"

God, I thought, if it's this difficult with Billy, and I knew he was trying hard to understand, then what would it be like at school, with members of my team, class, teachers?

"Sure, Billy, it's good. I'm okay. Honest," I lied, and went out to the car. In the bathroom, I broke a Thorazine pill in half and swallowed it. I hurried outside at the sound of the bell and was busy for the next twenty minutes, waiting for the tranquilizer to take effect.

By three o'clock, the pill had smoothed my rough edges of concern and nervousness. Calmed the old thoughts down to a regular beat, maybe like a slow Beatles tune. Billy and I talked some more, and his genuine concern and lack of understanding about mental hospitals caused me to smile sometimes and shake my head at others.

I told him about the camera in my room, and he stared and stared at me. "How could you stand it? Someone watching you sleep. It'd drive me buggy."

"I was buggy. I lost it."

"You're okay now," he said.

I nodded. "Practice starts in fifteen minutes. I'll see Bob and tell him I'm back working. You're sure that's okay?"

Billy had finished replacing the starter and had just cleaned his hands. "Sure. Sure." He gripped my shoulder. "If you're ready it's fine with me."

I left the station and squealed the tires a little up the hill to school. I met Lois in her car and she waved and waved, then I saw her brake lights after we passed, and I kept on going.

I knocked on the coach's door and went in, expecting a conversation like the one with Billy.

"Sam," he said.

"Hi, Coach."

"How's the arm?"

"I'm ready."

He leaned way back in his desk chair and folded his hands across his stomach. "Close the door." Then he said, "The guys on the team are concerned. They're worried, and to tell you the truth I'm not sure what to tell them. I've never had a player go to the mental ward before. Not that it's some sort of terrible thing. Well . . . can you tell me what happened? That is if you don't mind." He leaned forward.

"Too much stress. Something let go."

"Trouble at home?"

"No. I worried too much about George and it just got out of hand." I hated lying, but I couldn't very well tell him about Delores. A quick image of her on a cold metal table in the hospital flipped in and out of my head like a jack in the box.

Coach said, "Go change. Don't push it today. We lost yesterday against the Royals, in case you haven't heard."

I left the office, a tightening and twisting deep inside me about seeing the guys.

Most of them had already gone out to the field. I met Mike, the left inside, and we slapped hands. "Glad you're back," he said, over his shoulder above the noise of his cleats on the cement floor.

Paul, Emily's boyfriend, stuck his head around the corner. I figured he knew for sure about Delores' abortion. "Hey, Sam. Good to see ya."

"Howdy," I said, and opened my locker, not far from his.

"You okay, Sam?"

"Sure, right as rain." Now why did I say that, something my grandfather used to say.

Paul looked at me funny. "They treat you okay? Fix your arm up right?"

"Yup." I pulled on my jock strap and shorts, then sat down to put on my socks and spikes. Even though I felt a little sluggish, I wanted to get out and run, make a little contact. I smiled a little, and out of the corner of my eye saw Paul watching. And like a small limb bent under a large weight of snow I sensed the beginning of a break. I smiled directly at Paul and slid over on the bench. "So, Paul, tell me, what's everybody think about me being in a nuthouse? C'mon. Tell me."

He moved a few inches away. "They want you back. Like you used to be."

"Don't give me that bullshit, Paul."

"What else would they think? You're a good player, a senior, a starter. Basketball is coming, too."

"Sure. Right. Everybody thinks that."

"There's always a few assholes. You'll be angry all the time if you let them get to you."

"I guess. C'mon, let's go."

He waited while I finished tying my spikes, then we went out to the field.

I ran two laps to loosen up, then coach waved me over. "You taking any medication?"

"Some."

"So tell me."

"Lithium, and Thorazine when I need it."

He was surprised. "Powerful stuff, that Thorazine."

I looked at him. "Ever take any?"

"Stretch out good, then kick the ball around."

When I looked for him a few minutes later, he wasn't any place on the field, and I knew he'd gone in to call someone about the medication's effect on my playing. I tried to tell if the other guys were staring at me and that just made me feel stupid and paranoid, like after too much pot.

Coach came back and we did a few drills, then started a scrimmage. A couple of times I had to slow down. Once I took myself out of the game, totally winded after a sprint to save a ball from going out of bounds.

On the sideline while I caught my breath, Coach said, "It's going to take a little time."

"Don't I know it."

"Go back in when you're ready." He walked away and yelled something to another player.

In the showers after practice, two of the guys were talking low in one of the corners, looking at me from time to time. They were freshmen, benchwarmers most of the time. I lofted a bar of soap their way and it hit one of them in the head, a big stocky kid. When he looked to see who'd done it I waved, and his face got real red.

"Nice day," I said above the spraying showers, and the other guys quieted down.

"Not nice to talk about other people behind their back. Is it, fatso?"

"It wasn't nothin'."

I walked over beside him and picked up my bar of soap. "Remember that," I said, very close to his ear. "Or next time you'll eat this fucking bar of soap."

I walked out and grabbed my towel.

A few minutes later Paul sat down next to me. "Jesus, Sam, after you left the shower that fat kid, Ralph, was shakin' like a dog shittin' peach pits." He laughed and slapped me on the shoulder, and for the first time that day I smiled, and then I laughed, too. Fucking dumb freshmen anyways.

I changed into my extra set of work clothes and stuffed the others into a gym bag. At the station Billy said goodbye and left, just like always. Normal and not normal; I didn't think those words were very accurate at describing much of anything after I tried to figure out which one I was.

Mom brought supper, and an hour later Lois drove up to the pumps. She smiled and waved when I came out.

"Fill 'er up?" I said, then placed the palms of my hands on the window ledge and leaned down a little. She reached up and flicked a crumb from my chin.

"You're home," she said.

"Yeah. Most of me." And I didn't know why I'd said that, but it made sense. Lois rambled on about school and some college she'd applied for as if nothing out of the ordinary had happened, except for how fast she talked and the way she kept tapping the steering wheel in an uneven rhythm.

I looked at the gas gauge and the needle pointed to empty. "How much gas there, chatterbox?"

"Oh, two dollars."

She followed me to the rear of the car, and I flipped down the license plate and unscrewed the cap. I started the pump and inserted the nozzle. Lois vaulted herself up onto the trunk lid. "Sam. I did something wrong, only I didn't think it was wrong at the time."

I watched the numbers fly toward two dollars, then put in more for all the trips she'd taken to come and see me. She didn't notice.

"I love George," she said. "That's why I haven't slept with anyone. Couldn't."

I'd stopped the pump to listen, gasoline fumes clouded around my head as I leaned over the open tank.

"Couldn't," she whispered again, like it was some sort of a sin to be in love and not want to sleep around.

I stood up and placed the nozzle back in its pocket.

"Well," I said. "Well, I thought so." I touched her shoulder. "It certainly isn't anything to be sad about. C'mon."

She slid off the trunk and into my arms. We hugged each other tight, and I was glad to be able to return a little of the help she'd given me. Cars went past, and people stared, and it didn't bother me much at all. I lifted her off the ground, then set her back gently. "Go inside," I said, "and I'll move your car out of the way."

"Thanks, Sam."

We got sodas and talked inside for a little while. Everything seemed okay, and boy oh boy did I like that.

# CHAPTER 29

Lois stayed while I waited on several customers, then I mopped the floors. She told me about a postcard she received from George. He was fine, sick of being in basic and eager to go overseas. He didn't think there was much doubt that he'd go.

While I mopped the far bay of the garage, Lois paced up and down the other one. After a few trips I said, "So what else?" George used to pace like that when he had something to say.

"I know you just came home, but . . ." She paused for a second then paced up and back one more time. "I've been talking to Delores a lot lately, as you probably know." She stopped and faced me. "Delores is set on you, Sam, and it doesn't matter what her parents say about you. She couldn't care less about what anybody says about you."

"Listen Lois, I know already that I'm not fond of the nuthouse, and I'm sure jail appeals to me even less."

She stopped, placed hands on her hips, and I kept mopping in long back and forth strokes. "I'm telling you. She's in love. Not like a dumb little kid, either. She's been through a bad time and so have you. It stinks you can't be together."

"I know," I said, then the bell rang and I went outside to pump gas.

When I came back, Lois walked up to me, almost blocking my way out from behind the cash register. "Do you love her?"

I pushed buttons and pulled the cash register lever. "Jesus, Lois, I'm not too sure of much of anything. It's gonna' take a little time."

"I'm sorry. It's not really my business."

The next day, I saw Delores. "You look nice today," I said, and remembered what Lois had asked the night before about love. She had on my favorite skirt, the one with purple threads in it, and a beige sweater.

"Thanks. How are you?"

"Actually, better than I figured."

She touched the back of my hand. The bell would ring any second, and I still hadn't found the damn book. I pushed several others aside and saw a piece of paper with big letters written in black magic marker.

"You'll get yours, crazy man." Delores breathed in quick behind me and I knew she'd seen it too.

"Forget it," I said, and saw the history book. The bell rang.

"Can we talk at lunch?" she said. "Please."

"Okay." I turned and walked down the hall, and, of course, wanted to keep right on going. For a minute that piece of paper proved every fear true. I cursed under my breath and my anger must have showed when I walked into class. The girl on my left, Carol, leaned across the aisle and said, "Hello." She touched my arm in a sympathetic sort of gesture, and my conviction grew stronger that the whole thing would not work. I thought, in June it will all be over. Eight months that seemed like eight years away.

After the teacher's usual boring lecture, today about the War of 1812, the bell rang. "Sam, a minute of your time, please."

I stood beside his desk. He sat on one corner and swung his leg back and forth, waiting for the room to clear.

"Having a tough time?" he asked.

"Is there anyone that doesn't know where I've been?"

"Probably not. You'd better adjust."

I almost said, 'Fuck you. Adjust this.' But that might get me suspended.

"Also," he said. "I'm here to talk or do anything that might help."

"That's right," I said. "You're the senior class advisor. Wouldn't want some crazy person to ruin the senior trip, now would we?" I started out of the room, squeezing the history book in my right hand so hard it cramped up.

"Stop. Don't talk to me like that."

I turned at the door and gave a quick salute, then left.

Three doors down the hall, the guidance counselor stood in his doorway. Of course, waiting for me. Another asshole, I'd decided long ago.

"Come in for a minute. I'll call the study hall and tell them you're with me."

I sat down beside his desk and he tapped his fingers along the top. "I'll bet Coach is glad to have you back."

I nodded.

"Any more thoughts on college? Those applications should be going out. Or maybe join up like George."

I shrugged.

"Can you speak?"

"Yes."

"C'mon, Sam. Let's talk about it. I know this isn't an easy time for you."

"Oh you do. You been in a nuthouse, have you? Recently? Know how people treat you when you come home? Tell me all about it. Please."

"Nice attitude," he said. I could tell he had fears about mental illness, even though he tried to disguise them.

"Want me to tell you all about an old woman screaming, and all the injections of strong drugs and restraints and mean nurses and stupid doctors?"

He stared at the floor until I was finished. "At least you're back. You didn't have to stay long."

"Have any idea what a week is like in one of those places? My father wouldn't even come in to visit." I hadn't meant to say that.

"Have you made an appointment to see someone at the clinic?"

"I will."

"Please let me know how it's going."

"Sure, I will." I stood up. "Can I go?"

"Yes."

I walked down the empty hall to my locker and chucked the history book inside. What a pain in the ass this place is, I thought. I couldn't imagine it getting better.

At lunch time, Delores and I walked out back of the school to the elementary playground. The air was crisp and dry like the aging leaves under our feet. I sat down against the sun-warmed brick building.

"I have an idea," she said, and sat next to me. "An option for us."

"I'm listening." I figured after this morning I was ready for almost anything.

Delores crossed and re-crossed her ankles. "I didn't want to tell you so soon after you came home, but I don't think it matters."

"What is it, for Christ's sake!" I grabbed her hand. "No. I'm sorry."

"Lois and I are pretty good friends now. She's told me all about those people she met on Cape Cod this Summer." She gripped my hand tight.

"I'm not following this real well, Delores."

"I want to be with you, Sam."

"Be pretty tough if I was in jail."

"That's just it. We'll go away and they won't find us. We can live with Lois' friends."

Everything seemed to stop, the kids on the playground, the sun above, the leaves windblown paths across the grass. On Delores' face was a look of love and caring I'd never seen before.

"I don't like it here any more, either, Sam."

"We certainly are in a mess."

"It might be a way out. Lois says it's kind of a commune. Everyone pitches in and does their share. No one would find us."

"Let me think about it."

"Kiss me, Sam. Please."

We kissed for a long time, and I needed her more than I wanted to admit.

"Let's go to our place tonight," she said. "I'll meet you. Lois will pick me up and drop me off to you. Then pick me up later."

"You have it all planned out."

She bit my neck a little, then blew in my ear, touched it with the tip of her tongue.

"Okay. Okay. Have Lois drop you at our spot at seven."

"Oh, good. Good!"

# CHAPTER 30

That afternoon, classes went along pretty much as usual, and I hadn't even missed that much material. Between periods, the school nurse found me, and I walked with her to her small office and listed what pills I was taking, and said, yes, I'd already told Coach.

"Get plenty to drink when you're practicing," she said. "It's very important." She pointed a stubby finger at me. "Absolutely no alcohol."

"Right. I'm on the team."

She nodded. "No alcohol."

"Yes, ma'am."

At practice. another note had been slipped into my locker. I picked it up. In big red letters, WATCH OUT FOR CRAZY MAN. I tried to hold in my anger and crumpled the paper in my hands. Who would do this and why? I wanted to smash my fists into the lockers. It almost had to be someone on the team. No one else would know my locker number. Maybe it was Steve, the guy who'd played my position while I was gone.

The locker room was beginning to fill up. I waited for him, and uncrumpled the note, then folded it in half. He came in.

"Hey, Steve," I called, and watched him close. He waved and started down another aisle toward his locker. "C'mere, would ya?"

I gritted my teeth, and when he got close, held up the note for him to see. "Know anything about this?"

He backed up a step. "Nope."

"Maybe hoping they'd send me away for good so you could play more?"

The locker room had quieted down.

"No. Honest."

I turned around in a slow circle. "Then who, goddammit!"

Paul came over to me. "C'mon, Sam. I'll help you find out. This won't do it. C'mon."

Coach came in and everyone quickly went about their business. He gave me a look, though.

Paul followed me back to our lockers and I handed him the sheet.

"If they know it bothers you, they'll keep it up," he said, and handed the paper back to me.

"Well, they know."

Coach came over and I closed the piece of paper. "Let me see that." I handed it to him.

He glanced at it, then gave it back. "Any ideas?" he said.

"How many people know where my locker is except guys on the team? Anyways. Don't worry. I'll get over it."

"I don't want this sort of thing happening. We're a team." He turned and left, and I tried to think who might have done it. Then, of course, those two freshman assholes I'd given hell yesterday in the shower. Why hadn't I thought of that sooner? I decided to wait, and then I called Paul over and asked him to help me watch them. He agreed. No matter how badly I wanted to, I couldn't sprint as fast or turn as quick, and I knew it was the drugs. I hadn't taken any Thorazine since yesterday, though I'd certainly considered it a couple times during the day.

At the end of practice, my body seemed to sag on my bones, and my mouth was like sand paper. In the shower, I glanced at the two freshmen from time to time and thought about Delores and Cape Cod. What a decision. But if things stayed the way they were, I had to do something different. Run or tough it out?

You'd have thought I'd done something personal to these people. I was sick, sick enough to go to a hospital and get help. Why did they have to treat me like I was grotesque or that they might catch it, or I didn't know what.

As I started George's car, I did know what caused some of it: my unpredictability. If he'd try and jump out a window, what might he try and do to me for no reason? That must be it.

Those signs really bothered me. It was one thing to think people were looking at me for indications of craziness, and another to see it printed out on a piece of paper.

At home, Dad seemed quieter than usual while we ate supper; Mom chatted away as usual.

"Something wrong, Dad?" I asked, as Mom cleared the table.

"No."

Mom looked at him.

"What?" I asked.

"Well, we might as well have all this out in the open," Dad said.

"All right." Mom sat at the table again.

"I went to estimate a roofing job today. The woman wants it done before snow flies. I mentioned that I'd get you to help me and we'd be sure and have it done." He pushed a piece of boiled potato around on his plate. "She didn't like it, Sam. Asked if I could find another helper."

"What did you say?"

Dad stared at me. "I told her you were as good a help as I could find. She said she'd probably get another estimate and let me know."

I wanted to start packing. All this small-town bullshit sucked. "I'm sorry, Dad." And I wondered again what it meant if my problems were passed down in the family—from my mother.

"No. I won't work for people like that," Dad said.

And I thought, yet you wouldn't come inside the hospital to visit me. "I'm going for a ride," I said.

I drove the long way around to Delores and my spot, and still arrived early. The trees were definitely at peak, and the yellow leaves on the birches were so yellow and bright in the early evening sunshine they hurt my eyes when I first got out of the car. Behind the rock, I shook the old rubbers off the cedar tree, and I had to shake the damn thing pretty hard to remove them all.

I walked around kicking up leaves, mixing the old brown ones with the new red, yellow, and orange, and the smell caused memories of every other fall. This one so complicated: every decision a royal pain in the ass.

I wanted time to move back or ahead, I didn't care which, so long as now was over.

I wanted a beer and checked the trunk. Empty, except for a blanket and a pair of George's old Converse sneakers, the tongues frayed and the bottoms almost smooth. It seemed he'd been gone ages, but Sunday would mark the first month. I wished he would write, except I hadn't either. Probably because I didn't want to lie, or hold back the truth, which was the same as lying between friends.

I remembered something else and checked the glove box for rubbers. They were there, and I thought maybe I should wear two at once. Then I looked again to where the others had hung in the trees, and George laughing so hard.

Then that other bunch of memories flooded in, and as if someone had pulled a trigger I could feel myself coming unbalanced. Stupid cowboys and Indian thoughts. Upset beyond logic. Unable to calm down and try to consider all that had happened in the past two weeks.

Delores came walking up the narrow road, almost a vision, the yellow leaves and the bright white birch trunks framed her like some picture in an expensive kid's book.

"I love you," she said over and over, and I knew that love helped her live, and I wasn't worth it. I wanted to say it back but didn't know if it was true. Certainty was not a part of me.

I let go of her, then lit a cigarette and asked what was in the bag.

"Beer," she said, and handed me one. "I didn't think a couple could hurt. Okay?"

"That's great." I opened one and chugged as much as I could hold.

"Our spot," she said, and walked over to the leaf-covered brook, now full again, gurgling and splashing over a dam of colors.

Gray lichens and green moss, white birches and yellow leaves all fit, and now I wanted time to stand still. I walked up behind Delores and wrapped my arms around her.

"The brook is so pretty," she said.

"Yes."

We took off all our clothes and used them for a blanket. I was so happy everything worked, and afterwards, relaxation set in like the gathering darkness. The release of sex better than anything in the past two weeks. Delores got the extra blanket out of the car and tucked us tightly into it, our two warmths one. "What about going away?" she asked and snuggled closer.

I told her about the other sign and the senior advisor, and even though I hated how they made me feel, I wasn't sure if I was over-reacting, or this was how anyone else with a mental problem would be treated. I opened another beer and knew I shouldn't. How many people had told me not too? Yet it helped, and I decided it was better to have a couple beers than take more Thorazine.

"How can people be like that?" Delores said. "Don't they think you had a rough enough time of it already?"

"I think today was as bad as the worst day at the hospital. People treat me like I've changed into something scary and unpredictable."

I hugged her tight. "I feel so good now. I need you, Delores."

She told me she needed me, too, and that people wouldn't leave her alone either, parents still bitching about her stupidity, especially her wanting to get married, ruin her life, and the other girls at school a pain too.

"How? Tell me," I said.

"Some of them think I should stay away from you. What business is it of theirs, what I want?"

She raised her voice. "Who the hell are they to tell me what to do. I'm tired of people telling me what to do."

We sat up and talked about that for a few minutes, and it surprised me to understand how hard it had been for her since the abortion, and it pissed me off I hadn't understood that before now.

I saw the stars above in the cold black sky, but our heat and closeness kept us warm. All the bad things seemed far away, and I was like a child with no worries or cares.

I opened another beer, and we shared it along with a cigarette. A whippoorwill called from a long distance, almost out of hearing. Then again, and all was quiet except the movement of water beside us.

"Sam, we can't meet like this very often. You know that."

The light reflected from the small pool beside us.

"Why not?"

"They'll find out."

"Delores, if we run away, it's for good. At least for me. You thought of that?"

"Yes. And we'll stay together. Work at the commune, and if we don't like that we'll do something else."

"I don't think it's that simple."

"Okay. Then tell me this." She reached out for my hands. "How much longer can you stand what happened today?"

"Maybe it will get better. It's fear, you know. They're afraid of mental illness, craziness." I swallowed more beer, then handed the can to her.

"We have been apart for two terrible times when we could have helped each other." She finished the beer and threw the can away. "I don't want it to happen again!"

"Lay it on the line to your father."

"I have. Oh, have I."

"What's he say?"

"That you should be in jail already."

"But he doesn't want everybody to know you had an abortion, and people would find out that's why I was in jail."

"He doesn't want us together at all and he won't listen to anything else, especially now after . . ."

"Yeah. After Sam's been in a nuthouse. Goddammit!"

"No one can keep us apart when I turn sixteen next year. We can get married."

"I don't know," I said. "It's all too much too soon."

We didn't say anything for a minute and the silky water trickling over the leaf dams sent us a calming music.

"Let's give it a week, and then decide one way or the other."

"All right," Delores said, and hugged me. "I love you. And it's okay if you don't say it back, I know you do, and you're afraid if you say it you can't ever take it back."

"How'd you get so smart?"

She didn't answer, just gave me a smug look.

Lois drove in a few minutes later, the headlights blinding us. We showed her around the place and she liked it very much.

Lois said, "I called the commune tonight and Dennis said they could use two new members. I told them you were twenty, Sam, and Delores eighteen."

"We're going to wait one more week," I said.

"You'd like them. Either of you seen the ocean before?" Neither of us had.

"Oh, wait till you see it." She hugged herself, and said, "The dunes, and the color of the waves in the sun. I'll come visit during Christmas vacation if you go."

Delores squeezed my hand. "It's late," she said.

We kissed, and then they left. I sat against the big rock next to the brook and drank the last three beers and thought of what might happen if we ran away. Was I losing or regaining those bits of soul chipped away?

# CHAPTER 31

During the next week, all that had happened my first day back at school magnified from bad to worse. So bad at times that I longed for the hospital. Thorazine cut the edges of my awareness, but not enough to mask the obvious strange and sometimes mean treatment I received from those around me. I also had another run in with the guidance counselor; he wanted to know if I'd been to the clinic. He told me I should go, hinted that if I didn't I'd be kicked out of school, and I told him I could take care of myself.

But I did make an appointment and saw the psychiatrist on Wednesday, Dr. Randall. He thought I was doing fine and gave me another prescription for Thorazine. He thought I could discontinue the lithium in a month and take a less powerful tranquilizer. I tried to describe to him what happened every day at school.

"It's stigma, Sam," he said. "Seems like it always happens. A very unfortunate thing to go through after a stay in the hospital. I'm sure you agree." He leaned across his desk waiting for a reply.

"What can I do to stop it?"

"It should lessen with time. Try and ignore it as much as possible."

Not much help here either, I thought as I left his office. And right then and there I resolved to leave. I went home and wrote George a long letter telling him where I'd been, and what had happened since I'd come home, of Lois's help, and where Delores and I were going. I included, "I believe I'll go crazy again if I stay, and that is too horrible to imagine. Please try to understand, though I know that may not be possible."

The next day, a week from the day we'd said the decision to go or stay would be decided, Delores sneaked out of her house at midnight, a bulging suitcase in each hand. She tried to trot down the driveway, just like in a movie I'd seen long ago. I loaded the suitcases into the back seat, pushed the car silently down the road, then dumped the clutch and off we went, tuned exhaust purring into the night.

I'd changed nights with Bob that afternoon and took all the money from the cash register after I closed, leaving Billy a note that I'd start to pay him back as soon as I could. Several times during the week I'd tried to explain to him how everything had changed since leaving the hospital, and he kept saying I seemed fine to him. He obviously didn't want to talk about it.

Delores described the letter she'd left for her parents; she begged them not to try and find us, that we'd come back in a year, married and happy, if only they would leave us alone now.

We held hands in the darkness as we crossed the Hudson River, and less than an hour later we were in Massachusetts.

"I can't wait to see the ocean," Delores said.

"It's not too late to turn around."

"We'll be fine. I know it."

And really, for the first time, I thought we just might. A new start in a place where no one knew I'd been sick.

I pushed my back against the seat and stared down a long straight stretch of road on the Mass. Pike. Again that thought: she is so young.

I'd left a letter for my parents, too, and said I'd call from time to time, and asked that they try and put themselves in my place. Dad wouldn't understand. Mom would cry and be afraid for me. That caused a fear to grow in me, and I stopped at the next rest area and hugged Delores close. I was afraid that I was throwing my life away. Stigma and a disease maybe passed from my mother. Something triggered by stress.

"Maybe we should go back, Delores. No one will know we left. What about college for me, high school for you?"

"I don't want to go back. Isn't it enough we're together?"

"I want it to be."

"Good. Then it will."

As I drove down the ramp back onto the highway, Delores asked me about my supply of pills, and I told her the shrink had said he'd probably take me off the lithium in a month or so and I had enough Thorazine to last for quite a while if I took them only when necessary.

She gripped my arm. "I think we're doing the right thing." She went on to tell me how hard it had been since the abortion, and I told her I thought some of the stigma directed to me had gone to her as well. "We couldn't stay at home any longer," she said, projecting her jaw forward. But I think both of us knew it was questionable, and that a good many things could go wrong.

By four-thirty, light in the eastern sky began, and an hour later we caught our first whiffs of the ocean. The smell of salty air seemed to dry my nose, and I thought of the clean river water flowing over smooth stones. When would I see it again? Such a central part of my life. Running off to live with a fifteen-year-old in a commune. If we were caught, I was caught; they'd probably lock me up and forget I ever existed.

Delores had fallen asleep. I slowed the car and took long looks at her in the brightening light of dawn. The fact that she wanted to run away with me, be with me, was difficult to understand, unless she was just too young to know what she was doing, or maybe she hated people knowing about the abortion as much as I hated the stigma of mental illness.

I wished I knew what love really was and began to remember the past as the sun peeked over the horizon, a blinding light. I squinted and flipped down the visor. Maybe all I'd ever done was want, and want unfairly, unreasonably. I wanted George to be my best friend, but at first the years between us stopped that, and then when we overcame that problem, I created another by wanting to pay him back after he saved me. And Delores. First, I wanted her for my girlfriend, then I wanted her to have sex with me, then she was pregnant, and not long after that I couldn't decide whether I wanted her to have the child or not, then I was so sad after the abortion and after George was gone that I think maybe I wanted to go crazy. I'd certainly fulfilled that wish.

Another smell of ocean came in through the slightly open window, more of a decaying smell, I thought. Maybe I didn't know what I really wanted, but I certainly was sure of what I did not want: to be treated as different, an outcast, a mental patient, a crazy person. I hated those labels.

From time to time during this week I'd felt like I was being stared at through binoculars from the wrong end, scrutinized to see if I would do the expected or unexpected. Is he normal or not normal? Predictable or dangerous, and I'd really tried my best to absorb all this scrutiny by ignoring it; business as usual. You know, Sam the senior, the soccer player, the guy with a pretty girlfriend that plans to go to college next year. A regular guy. Impossible though, when the stigmatizing judgments came from all directions. Except for two people: Delores and Lois. They acted like I'd had a problem, went to have it taken care of and was on my way back to normal. That was the truth, and I believe that is exactly what would have happened if others hadn't surrounded me with fear and mistrust and treated me with a strangeness that I'd done nothing to deserve, except go to a mental institution.

Now Delores and I were running away. We crossed a small stream and the brackish smell of the water came through the window so strongly it woke Delores.

So pretty. She rubbed her eyes with the backs of her hands, then sniffed the air. "We must be close, Sam." She gripped my thigh. "Aren't you tired?" She brushed back her hair.

"No. I want to see the ocean."

We'd been off the turnpike for perhaps twenty miles and a few minutes later we went over a bridge that connected the Cape to the main land; in the distance we could see a vast expanse of water. Ocean. I wanted to stop. It kind of took my breath away, but morning traffic surrounded us, and they didn't have shoulders on the roads, but concrete lips and I didn't want to chance messing up George's car.

We took the next exit and not long after that I parked in an almost empty lot, the nose of George's car pointing at the ocean. The blinding sun was directly in our eyes as we walked down the beach holding hands. The whispers and crashes of the waves became more distinct the closer we came to the water, and the gulls cried overhead as they searched for food.

This will heal me. So much more complicated, but simpler, too, than the river. The river back home, a home I'd never been so far from.

At the water's edge Delores and I stood and stared across the tops of the waves. I tried to imagine Viet Nam and George there in not so long a time. Even though the ocean was loud, it was very peaceful. It's rhythm like a mystical music; river waves magnified a hundred times. A music for healing me. Delores was captured by it too, and I couldn't believe we were the only ones on this beach. She shielded her eyes from the sun, then bent and reached her fingers into the foamy depths of a small wave.

"Cold, Sam." She touched the salt to her lips and smiled. "Taste it," she said, then kissed me with her cold salty lips.

We laughed and walked along the beach, arms around each others' waist.

"We will want to see the ocean every day," she said. "Lois told me from the place we'll live the beach is a five-minute walk."

"If we went home now the memory of this short time here with you seeing the ocean for the first time would probably be worth all the trouble."

Delores answered by pinching my sides and giving me a kiss, and that reminded me how much weight I'd lost, how little I'd eaten since going into the hospital.

The beach remained almost deserted except for a few people out jogging or taking their dogs for a walk. I went back to the car for a sleeping bag, and, at the foot of one of the dunes that Delores said looked like cookie dough mounds, we fell asleep.

I woke up to Delores snoring; quick little gasps, then a long wheeze. I wanted to stay alone with her for a few days. We might be able to find a cheap motel at this time of the year. And that's what we did.

Up the coast a ways we found a cottage with a kitchenette for fifteen dollars a night. I paid with Billy's money and was quite sure he would understand. Still, as usual, those twinges of guilt bothered me.

Those two nights and three days were like every honeymoon should be. We didn't talk about the past very much or why we were really here. We acted adult, like kids playing house maybe, but under quite different circumstances. Delores cooked our dinners on the small gas range. The first night we had steamed shrimp and hot dogs. We slept till ten the next morning, our first night ever sleeping together. We walked in bare feet on the beach and splashed in the water until our feet were numb with ocean cold.

I fell in love with Delores Prairie during three short days. Maybe I'd been on the edge of it for a long time, or maybe this was the perfect situation for it to happen, but an instinct pegged this as love, a truth I'd been searching for all my life.

While she slept, I wrote a letter to George about the ocean and my new found love for Delores. And other things, like what kind of rifle he carried and how much I wanted to see him before he left.

# CHAPTER 32

On the third morning, Monday, we packed up and checked out. Delores said, "One of us had better call home, don't you think?"

"I guess," and that spoiled the spell of the last few days, since we'd left really it had all been like a fairy tale, and now the true situation came back, the uncertainty of it all.

I stopped at a small store, and while Delores went into the phone booth, I went inside to buy a pack of cigarettes. Then I sat in the car and smoked and waited. The scrub brush and sand, air and sky, everything about the Cape Cod landscape so different from anything I'd expected, almost moonlike, alien.

Delores got into the car. "That bad?"

She nodded. "Mom is very very upset, and Dad hired a lawyer. They've got the cops looking all over for us."

I slid down in the seat and felt conspicuous in George's souped up Mustang with racing stripes and New York plates.

"Did your Mom say anything about my parents?"

"That they're worried and your father blames himself."

"Sure he does," and then I knew that wasn't fair.

"Should we go back, Sam?"

"No," I said and stared into the weather-twisted-limbs of a small tree in front of us. I turned to face Delores. "Do you want to go back? Do you think it will be any better?"

"No. I want us to be close like the last few days."

"I'd like that too, Delores. Let's go to the commune and see what that's like."

"Okay." We awkwardly hugged across the bucket seats and shifting lever, then went on our way, sure a cop would zoom up behind us at any second.

I didn't think Delores was telling me everything that had been said on the phone. She had her chin set in that stubborn way. I reached for her hand.

"You haven't told me everything."

"No."

"C'mon."

"Dad says you kidnapped me."

"What?" If I hadn't been on a four-lane highway I'd have skidded to a stop. "What?" I yelled.

"Mom said if we didn't come home immediately he was going to file charges."

"Well, Jesus Christ! Didn't you tell them the truth?"

"You know my father."

Now I knew what I'd hear from my parents when I called. Shit and damn. I couldn't imagine sitting in a jail cell, going to court. Kidnapping. I'd get years. Holy shit.

"They'll never find us if we hide the car," she said. "Lois won't tell."

"Let's get to that commune and see what's up, then we'll call Lois."

Half an hour later, Delores saw the exit for the town and then we found the street. We weren't far from Provincetown at the end of the Cape. The old two-story house was exactly as Lois had described it, in need of paint and many other repairs. We parked around the back. On the back porch, a guy I guessed to be in his thirties sat in a rocking chair, his hair to the middle of his chest. He looked exactly like every hippie I'd imagined. Cutoff jeans frayed and paint-spotted, love beads, copper bracelet. It didn't seem possible. We got out of the car.

"Welcome," he said. "I'm Dennis. You must be Sam and Delores." He gave us the peace sign, kind of reverently I thought. I waved, and Delores said hello.

"Lois called a couple times and sounded a little worried that you hadn't arrived yet."

"Can I use the phone?"

"Right inside on the left." He began rocking back and forth slow, smiling at Delores as I walked past and inside. I saw a wooden bowl beside him full of pot and rolled up joints.

"Hello, Lois?"

"Yes. Oh, God, Sam. What a mess."

"Tell me."

"Both Delores and your parents think I know where you are."

"Why?"

"Because lately Delores and I have hung out together so much. Sam, they even called George and asked him if you'd written him about it."

"Great."

"It's worse than we ever thought it would be. Everyone's talking about it in school. The cops even went to see Billy."

"Shit. Shit."

"Sam, you better come home."

"To what, Lois? Now I'm a nut and a criminal. Come home to handcuffs and the jail, or the nuthouse?" Another piece of soul vibrated with anxiety.

"Sam?" she paused.

I thought of the distance Delores and I had come, the fun and feelings of the past three days.

"Sam, are you there?"

"Yeah."

If you sent Delores home, everything would be much better. I'm sorry. I'm the one who suggested you leave."

"You really think they'll find us."

"Not for a while. They seem to think you haven't gone far from here. You know her father is a sonofabitch. You wouldn't believe the way he talked to me. Cursing and yelling that he'd get me too, if I didn't tell what part I had in it."

"I don't think Delores will go."

"She'll do what you tell her. Have her call me if she won't."

For the next few seconds all I could think of was the Thorazine in my knap sack. Too much. It all hit me like the roar of a train coming into a station, noise blotting out all thought. A wave of instability, bordering on insanity, sank into me and I didn't have any answers. Anger, pain, love, all combined into madness. "I'll call you back, Lois."

"I'll wait," she said.

I pushed out the door, past Delores and Dennis who stood there talking, smoking a joint. I reached through the car's open window into my knap sack for the pills, swallowed a whole Thorazine.

Delores came up behind me, saw the pill bottle in my hand, the expression on my face.

"What did Lois say?"

"Never mind for now."

I walked back to the porch, stared up at the guy, Dennis. "Where is the ocean?"

He pointed his thumb in the direction of the front of the house, and I started walking.

I heard him say, "Far out," to Delores, who'd started to follow me.

"No," I said. "Please. I have to think by myself."

Two blocks away, the ocean came into view, and a few minutes later I sat with my back against a dune, out of the wind. I stared out over the waves, and again imagined Viet Nam and blood and guts and the racket of gunfire. I'll sign up, I thought.

Then it came to me that I was probably ineligible because of being a nuthouse convict. I'd be labeled defective or something like that. Incompetent. Manic-depressive.

The Thorazine started to work. It was the first whole one I'd taken since I left the hospital. Like the way water and powdered Jell-O firmed up in the fridge, that's the way it worked. Yeah. I smiled a little, felt my body weight kind of sag on my bones. I must have sat there for half an hour and the options got fewer and fewer, and what it came down to was I had to save my own ass. I was eighteen and had kidnapped a fifteen-year-old.

What a mess. Just when a spark of love had really got a good start, I had to send Delores away. Squash it before it squashed me in a prison cell somewhere. Send her back.

I stared at the ocean, loving it, too, and wanting Delores to stay, and I imagined all of the likely consequences.

I walked down to the water's edge. All the bubbles that remained after each wave receded fascinated me and I knelt down and could hear their popping. What a wonderful place, I thought, as I rested my knees on the cold, water-saturated sand.

I stared out at the waves, huge from this angle, and I did not want to go any place for a long time, and imagined myself toppling over, lying on the beach in a curled-up position as the tide came in. No more stupid decisions. When was the last time I'd made a right one?

I sat back on my heels, hands clasped below my knees. What about Delores? I'd fallen in love and there must be a way to stay together. I tried to extract myself from the Thorazine haze, and it was very difficult. I moved up the beach, the salt breeze strong against my left side. Alone, like this. Maybe I had to do whatever it was I had to do alone, and I laughed at that. So hard to make good sense. George had gone away, and now Delores would have to ride a stinky old bus back the way we'd come. I walked into the ocean up to my knees. Naturally, I had to save my own ass, an instinct like that of some crazy cave man searching for food in the dead of winter. Or a young man considering suicide. The truth.

# CHAPTER 33

I walked back and forth on the beach for over an hour and remembered part of a Frost poem from elementary school, "And miles to go before I sleep." Then I sat on the same dune where I had when I'd first come down to the beach, my position in the sand eroded by the wind, blown into a weird shape. I smushed my butt around and tried to remember how long George had been gone, and decided five weeks, and I wanted to talk to him so bad, hear him bitch me out.

Later at the house, Delores and I sat in the car. Dennis had gone inside.

"You have to go back, Delores. They'll find us and put me in jail if you don't. I can't be on the run forever." There, I'd said it, and I could tell already by the way she stared out the windshield that she knew we had no other choice. I started the car and drove toward the town.

"I'll never see you again."

"That's not true."

It might be, though, and I remembered my attempt to leap out the window, and the urges at the beach.

"Can't we go home together?"

"I prefer the ocean, at least till things calm down."

"I'll make him promise not to do anything."

"You could try, but we both know it won't work."

This had been a hopeless idea from the start. What parent would allow their fifteen-year old daughter to run away with a mental patient who'd recently gotten her pregnant. They'd search for years. Shit and shit and shit, those stupid words skipped through my mind with their endless meanings. A bus crossed in front of us at the next intersection and I followed it. It stopped at the Provincetown bus station.

"What will you do?" Delores asked, then hiccupped.

"Stay at the commune for a while, try and find a job."

She hiccupped again.

"I still have over two hundred dollars."

She dug in her purse. "Here's another hundred."

"Where'd you get that?"

"Mom's 'pin money' she calls it."

"No. Give it back."

"No, Sam!" she yelled, and I parked a little way down the street from the bus station and shut off the motor. She hiccupped and covered her mouth. "I'm worried. I'm sad. I'm scared. And these damn fucking hiccups!"

I don't think I'd ever heard her use that word before. "Wait here," I said. "I'll go find out about the bus."

One left in ten minutes for Albany, the man behind the counter said, and I bought a ticket.

Back at the car I said, "Ten minutes."

"I want more time."

"You'll be home by nine or ten and back in school tomorrow morning."

She stepped out of the car.

"Seems hard to believe," I said, more to myself than her.

"Sam, will you be all right without me? Please call Lois and let her know what's going on."

She stepped out of the car and hugged me so tight I was sure it had gotten rid of her hiccups. Then she kissed me and hiccupped against my lips.

"I love you very much, Delores."

"Oh, Sam. It's so good to hear you say it. How has all this happened?"

"I wish I knew." From inside me deep rumblings seemed about to erupt.

"Let me know when the heat is off from your parents. I'll come home and play basketball and you'll be on the cheerleading squad. All like it's supposed to be." I laughed a little and she smiled, her hazel eyes bright, and the whites surrounding them like the tips of a breaking wave.

"We'll never have it like it's supposed to be," she said.

A bus pulled in belching black diesel fumes and we knew it must be hers. We walked through the station holding hands, each of us carrying one of her suitcases.

"Tell my parents I'm fine," I said. "I may not call them for a while."

"I hate this." She stamped her foot.

"I know. I sure do." One more hug and a kiss, then I watched Delores step into the bus and I helped the driver shove her bags in the underneath compartment. As the bus pulled away I could barely make out Delores' face beside the fingers of one hand. The green-tinted glass reminded me of the ocean's color.

I wanted to go back home.

The people at the commune were nice to me, except I couldn't ever quite figure out what they meant most of the time. "Cool" could be good or bad, depending on how you said it, and so could "far out." It was difficult for me to figure out because of their Boston way of speaking, and the fact that I didn't know them very well. Their free love thing didn't seem to be working that great either. Six guys and four girls lived in the house, and at times the tension between certain individuals was quite visible. Someone would say "wow," and that might mean bad things were happening, or just that they were stoned.

I bought a bag of groceries every two or three days and helped with the cleaning and stayed away from the women.

The ocean was a better listener than the river at home because it drowns out my spoken words and some of my thoughts; at home the river seemed to send them back. At times I thought the ocean was trying to tell me something, the waves punctuating my words like exclamation points or question marks at just the precise time. I spent almost every afternoon in all kinds of weather down at the beach. Talking and listening. The craziness a black shroud. I became absorbed with thinking about my soul.

After I'd considered and re-considered the past, what it all came down to was trying to figure out mental illness. By now I was sure I had it, this unbalanced, at times petrifying fear, and an almost itchy longing for death at times. I'd been on Cape Cod for a week and taken Thorazine three out of the seven days, and I didn't think that was too bad. Six of the pills still rattled in the bottle, and it was like a race to get my head together before they ran out.

I'd called home and talked to Mom, and surprisingly she'd seemed to understand, and I think both her and Dad knew the pain of my illness in their own way. Before we hung up, Mom said, "I love you," and said she would send a little money if I needed it. She also added that Billy had called and said not to worry about the money I'd borrowed.

For the next few days I had a pretty good grip on what had happened, was happening, the ocean like a cherry lifesaver that never dissolved. The worst times were when I thought about going home. The lithium had run out, and I took the Thorazine at the worst times only, and unfortunately during the next week they started to increase. I'd talked to Delores twice when she was at Lois's and the distance overshadowed the love I'd felt when we were together.

After my first time, I kind of knew what going crazy was about, and to a degree could control it, at least in certain aspects. I let go a part of the craziness when I talked to the ocean. It was so new to me that my memories and thoughts, when directed toward it, twisted, and exaggerated in strange ways. I'd sit and dig my heels into the sand and mush my ass around and imagine I was in a special chair ready for a rocking journey. Then I'd let it begin.

Maybe I'd start thinking about something George and I used to do, like damming up the ditches in the spring, and from there it would move into us riding our inner tubes down the river. I'd rock back and forth on the beach, imitating the swells in front of me, and call out over the ocean to George, imagining him in the stern of a life boat and Delores at the oars. Or I'd imagine the waves frozen still, the peaks and the froth, everything brittle: me and George playing tag on the steep sides, whooping, and leaping over the crests. Jump and slide. Jump and slide. And those damn whippoorwills.

When I'd come out of it, the ocean in its October coldness seemed positive, if unpredictable, like a constant friend, capable of anything. And I wondered what George thought of me now, and what he'd say in his next letter, or when I next saw him, and the possibility of never seeing him hit me with the force of a huge wave.

I'd again imagine playing cowboys and Indians, and my near loss of life. That usually snapped me like a bowstring pulled until it broke, stinging.

Several days later all the pills were gone, and I started to spend money on beer and whiskey. The next week seemed like one long day, and the people at the commune knew I was not with it, but they were in such a mood of 'do your own thing' that they didn't bother me.

One of the guys, Amos, tall and skinny in his mid-thirties quizzed me one day for about an hour. We smoked joints continuously. He thought mental illness must be a weird "trip" and asked all about it. I described how I talked and listened to the ocean and after the inevitable "far out" he stared out the window for a minute, then said he thought I should just let the brain "do its thing, man."

I couldn't sleep for more than two hours at a time and had to do what Amos suggested. Irrationality took over like the nor'easters the hippies said would hit any day now that November was here. Was it? Must be. Someone had flipped the calendar in the kitchen.

One day I started to count the grains of sand on the beach, tired of this, and started counting handfuls, digging in the sand like a dog searching for a bone.

After maybe five more days of drinking and no food, little sleep, Dennis asked me if I needed help, and I couldn't speak; I was that fucked up. He called an ambulance. At the public hospital they thought I was on drugs—LSD or peyote—parts of this time gray.

A doctor examined me, and then they led me to the mental wing, took all my personal stuff and asked tons of questions. I admitted I'd gone off the lithium and ran out of Thorazine and the nurse went away with a satisfied expression on her face, like she'd solved a puzzle.

That first night after they'd given me an injection they asked if I wanted to call anyone, and at first, I thought of Delores, but she seemed far away, and then I called Lois because she seemed so close.

"Hello," she said. "Sam, is that you?"

"It's me. How's things?"

"Sam, George is coming home. Only for two days. He'll be here tomorrow!"

"No." I looked around for an escape, then tried like hell to act normal, push the heavy block of unreason away.

"Let's meet halfway. He wants to see you before he goes. He's . . . he's different now, I think."

I laughed a little, then said, "Well, he'll be surprised to see me." I faced the wall. "If I can get out of here."

"Where are you, Sam?"

"Don't worry."

A nurse tapped me on the shoulder, then tapped her watch. If she'd been blond I'd have told her to go fuck herself and could clearly see that bitch Alice from the other hospital.

"I'll call you tomorrow morning, Lois." I hung up.

"Everything okay?" the nurse asked, her clothes so white and stiff she seemed fake.

"Fine. Thank you," I said, and went to sit on a couch and try to think this over logically, carefully. Why couldn't I have known this yesterday?

It was after dinner when I'd called Lois, and now I had to find a way out. The shot they'd given helped. I needed information. I asked a guy in the chair next to me for a cigarette, then asked what his troubles were, and how long he'd been here; the usual line of bullshit. Then the big question: what happens when they close the place up for the night. He moved away a little. "They hook all the doors up to alarms."

"Oh," I said. "To hell with it."

Then I decided to go home. Fuck 'em all, I told myself. At least I'll see George, and afterward they can lock me up for as long as they want. In either place.

I walked to the main desk and asked a nurse if I could have my wallet a second, so I could copy down a phone number. When she wasn't looking I took all the money out except a few ones and handed it back.

Shit, I thought. Should have taken my license. "Could I just check that again." She gave me a sour look but handed it back and I removed the license.

Ten minutes later I was out the doors and down the stairs, running faster than I imagined I could, almost expecting to be shot in the back. "I'm coming, George," I whispered and pumped my knees higher, really stretching out my strides.

Twenty minutes later, after running and walking, dodging into hedges and behind trees, I made it to the center of town and flagged a taxi. He let me off a block away from the commune. I reached up under the front bumper and found the extra ignition key in a little magnetic box. An hour later, I was off the Cape, wide-eyed, drinking beer and ready. For what, I wasn't sure.

I just felt ready.

# CHAPTER 34

Great lengths of straight road on the Mass. Pike stretched out before me. To hang on to some sense I had to keep drinking beer, and I tried to pace myself. So many things had happened so quickly that it seemed a hole of some sort opened up in every direction I tried to figure out. Nothing sure. That hospital probably had the Massachusetts State cops looking for me, Delores father had the New York State police out to get me. George was coming home, and I had no safe place to go. I just couldn't think, and slowly and steadily drank one beer after the other. Looking for something, an answer, a way out, and though I knew it was useless, I had to go back home.

Later on, I didn't know what time, I got off an exit and paid my toll, expecting trouble. But the toll booth attendant was half asleep, and I took the first dirt road I could find, then a logging road and finally shut the car off in a grove of beech trees, big ones. The beer had done me in, and finally, gratefully, I slept.

Something woke me up, and the ghostly light of dawn came in through the breath-fogged windows. Two whippoorwills, one on each side of the car, and not very far away. Was I dreaming? I rolled down the window, wiped the windshield with the back of my hand.

At first their cries reminded me of home with George in the tree house, then a third one landed on the hood, and its song was so loud it hurt my ears. I couldn't move. It went right through me and its cadence, along with the other two that joined in, sounded to me like the rounds we used to sing in elementary school: Row Row Row Your Boat. I heard it as different groups singing, "Whip or will," and "Whip your will," and "Whip will," and the fact snapped into me that I'd been whipping myself, my will, my soul.

It drove me out of the car screaming at the top of my lungs for them to shut up. The one flew off the hood and the others stopped, but not for long.

I leaned against the car, thinking and thinking, and hating the insanity that overwhelmed me. Whip your will, and it is truth, and I knew it was truth, and I wanted to laugh and cry and scream. If there had been a window to jump through, I'd have been gone.

Three beers left. I chugged the first two so fast the beer dribbled down my chin. "Whip or will," the birds sang, and then it made sense in another way. Either whip yourself like I'd been doing over things I'd caused myself or with someone else but could do nothing about now; or use my Will to control and move ahead. I sipped the last beer. A whippoorwill's truth? No way. This was crazy.

I smoked cigarette after cigarette as the day lightened, and the whippoorwills sang on. What will George think of me? Lois had said he'd changed and I couldn't imagine that. Then I did have to laugh, as I stared at myself in the rearview mirror, hair in all directions, streaks of sweat through dirt on my face. Hell, since he'd gone, I'd been crazy twice, and now I was coming home, too. Had I changed deep inside, or was it just the illness?

The birds stopped their chant as the sun broke over the ridge, and their flutter of wings almost seemed fake, like flipping a deck of cards back and forth for sound effects. I'd wanted them to stay. Could they mean so much? My grandfather had told me that if you spread a white sheet on the lawn when you heard a whippoorwill it would come and sing on it.

We'd never done it though. I'd never heard more than two whippoorwills so close together, and any of the strangeness in my life that had seemed about to straighten itself out folded up into a complicated mess of wrinkles and bends. My mind seemed headed for a blackness like the tiny hole of a railroad tunnel from a long ways off. More beer.

By nine o'clock I was twenty minutes from home in a gas station. I figured Lois had stayed home from school to pick up George. I was right. She answered on the second ring.

"Where are you, Sam?"

"Not far. What time is George coming home?"

"Noon. Listen, Sam. You didn't give me a chance to tell you last night. Delores' father has decided not to press charges. Something happened."

"Like what?"

"Delores told me her mother threatened to leave him if he didn't drop the whole thing."

"Can I see Delores?"

"I'm not sure."

"Jesus, something good," I whispered, and wanted to see Delores.

"What did you say?"

"Nothing. Can you get Delores out of school and bring her to the birches?"

"I don't know. Where are you?"

"Twenty minutes from home."

"Holy shit. You really took a chance. Well, I'll try and catch her in math class. I'll have to hurry."

"Great. I'll be waiting."

I picked up a case of cold Budweiser then drove the back roads slowly toward our spot and imagined cold yellow beer waves running far up the beach, scooping them up by the mug full.

So much had happened in such a short time. A trip with a girl and love found after so long, only to end with the threat of jail, again. Then the ocean, its impossible vastness and beauty and a reprieve. It did not seem possible that anyone's life could actually be like this, that a mind could take such control. I wanted it to stop for one week, or even a day, to see what normal was like. But my mind raced on up and over, back and forth over all the things which had happened and ended where I was now, and it wouldn't stop, like old black and white film chattering too quick through the projector. And the cries of those whippoorwills seemed to penetrate everything because at every instance I had been whipping myself, willing myself to the impossible: pay back George, undo Delores' pregnancy, abortion. Yet, too, in a way this bird encounter was a good thing because it helped me distill all the problems into something simple like a whippoorwill song, which I'd known my whole life.

Lois' car was already parked in the birch grove as I drove up the narrow path. She opened the car door and got out, then was in my arms. For the brief seconds I'd seen her face she looked different, older, worried.

"Sam, I'm so sorry. I just missed her, and I didn't know how I could get her out of Math class." She gripped my shoulders and stared at my face. "I'm glad to see you," she said.

I offered her a beer and she shook her head, no. I opened a fresh one for myself. "Medication," I said. "Ran out of the other stuff."

"Delores said she liked the Cape."

"Too bad she had to leave."

We couldn't seem to talk, and I walked around the birch grove, almost all the yellow leaves off the limbs, then at the same time we said each other's name.

"I'm so worried, and so is Delores. You hardly ever called, and you weren't at the commune most of the time when she did call."

"I needed time to think. Most of the time I was at the ocean."

"I'm sorry," she said. "That's not a good enough excuse."

I thought she was kidding. "So you're mad at me?"

"Yes."

"Delores?"

"Yes. Can't you imagine what it's been like for her at home, and then the person she loves acts like they don't give a damn."

"You're right." I lit a cigarette and walked up behind her.

"I called you from a nuthouse last night, then ran away after you told me George was coming home."

"Are they after you?"

"You mean the men with the white coats." I laughed. "No, I don't think so."

"How did you get there in the first place?"

"I think I had another psychotic episode. I couldn't speak for a couple hours." After a long swallow of beer, "This mental illness stuff is not easy to explain. I wish I could, especially to you and Delores, and George.

Anyways, I think I'll be all right when I go back on the pills. For now, the beer will do."

I pointed the top of the bottle at her. "I'm not telling George. If I can keep it together for the next two days, he's home, he won't have to go off worrying about me locked up in some mental ward."

"You're going back to the Cape?" She reached into the car for a beer.

"Being crazy is awfully strange. The first time was easier because it snuck up on me like a ghost, something unbelievable, unknown. But now, I can kind of explain it, see it almost, and chug beers when it gets real close." I kicked the tire, drank a little more beer. "I'll probably have to go to the state hospital after George leaves. That private one, I don't know, it didn't work."

She leaned against me and hugged me again.

"Thanks, Lois."

"You're welcome, Sam." She stepped back and stared at me, shook her head a little.

"Do I look that bad?"

"Not good."

"I'll wash up in the brook."

"Are you going to stay here until George leaves?"

"Sure. Where else?"

"Can I suggest something?"

"Sure."

"You might want to clean up the car a little."

"Jesus, you're right. George will kick my ass." I started by heaving out beer cans and other trash, then tried to sweep out the beach sand and ashes with a rag, and of course, it was hopeless. I couldn't stop the tears then, and the thought of a wrist-size tree limb in my hand, bent double to almost the breaking point fit my tension. I leaned against the car, gazed along its salt grimy side.

"Don't worry," Lois said, and patted my shoulder. "Wipe it off with a towel. I won't be back for two hours."

She left a few minutes later, and I gave up on the car five after that. I sat down next to the brook. Back again. From this to that to the other. Brook to river to ocean. Tiny slivers of frost ice clung to the banks still in shadow, and again I imagined ocean waves frozen tight, at the breaking point, white foam as white as Delores' eyes, caught, stilled in bright sunshine. Then slowly melting.

I must have slept for a while, and the next thing I heard was a car coming up the narrow road and George's face peering out the windshield, his arm at a crooked angle on his head.

I stood up and waved, then swiped at the water and rubbed my face with the dirty wet palm of my hand. The water, numbing cold.

George got out of the car, Lois waved, then backed out.

We shook hands then awkwardly put our arms around each other and patted backs, like old men in Italian movies, I thought. I could smell myself and knew he could too. I couldn't remember the last time I'd showered.

"Holy shit, Sam, what's going on?"

"Sometimes I'm not real sure." I half smiled. "At other times I do okay. What's with you? All dressed up in your soldier suit."

I walked to the passenger side of his car and tossed him a beer and opened one for myself. He ran his finger through the salty haze on the car. "Fuckin' A, Sam, is this the car I loaned you?" He looked at me and I tried to smile, and knew he was thinking I wasn't the same person he'd last seen either.

"Tell me about the army," I said.

"It sucks most of the time. I'm glad I joined, though."

"Good. They wouldn't take me now. Maybe if I lied."

"Probably not." He tilted his head back to drink, and under the brim of his hat I could see where they'd buzzed all his hair away. He looked more compact, tighter and sinewy.

"Tell me how you ended up in the hospital. I won't be here long, so none of your bullshit. Truth."

"I snapped. Nervous breakdown. Too much stress." I wanted to pound my fist into the car roof. "All of those, maybe none of those. It may be genetic. The fucking doctors don't know nothing."

"Well, you look like hell. That's the truth, and you smell, too."

"Thanks. Any other helpful comments?"

"Maybe. Running away with Delores. What were you thinking? Lois tells me now you're off the hook again with her old man. You are one lucky sonofabitch."

"I suppose you'd throw me in jail."

"No. You know how a redneck like her father can be."

"Sure do. My father wouldn't even step into the hospital to see me."

"I saw guys in basic lose it under the pressure. The sergeants are relentless. You don't want unstable people in combat."

"That definitely lets me out." And told him I was fighting on two fronts, the illness and the stigma.

George stepped closer. "What's it like?" he whispered, then swallowed the rest of his beer.

I sensed our friendship coming closer, like magnets attracting.

"Very confusing. Pretty lonely," I said.

"Can't they give you medicine?" He reached up to push back hair he didn't have, then took off his hat.

"They did. It helped. Going back to school was quite the experience."

"Lois wrote me about the signs in your locker and other stuff."

"You can't imagine what treatment like that does to your insides. Like ripping a piece of paper into a hundred pieces, knowing the impossibility of ever taping them all back together."

"So what's next?" He reached past me for another beer. He reminded me of a professional soldier, like the ones you see in TV ads. Professional. Older.

I whispered. "State hospital."

"You don't seem in that bad shape."

I could see he was trying to resist that idea. Probably didn't really want to have a friend who'd been there. "This helps disguise most of it." I raised the beer can. Is stigma inevitable? I wondered.

"George. I've been out of pills for days. At times I'm so fucked in the head nothing makes sense, or the weirdest things you can imagine do." Then I told him all about the whippoorwills and he stared at me like I was a stranger.

"How do you find all those meanings from a few birds singing?"

"I think that's why they call it manic."

"It almost sounds like what they described to us as battle fatigue."

"That about describes it for me. I've been fighting since after the first week you left, almost non-stop."

"Okay. Now I want you to listen to me," he said. "I haven't told Lois yet, but I have to go back tomorrow."

"She said Wednesday. Today's Monday."

"I know. They changed the orders last night. My ship leaves tomorrow night."

"How long a trip is it?"

"Ten days maybe."

"So many killed every day, George."

"Not that many when you think of all the guys over there. I'll make it. Promise me you'll believe that and be the way you always were when I come back." He laughed. "Christ, look at the floor of my car. You brought the beach home with you."

"Delores and I had three great days. You'll love the ocean. Please write and tell me what your first thought is when you see it. Promise?"

"All right." That strange look again. "Do you love Delores?"

"I think so some days, other days I'm not sure. I was sure of it at the Cape. She's young." I waved my arms in the air. "Hell, I'm young. You're young. You're going to war, I'm going to a nuthouse, and Delores had an abortion a month ago."

"Why don't I take you over there today? I'd like to do it and know you were getting some help."

"I'll go after you leave." I reached for another beer. My best friend taking me to a mental hospital. No way. His last day home with his girlfriend for two years.

I popped open the can, raised it high. "To us!" Then quickly put it to my lips to catch the foam.

"To us," George said, and we chug-a-lugged to the shiny wet bottoms of the cans.

"It would make me happier to know you were safe after I leave. No more cowboys and Indians, Sam."

"I shouldn't have written you about that."

"I know you. That letter helped me understand what was going on, at least a little better. I think you been coming to this since we were kids." He opened another beer. "It must be as scary as where I'm going."

"I don't doubt that."

"Then let's get a quart of whiskey and I'll take you to where they can fix you up."

"You really want to do this."

"Actually, I just want my car back." He slugged me on the arm and laughed, then stood close to me. "All your life you've worried about what I think about you and what others think. Fuck everyone, Sam. Get better for yourself. Go back to school. You can be done in June and go to college." He gripped my collar bone tight, and it hurt. He said, "Bluntly, I'm telling you not to be an asshole. If you need the state hospital, let's do it today."

I walked one step away from him, then walked around and around in a tight circle.

"All right. All right," I said.

He slapped me on the back, and we heard a car coming up the road. Cops. We stood there and watched the cops get out of their car and slide night sticks into holders at their side.

"Hello fellas," the older of the two said. He pointed at me. "You're Sam Caster."

"Yes." What the hell, I thought, and held out my wrists for the cuffs. "Sorry, George," I said out of the side of my mouth, "I thought Delores father had called them off."

The younger cop, tall as hell, lifted up his right hand. "No problems," he said. "We saw all the tire tracks leading in and out of here and thought we'd check it out. Didn't know it was you. Sam, I will say this, if it had been three days ago you would be coming with us."

"We can go, then?" George said.

"Yes," the older one said. "Been overseas?" He pushed at the creases of his high forehead.

"Going."

"Good luck." He held out his hand and George shook it.

They turned to go, and I couldn't help but ask, "What were the charges?"

"Kidnapping, contributing to the delinquency of a minor, and maybe rape. You're lucky he changed his mind. Also lucky he talked the county attorney out of charging you." He opened the car door, then paused. "Straighten up, Sam."

"Holy shit," George whispered, as they backed down the narrow path. "They could have put you away for years. Do you know why he changed his mind?"

"Delores' mother threatened to leave him."

"That cop was right. You're one lucky bastard."

"Why don't I feel that way?"

I chugged the remains of the beer I'd placed behind the tire and opened another. "I could use that whiskey. My nerves are really shakin' after talkin' to those cops."

"Lois should be back any minute. Tell me more, now, before she does."

"Oh, Jesus, I don't know. Maybe I'm like a glass of water balanced on a tightrope and an earthquake is shaking everything, and someone is doing jumping jacks in my stomach. I need those pills, George."

"Will you have to take them forever?"

No one else had asked me so many questions, and talking helped a little, and just being with him did, too. So many good times. He had to go away tomorrow.

"One doctor told me that if I went off the lithium and something like this happened my problem might be hereditary, and I would have to take the stuff for the rest of my life."

George swallowed more beer. "You know," he said. "This might not be so bad as you think. I mean you can't do anything about what's been passed to you, and if the pills help compensate, that's good. Do you see?"

"I don't think so."

"Well, if it's in your blood or your brain, or whatever, then you couldn't do anything to prevent it. It's not like you're emotionally weak because you couldn't handle something."

"You mean it's not like having a nervous breakdown because you lost your job or something like that."

"Exactly."

"You should have been a therapist." Then I walked over to the brook and thought, if it is just taking a few pills, maybe I can lick this thing. It wasn't that easy though, not when your brain feels like a bowl of mushed around spaghetti. The pills take time to work, and they obviously wouldn't let me drink at the hospital, but of course there was my old friend Thorazine. I still couldn't be sure if it was genetic or emotional. Talking to George had confused me, and helped me, too. I was beyond really clear thought. I sat beside the stream, then leaned out over, down to it, my nose inches away, and stared at my reflection, then at the yellow birch leaves that lined the bottom of the brook, plastered there by the current. Pressured there like I'd been so long ago. I dunked my face under and tried to bite a bright yellow leaf, then pushed myself back into a sitting position, and George came over to see what in hell I was doing. I tried to tell him about the brook and the river and the ocean, and he stared with wide eyes, obviously not comprehending my madness.

# CHAPTER 35

We could hear another car coming up the road, and I half expected to see my parents. So much for our birch grove and brook being a secret. It was Lois, and beside her I could see Delores' face up close to the windshield. I waved.

She was out of the car before Lois stopped, then in my arms smiling. "It's so good you're home. We can see each other."

George and Lois walked off into the woods, Lois carrying a blanket and George two cans of beer.

Holding Delores like that again at our spot, and a glimpse of George's back, olive green, every now and then as he and Lois walked through the white birch trees, acted like a trigger. The ups and downs, the pills and no pills, the ocean, now the brook, with Delores, without Delores, and always George maybe living or dying. I cracked open in Delores' arms like a broken egg, the yellow yolk my brain, a gooey mess, and those fucking whippoorwills.

Without knowing until I heard the sound, I screamed as loud as I ever had in my life and pushed Delores away from me. The last thing I saw as she tripped and fell backwards in slow motion were the great whites of her eyes, and I imagined they were all the sanity I had lost. Now an insanity overtook me that no alcohol, no love, no friendship, could cure. I ran into the woods dodging the trees, imagining a thousand North Vietnamese were after me. I jumped over fallen trees and rocks higher than I ever had before, and an image of myself as a child wanting to jump up so high I'd be in space overcame me, and I scrambled up the side of a ledge at least forty feet high, and there was George looking so small on the other side, an almost sheer drop to the ground. He held up his hand. "No!"

Before he could say more, I turned around with my back to him and somehow found foot and handholds enough to let me down, then around the outcrop of stone. I tried to run past him, faked one way like Coach had taught us, then went the other. He tripped me. I grabbed for his legs.

The next thing I knew I was in the back seat of his car tied up by the seat belts. My left cheek hurt.

"Take me home," I said.

Delores was next to me. "Have a beer," she said.

"I love you. No more nuthouses for this boy. Those whippoorwills will get me. Won't they George?"

He turned, and I could see the side of his face was bruised. He drove faster away from our spot. Delores climbed over my legs, into my lap, her skirt riding up to her sky-blue underwear. Lois turned and smiled at me, then scooted closer to George. Delores caressed my forehead.

"Let's get whiskey. George, you said before."

"All right. That will be our next stop. Jesus Christ. "

We looked at each other in the rearview mirror.

"I love you," he said, and I thought he meant Lois, because she inched closer, then George took his right hand off the wheel and reached back, I knew then, for one of mine, and we gripped hands for a few seconds.

Lois said, "I told you he'd changed, Sam."

"You did." That helped the insanity to recede, a little, like a pill going down and you start to feel the effects before it can possibly happen.

"How far to go?"

"Hour," George said. I tried to loosen an arm to touch Delores but could barely move.

It almost hurt to realize how much these three people cared, how hard it must be for them to understand—that they could not understand. I wanted to hug Delores, all the rage gone, but George had me tied in good with all the seat straps and buckles.

Delores stared at me and started to let me go. "He's okay," she said. I could tell George wasn't so sure, and I wished I could remember what had happened after he tripped and tackled me but didn't want to talk about it at all.

George said, "I don't want to cold cock you again."

"No. Me either."

We stopped at a liquor store a few minutes later. "Jack Daniels," I said, and Lois got out and trotted inside.

"What happened?" Delores asked.

"I'm not sure I know or want to know," I said. "It's embarrassing for you to see me like this. I'm sorry I pushed you down."

"I landed in leaves. It scared me is all." She massaged my knee in slow circles and I rested my head against the back deck and stared up at the sky. The madness still very close, and I fought the urge to jump and run. "C'mon, Lois," I said. Then to myself, "Think of something else."

"What's this big change with your father?" I gripped her hand tight.

George sat half-turned in his seat watching me and the liquor store.

"It was Mom. She and I talked, and I told her that no matter what they said or did, I would still love you. She kept saying I was too young and I'd get over you in time, and then, I guess it was a week ago, I asked her what she'd have said if someone told her that Daddy was sick and might die, but she could not see him. Would she get over that?"

Delores sang our song, "Closer to You," and her soft voice comforted.

Lois came back and handed me the brown paper wrapped bottle, and before George started the car and pulled away from the curb, I was chugging, and at first it burned, and choked me, then warmed, then felt very very good. I offered, but no one else wanted any.

Delores continued. "A few days later Mom told me she'd talked to Dad several times and he wouldn't change his opinion. He said he'd track you down himself if the cops didn't find you soon."

"Shit," I said, and tipped up the bottle. George put in a Doors tape and rolled down his window a little farther. The sound of "L.A. Woman" surrounded us.

Delores took the bottle out of my hand. "That night she told Dad in front of me that if he didn't call off the cops she was taking me and leaving until he did. He didn't believe it until Mom put an already packed suitcase for each of us in the car trunk."

Lois passed back two cans of beer.

"Sam, you should have seen him standing on the porch when he realized she wasn't kidding." Delores opened the beer and took a small sip. "Then Mom followed him inside and they hadn't talked twenty seconds when she handed him the phone, and half an hour later the cops came with papers for him to sign, then he called the county attorney." She took a big swallow.

George said, "Luc—ky."

"On certain days, maybe." I took another swallow of whiskey and no one said anything for a few miles. I thought, the thing about going crazy is that you drag other people into a really crazy situation, and James Morrison sang into my right ear when I leaned back, "I been down so goddamn long that it looks like up to me." The blues. Then the rain sounds of "Riders on the Storm" began and we all listened, and the double yellow strip on the road led us around a long sloping curve.

On the grounds of the state mental hospital, George stopped next to a man on the sidewalk and asked him where the admissions office was located. The guy, probably in his thirties gave us a wide-eyed look, and said, "Follow me," then posed as if he was seated on a motorcycle, yelled "vroom, vroom," and away he went across the lawn, going like a sonofabitch.

"Wow," George said, "Far out," and drove ahead slowly, and then we all laughed. I wanted to go home so bad and see Mom, and George drove a little faster. He finally stopped a few minutes later in front of a big stone building, over the front door a sign, its background brown, the letters, 'Admissions' printed in yellow, just like all the state forest signs where Dad and I had gone fishing all those years.

George shut off the car and my ears rang, too quiet; I knew there was screaming behind the stones.

"Just me and George," I said, and hugged Delores, and gripped one of Lois' hands. "I'm sorry I've spoiled so much of your time with George."

"It's brought us all closer," she said. "Please get well, Sam."

"I will." Then George held the bucket seat forward and I got out, Delores' hand steady against my butt.

We walked up the sidewalk like we were on our way to a funeral. His or mine? It's all in the timing, I thought.

The woman at the desk looked at both of us like we were nuts, and I smiled at her and remembered all the things that had happened at school and was surprised to see a similar expression at the admitting desk of a mental hospital.

"Can I help you?" she asked.

George pointed at me, then looked down at his uniform.

I said, "I was recently at the hospital in Steadville and stopped taking my lithium and Thorazine almost two weeks ago. Not doing so well."

"Your doctor?"

"Dr. Fianco at the hospital, Dr. Randall at the clinic."

"Have a seat in the room across the hall," she said, and picked up the phone. George and I sat in straight back wood chairs, and I stared at the grayish-beige highly polished linoleum.

"Were things really that terrible at school you had to run away?"

I looked at him and he was staring out a tall almost floor-to-ceiling window at the fall brown grass and large elm trees, their limbs nearly bare.

"Before I left you said you weren't going to let the assholes bother you."

"I didn't know there were so many, or that they could be so big."

"You don't have any tolerance."

"Do they teach you that in the service?"

"Some."

"Well, I either got sympathy, or sarcasm, which are both negative in my book. Only a few treated me fairly, like I'd gone to have a problem fixed and came back. Everyone is curious and afraid of mental illness at the same time."

"It's beyond me, I guess."

"What's that mean?"

"Because I don't understand something doesn't mean we're any less friends."

"What about you. You leave tomorrow. Ready?"

"They give you good training," he said, and squared his shoulders a little. Then he lit a cigarette for each of us. "Sure I'm scared, but I'm a good shot, better than I ever thought."

"I can't imagine it."

"Any more than I can imagine staying here."

I hung my head. "If you felt like I do at times, times without pills and whiskey, your insides like a big bear trap all set to go, and the tiniest touch will set her off." I flicked my ashes on the floor. "You might be glad to be in this place, as much as you'd hate it, too."

He didn't say anything.

"Why does Lois say you've changed?" And even though we were in a closed room, a long low moan, almost like a cow, came to us.

"It's death, Sam. I think all your problems started when I saved you, and you were too young to be able to understand it, and I was, too." He touched the bruise on his cheek. "Everyone at boot camp was affected by the possibility, very real, of death. Bullets kill people. Everyone knows everyone is headed for it, but they don't accept it for themselves. Not like I do now, because of war, and not like you have since we were kids and you almost drowned. A little kid shouldn't be faced with it, at least not you. You've twisted it all around. Beyond knowing."

"I'll think of you every day."

"And screw yourself up even more."

"No." I stamped my foot like Delores had done at the bus station. "This time I'll stay on the pills, and the bad will make me stronger. I'll fight like Delores. Her strength is unbelievable."

"Some day I'll let you read the letters Lois has written to me. They're a part of you and Delores and she and I. I never would have believed I could feel so strongly about someone in such a short time. And we're so different."

"I'd like to read them."

A nurse came to the door. "Come this way, Mr. Caster."

"Should my friend wait?"

"No, that won't be necessary. We'll take good care of you now." George and I stood, gripped hands, then hugged. "Come back, George. Please come back."

"More years left, Sammy ol' boy. Many more," and he snapped his right hand to his forehead and I did the same, except not quite so crisply.

I watched him go through one set of heavy doors, then another, out into the open air, down the steps, only the back of his shaved neck, then the top of his hat visible for another step or two. He was gone. And one word, 'okay', echoed in my ears as I walked beside the starched white form of the nurse to a door marked simply, Doctor. I could only wish for 'okay.'

I sat down in front of a gray-haired man and thought, I didn't even tell George much about the ocean, and remembered the long days at the beach, almost in a trance as the waves kept rolling in one after another, then receding. George would see the ocean for the first time tomorrow. He better write and tell me like he promised.

The doctor looked up from his papers. "Well, young man, you've quite a history for such a short time."

I sat quietly, the ocean rhythm leaving, intruded upon by this old man's voice, raspy and irritating. What did he know? I wanted pills and a place to rest.

He asked me all sorts of questions about where I'd been, about when I'd stopped the pills and other things. I told him I didn't feel very well.

"You'll get no medication for twenty-four hours. Not until the alcohol has had a chance to leave your system."

The weight on the trigger increased as that sunk in.

"Please," I said. "I only drank so I wouldn't lose it. Don't you understand?"

"We have rules here. Try and control yourself."

I sensed the hopelessness of running in this place, and tried to sit still, think of something. No way. Twenty-four hours with nothing. Shit. Okay?

"I won't make it."

I thought his eyes softened, their light bluish color brightened a little. He said, "Inner strength is the way out of mental illness." He pushed a button on the top of the desk and two men came into the room: the inevitable men in white coats and pants. "Admitting Ward," the doctor said, and closed the file on his desk.

We walked down long halls and around sharp corners, constantly opening and closing doors, and still I didn't hear any of the expected screams.

They took my clothes and gave me cotton pajamas, and a thin flannel robe. The only thing they let me keep was a nearly full pack of cigarettes and told me matches were available at the desk. I sat on a couch and stared at the television, secretively glancing at the other fifteen or so men in the room, some playing cards, others flipping through magazines, or watching television like me. Several banged balls back and forth on a bumper pool table. They all seemed oddly content.

Brain sick, I thought. That's all. Brain sick.

Then I remembered those whippoorwills around the car. That had only been this morning around four-thirty. How many times had I gone crazy since then?

I stood up, selected a route, and tried to pace the craziness away.

# CHAPTER 36

The pacing helped, a little. The other patients glanced at me when they thought I wasn't looking, the same way I checked them out. I could see they were afraid of me, even if just a little bit, and I imagined if you stayed here long enough you saw people do some awfully strange things. I remembered the students at school, the teacher, even Billy—like animals—they sensed I was different, unreliable, unpredictable. Like a bad smell.

I am afraid, too. I am fear. As my paces quickened, I imagined at each turn I could be George marching to war, and I did crisp about face turns, and even saluted sometimes. George, Delores, Lois: the look in each face different. Worry. Caring. Love. George said he loved me. I hadn't said it back. He'd always known. A struggle between those three people and the rest who treated me different tore at me and the craziness; a wicked and total confusion took over. A fear of living . . . of dying I wasn't sure.

It was dark outside when I woke up, and the straitjacket gripped me tightly. No drugs. How could they be so cruel. So I struggled and tensed every muscle, fighting, while an attendant's face watched me through a small window. For a while I imagined myself as the greatest escape artist ever, and hopelessly, so hopelessly, I squirmed and shoved. Soon the sweat-soaked restraint gripped even tighter, and not long after I cried myself to sleep.

Later, a woman bathed my face with a towel.

"Let me out of this fucking thing!"

"None of that talk, or I'll go."

"Get the fuck out!"

She left.

I wanted water. So important, water. George and I splashing in it, drinking it, pissing in it, swimming in it, drowning in it, saved by it. Staring at the water down on the riverbank on my rock while its smooth cleanness helped clearer thoughts come to the surface. Then, Delores' and my spot, making love so many times, the brook gurgling happily, like a baby that hadn't died. And finally, ocean water.

For the first time, really, I thought about all the water, all the time I'd spent in it, near it, looking at it, asking it for help. I couldn't quite make sense of it, as I lay there so badly wanting a drink of it. Water might be the solution to my insanity. Water and whippoorwills. How?

"Water!" I screamed. "Water!" Half expecting they'd gag me. No one came.

"Water!" I yelled. "Water time."

Still no one, and my throat hurt, like coughing up whiskey.

Then, like ice cracking open against a rock, a quick shatter, it came to me that water helped because it relaxed me. For so many years when the stress had got to me, or the craziness, or whatever you wanted to call it, even the thought of going to the river had helped. That's it: more water time, and it seemed my mind had solved a problem without hardly thinking about it. But I had to know why I went to the water, not only that I always wanted to go, that it always helped. Close. Closer. I lay panting and sweating, and wanted a drink worse than ever, but that was part of it too, had to be, the patience to wait for water when you could not have it, like having to wait for George to return. Maybe a year. He hadn't been like the others, and he'd seen me for the first time at my worst. Wait for the irrational treatment by the others to go away, like a slow ice melt in the spring so I could see the clear water again. Tolerance, George had said.

I must have slept.

Other people moved around behind that window and woke me up from a dream I was at the ocean, and I did remember my thoughts before going to sleep. My mind is not totally gone. No. Not totally here either.

They gave me an injection and half an hour after that unstrapped me and led me to the showers, quite similar to the ones in our locker room at school. I decided I'd rather be here than there.

The rest of that day, and the next, and the next, I alternated between knowing and not knowing. Knowing who I was and why I was here, and not knowing a fucking thing. Craziness could be the exact opposite of what you think of as normal, magnified.

In periods of murkiness I'd think, why aren't the pills working? And each time I lined up with all the others for medications it seemed like they'd added more pills. Half the time I was in a sort of brownout like I imagined New York City in a heat wave.

Friday night, the calendar behind the desk kept track, the only way I could. Delores called.

After she hung up, I held the phone and looked at the receiver, waiting, waiting. Delores had said she would come and visit on Sunday. Lois would drive. I wanted her now and didn't think I could wait two days, because somehow time was mixed up with minutes which had become hours, and I wasn't good at math.

I placed the phone on the buttons, looked at the attendant; he smiled and asked how everything was at home, and then I turned away, confined where I was, and that was one of the very last things I remembered for what they later said was two weeks. Those two buttons going down on the receiver, like the plunger on a bomb.

At times I'd rise up out of the madness blackness like a tortured ocean swimmer, see no sight of land, and sink again to pressuring depths. Oh, I came up many more than three times, and that only worsened the whole situation. No one, no drug, could get a grip.

For a long time afterwards snatches of that time would return, little bird shit episodes of deeply etched memory, scratched in like a hit from a sharp rock, healed, then opened again.

I sometimes sat in front of a barred window, the sunlight entering through filtered dust, and I'd think, Crazy dust, and move my hand through it in a weaving motion. Lighter than water, heavier than air.

One day, as I came out of it for a few minutes, I was in a dim room with a priest and rain poured down the window and it thundered from time to time. I'm not Catholic. What's this? He talked to me about letting

go of the past, of redemption. I asked what he meant, and he said he had
spoken with Delores about the abortion, and I wondered when because I
hadn't seen her and why hadn't she okayed this with me, and then I sank
back down wherever it was I went. At least there my unknowing was safe.

On a Sunday evening during the *Quick Draw McGraw* show, I
watched Quick Draw get shot full of holes, take a long drink, then spout
water like a sprinkling can. He said something stupid to BaBa Looey, and
I was back. For good.

I asked the guy next to me for a smoke and lit mine from the glowing
tip of his. A different existence, and the world seemed like a new place,
part of my mind healed, like when you take off a long-attached Band-aid.
Fresh air.

I stood up and walked around, surprised to see I was dressed in jeans
and a flannel shirt that weren't my own. State issue. The attendants on
duty looked at me with a surprised, welcome kind of look, and it
embarrassed me. Did I look that different? I asked the attendant behind
the desk if somebody had messed with the calendar, and he said no, it was
correct. December 5, a Sunday. I'd been here sixteen days. It was after
supper, and I stared at the television. "Cartoons at night?"

"It's a special. How do you feel?" he asked and touched my sleeve.
And I liked him right away for that gesture, and the friendly tone in his
voice. He said his name was Brian and his hair was a dark red rust, and
his face all freckles. Bright blue eyes. He was built too, and I imagine he
had to be to work here.

"I'm hungry," I said, "and could I call home later?"

"Good. Sure. You're better."

I laughed a little uncertainly. "Boy," I said. "Where did the time go."

"Do you remember anything?"

"Some. A priest."

"He comes in and talks to patients once a week or so. Don't bother
yourself about the lost time. Be glad it happened here." He opened a
bottom drawer and pointed at two cartons of cigarettes. "Yours," he said,
then reached for a pack and handed it to me.

"From who?"

"You have a friend named George?"

"Sure."

"Him. He must have sent them from a PX. No tax stamps."

"Shit." Where was he now? Brian looked at me like I was leaving again, and he had more to say.

"Sam."

"What?"

"Where is your friend, George?"

"I can't figure. Maybe in Viet Nam. He left on a ship over two weeks ago."

"Fucking war," Brian said, I think more to himself than me, and I liked him that much better. Then I walked away and lit another cigarette from the one almost gone in my hand. George will take care of himself. George has to take extra care of himself. He promised. "Goddamn communists," I whispered, and a guy standing next to the small bumper pool table looked at me funny.

The place was clean and shabby. Stuffing leaked out of the couches and chairs in small pieces, and the wooden chairs were all scratched and marked by cigarette burns, but the floors were clean. All this stuff old and used by crazy people. The ceiling must be twenty feet above us, a high stucco dome and tiny round windows placed at intervals. It made me dizzy. Hadn't someone told me about these ceilings, then I remembered the guy at the other hospital.

A patient came up to where I stood leaning on the back of a couch staring, thinking, and asked for a cigarette. I shook one out and he reached and took two. "One for later?" he asked.

"I guess." Did they know about the cartons George had sent? Was he crawling in the jungle with snakes, or in a bar, or in bed with some whore? Or dead? I knew I couldn't think like that, could almost sense the veils of non-memory creeping, descending.

"Can I call my mother?" I asked Brian.

"Okay. Not for long."

"Thanks." I dialed and waited.

"Hi, Mom, it's me."

"You're okay now. I know it. You called," she said all at once.

"I think so."

"That's so good, Sam. You've been away for so long."

"I'm sorry, Mom. It's all been a mess."

"Delores called just a little while ago."

"When can you visit? I miss you."

"I'll ask your father. It's so good to hear your voice." Then very stern, she said, "Don't you ever go away and not tell me where you're going. Promise?"

"I won't, Mom."

Brian tapped his watch. "I gotta go, Mom."

"Please get over this." She laughed a little. "You're giving me gray hairs."

"If that's what mental illness does, Mom, I'm probably forty and bald. Bye."

"I love you," she said. "We'll visit."

Brian asked, "Everything all right?"

"This stuff is rough on the family."

"No doubting that. Time for meds," he said to me, then louder, "Meds." Everyone headed for the dispensing room.

In line, the guy behind me asked how I felt. "Not so out of it," I said.

"One night I thought you were going to fly right out of here."

"Why is that?" Knowing I did not want to know.

He pointed at the wall beside us. You kept trying to run up the walls, and by Jesus one time you must have gone three steps up before you made a nice little turn and came back down."

"Really climbing the walls," I said, and we both smiled. "You kept saying something over and over."

"What's that?"

"Something like 'whipper will'? Could that be?"

"Yeah."

The line moved forward, and we shuffled ahead. "What is it?"

"A bird. I hate the fuckers." And I wanted the pills badly.

"Oh," he said. "Must've been chasing them."

"Rather not talk about it."

"Okay. Name's Ralph."

"Sam." And I remembered that other Ralph on the soccer team, one of the fuckheads that had stuck those notes in my lockers.

After pills and a half hour of television I went to bed, oddly knowing where my room was, but not remembering ever having been there. Last place I remembered was the bed where I'd been strait-jacketed. This room was more cell-like: brown metal locker, thin-mattressed single bed, almost a cot, a night stand, plain lamp, and nothing else, except of course the bars on the window. Cold brown linoleum under my bare feet and a stale smell of old clothes in moth balls.

I sat and tried to figure out if mental illness was some weird kind of forgetting, and if when the mind becomes too sick, at some crucial point it shuts down. It seemed like this is what had happened. Maybe it was like shock. I'd heard of people with broken arms and legs from car accidents that remembered the accident in slow motion, tiny details, but not the pain until some trigger brings them back. Mind shock, maybe that's how I'd lost two weeks, a short circuit, two crucial mind wires touching in the mass of all the jangled-up nerves. A break so I didn't know a goddamn thing while they healed enough to function again. "Bat shit," my grandfather used to say when something confused him. Definitely bat shit.

# CHAPTER 37

In the morning the head nurse questioned me about the recent past, and seemed satisfied I remembered little of the last two weeks. Did she think I was faking?

She told me to go along to Occupational Therapy when everyone returned.

"What?"

"You went every morning last week."

"Not that I know about."

"Go along."

The other patients came back from breakfast, and for the first time in my memory I walked out of the ward, and immediately wished they'd let me stay in it. Prayed, even. I'd heard noise from the other side of the short walls, I mean the ceilings were twenty feet high and the partitions only eight, and from the moans and occasional screams I'd been prepared for something unpleasant on the other side, but nothing like what I saw as we went from our ward and through a corner of the next. All old men. Some shuffling along, others tied to chairs with sheets. Blank looks, crazy looks. Pleading stares and waving hands. It only took perhaps fifteen steps to walk through and the smell of piss and shit almost made me puke. I'd walked through this all last week?

To the others, this all appeared normal, and they just kept walking, then a very wide metal door clanged behind us, and it was quiet and the air smelled of bleach.

How could I have ever gone through there and not known? Mind fucked, was my only explanation. Those poor old men. Absolutely mind fucked.

"What was that?" I asked the guy in front of me.

"Huh?" A strange look. "The geriatric ward."

"Oh."

"Get used to it," he said. "We walk through there for every meal, and to and from almost everywhere else." He paused, a half step. "Where have you been?"

"No way around?"

"Not unless you have outside privileges."

"When does that happen?"

"Am I nuts, or did you just get here today?"

"I, ah, don't remember too much."

"Just kidding." He smiled and the tips of his top front teeth were black. "You'll get outside privileges when the powers that be decide you probably won't run. I'm Steve."

"Sam," I said, and we kept on walking, me hoping he wouldn't start telling me a story about something I'd done in the last two weeks.

Occupational Therapy wasn't so bad. In one room they held group meetings, group therapy, I guess, and those who weren't invited to that sat around drinking coffee and smoking cigarettes in the adjacent room. Both men and women attended these morning and sometimes afternoon sessions; otherwise, we were kept separate, except if you happened to meet them outside or in the cafeteria. I figured all that out by asking questions on this first morning with memory, and many of them stared at me strangely as if I was crazier now than when I couldn't remember, and that took some getting used to.

I was pretty whacked out on the Thorazine, and my eyes didn't work well enough to read, and when I asked several of the others about it they said that was normal. The whole time I was in the nuthouse I rarely saw anyone reading.

After two hours of sitting and smoking and staring out the windows I started to wonder why they let some into group therapy and others had to stay out here. Were we the misfits of the misfits? A guy came over to where I sat and asked me for a cigarette, and I asked him if he knew.

"Give life experiences. If they let you go in and you don't do that you have to stay out here."

"Oh." He sounded a little pissed about my asking, and I watched him walk into the tiny, narrow kitchen where we were allowed to make terrible-tasting instant de-caffeinated coffee.

I tried to figure out what was wrong with the others. Most of them seemed depressed, but that could be the pills; I didn't feel real perky myself.

Several of the women seemed to move something all the time: a finger, head, foot, leg. Always in motion. Nerves bad, I guessed. Some of them were as old as my mother, and their teeth were bad, stained from smoking, and they wore dresses that fit like old flour sacks.

At eleven-thirty we all left for our wards, perhaps thirty-five of us, then at a T in the corridors the women went one way and we the other. I wanted to know what was behind all the closed doors we passed. Nothing on them gave any indication. Chocolate brown wooden doors, the walls a tan-beige, and the linoleum some of each. Boring.

Now that I knew where I was I wanted to go home.

Back at the ward I stood in front of a window: George, Delores, Lois, Mom, Dad—all out there, and me here. Even through the Thorazine the thought of jumping came. Air. Out in it with no sense of weight. The sense of flight, then a sudden end.

The phone rang, then the attendant hollered, "Lunch," and off we went back past the smelly old men. Abused men. No one should have to live like that, corralled like diseased animals. I'd rather be shot.

Steve, the guy I'd talked to at O.T. walked behind me down the cool, footstep-echoing corridors. Now I was going to another place I must have been a number of times and couldn't remember. The cafeteria. I didn't want this guy Steve to know I didn't remember, and I said, "Another wonderful meal."

"I hate the place," he said. "If it wasn't for Thorazine I'd probably kill somebody." He glanced at me like I was a likely candidate if I said one wrong word. Then he added, "Just kidding."

"Yeah." We rounded a corner and the women trickled in beside us, and we could hear the sound of silverware and trays. Then a steamy, slightly rancid smell came to me.

"Oh, boy," Steve said. "It's stuffed cabbage day."

"That's bad shit," I said. "How long you been here?" We stopped behind a short line of people from another men's ward, most of them older, several day's growth of beard over slack looking facial skin, like prison camp pictures I'd seen.

"Four months," Steve said, tapping me on the shoulder to regain my attention. "From admitting they sent me to ward six after three weeks, then I spent four there, then back to admitting. Maybe home soon."

"Good for you," I said. "And good luck."

"You must have quite a bit of that."

"Why's that?"

"You were allowed to stay in admitting in your shape."

"Yeah, must be luck."

I kind of followed Steve's lead. We picked up trays, then silverware and baby-stepped through the line, attendants from our ward and others all over the place, watching. For what, I wondered.

A gray-haired woman pushed a plate across the top of the steam table and I heard screaming and yelling behind me. I took the plate and turned, took another baby step. An attendant stood over a woman and yelled, "No more! I mean it!" then turned away and the woman stuck out her tongue, just like in elementary school.

All the wards ate together, except the closed ones, Steve told me, and after another quick look I didn't feel very safe. Several guys not much older than me had thick plastic helmets permanently riveted by several chin straps to their heads and I asked Steve about that.

"You'd think you'd never been here, Sam. What the fuck? You must've seen one of those guys beat his head on the table or the wall in the last two weeks. You playing games?"

I pushed around the vile smelling cabbage.

"You don't remember. I'll be a sonofabitch. You don't remember having eaten here before? Ever? Is that possible?"

"Tiny parts are coming back," I whispered. "Most of the last two weeks are like the most difficult jigsaw puzzle you've ever seen, all off-white to black, so many pieces missing."

"You poor bastard."

"I don't mind missing two weeks of this cafeteria. It's enough to drive you nuts." The noise around us was like someone fiddling with the volume control, up and down in waves of strange laughter and shouts, occasional screams and moans, and it all smelled like soured pissed-in pants. People ranged in age from fifteen to fifty. Every imaginable description of crazy was in evidence. Blank stares, drooling mouths, anger, almost tears, dead pan, maniacal smiles, and it was clear many of them had accepted these selves as themselves, and I guessed fifty per cent of them were here for good. This scared me awful, and I imagined my face had matched some of their expressions during the last two weeks.

I had to go home, and I knew they wouldn't let me for quite a while, and that it wouldn't do any good to run away; they'd lock me up. As I sat trying to eat something of the sour cabbage stuffed with fatty hamburger, I came to the decision that I wanted to live and try to be normal, and although jumping might always be a possibility, it wasn't as serious a consideration, only a glimpse I took from time to time of weightlessness, freedom, and lightness that could take me away for good, like even the thoughts of it now took me away from this horrible place where I sat, where I'd been for two weeks and couldn't remember.

I heard, "Jesus, Sam, you're way out there sometimes."

"Sorry, this is all so strange."

The tangled brush of my thoughts weaved and snarled in my head as Steve and I dumped most of our food into an open garbage can, then placed the trays on a conveyor. "Pig food," I thought.

As soon as I came into the ward the head nurse walked up to me. "Doctor wants to see you in ten minutes."

"Okay."

"Go comb your hair," she said, then walked to the desk and opened a drawer. "Use this." She handed me an electric razor.

I couldn't remember when I'd last looked in a mirror. The peachy fuzz of my beard had a tiny curl to it, and the razor's dull blades did more pulling than cutting. In the shiny piece of sheet metal that served for a mirror, I stared at my face, and it was a person I did not know. Hollow cheeks, sunken eyes, big ears, just like you'd expect a crazy person to look. Manic depressive, I reminded myself. I stood back a little. For Christ's sake, I looked a little like Dumbo, and I remembered thinking something like that before my first dance.

The electric razor whined. George and Delores hadn't said anything, and the sight of me explained more positively how much they loved me. This look couldn't have happened in two weeks.

I couldn't let Mom see me like this; I had to eat.

The doctor, an oriental woman, motioned for me to sit in a chair to the left of her desk.

"Do you remember ever talking to me?"

"No, Ma'am," I said, and folded my hands in my lap. An image of myself sitting like a prisoner of war being interrogated seemed exactly right.

"I didn't think so," she said. "What do you remember since you came here?"

"Coming here with my friends, then George leaving, and walking to the ward. A straitjacket. That's about it."

"Don't think it unusual," she said, and pushed back a straight black lank of hair from her incredibly smooth forehead. All her features very small and attractive.

"Dr. Schella. Do you remember my name?" She sat forward a little, as if interested.

"Not really."

"Mr. Caster, you've had a psychotic episode, and not your first, if the other hospital's records are correct. It began the first day you were here, and since then I've prescribed Thorazine, and as of two days ago you have been taking the maximum allowed by state mandate." She smiled a little. "I'm very pleased you have begun to recover."

"You'd have sent me to another ward soon."

"Yes. In a matter of days, actually."

"I want to get better."

"Why don't you take the lithium?"

Now I sat forward and gripped the edge of the desk. "You mean when I was on Cape Cod?"

She shook her head no.

"Here? I swallow every pill they give me. Except I don't remember so good."

"It's been two weeks and your blood level is still very low."

"That happened at the other hospital, longer than they thought, too. Honest."

"I'll check." She stared out the window for a good ten seconds, then leafed through a folder, mine, I assumed. "Since you've been ill," she said, and sat back, "how has it all seemed? In general, I'm asking."

"Well." I didn't expect her to ask that sort of question. I said the first thing that came to mind. "Like a long journey where ninety percent of the stuff that could go wrong has gone wrong."

"Could you control anything?"

"Now?" It seemed her perception and my perception of English were different, at least the way she asked some questions.

"No. Before you lost your memory."

"Most of the time I'd decide something and then do it."

"Okay. I'm trying to determine how long you have been psychotic."

"I remember everything except for the last two weeks here. I hate not remembering, and even here, going places I've been, not knowing, well, it's embarrassing."

"You are recovering, I think. I'll see you again in a few days."

When I was halfway to the door, I was thinking about whippoorwills when she said to my back, "Do you think of jumping?"

"No," I said, still facing away from her, then I took another step, gripped the door knob, glanced at her for a second, "not so much," then closed the door behind me, very softly.

# CHAPTER 38

One week passed and then another, and some days were good and others not. Memory in and out like the cash register at Billy's. I'd lost Thanksgiving and now Christmas was coming. Only five days away. In this place for over a month and the doctor would not let me go home for one lousy day. Christmas day.

I'd had two letters from George, and it was hard to tell just how things were with him. The letters were too upbeat to be real, or Viet Nam was like Disneyland. He wrote about whores and gooks and said that he hadn't really been in the bush yet, and they expected a ceasefire at Christmas. The last letter had come a week ago and I kept it with the first, under my pillow, and their soft crinkling noises, as I shifted my head, helped me to sleep.

Delores and Lois visited two days after George's second letter arrived. Lois said her letters were positive, too.

I decided he was lying for my sake, and even though Lois wouldn't admit it, I think that's what she thought too, and I wondered what he really wrote to her.

They'd given me outdoor privileges during the last week, and every day I'd gone to the snack bar and bought candy bars and hot chocolate, then sat on a green metal park bench under a big maple and tried to gain weight, guessing I'd lost thirty of my original one-sixty. It had been a bitterly cold winter, yet I stayed outside as much as possible; they kept the entire hospital at a stifling eighty degrees.

Delores and Lois could not contain their surprise at how much weight I'd lost. Delores hugged me, and I could feel her fingers grip my fatless ribs, and she with that thin layer of baby fat all over. She was my baby, and the one we'd lost. Even though almost every trace of sexual desire was masked by the Thorazine, I badly wanted to lie down next to her naked in a bed, like on those few honeymoon-like days at the Cape.

We sat on the green metal park bench under the maple, me in the middle, and I said, "I'm sorry I look so bad, Delores."

She put her arm through mine and leaned against me, pushed me against Lois.

"You've gained weight since we were here last time," Delores said. And I couldn't bear to tell her I had no memory of that, and then wondered if I would remember today, tomorrow, or next week.

"The bastards won't let me go home for Christmas," I said.

"We'll be here," Lois said.

"Oh, no. Uh, Uh. You two stay home with your families."

"It's all settled," Delores said. "No more arguing."

"My parents will come. I'm sure of it." I wasn't though. If Dad wouldn't come, Mom wouldn't drive this far alone.

"Are they helping you, Sam?" Lois asked.

These two are the greatest, I thought, and have helped more than they'll ever know. They cause good thoughts.

"The pills help the most. The rest of the place is just there while the pills do their thing, and it's almost a constant reminder that you better get better or they'll send you some place worse."

"You'll be home soon," Delores said. "I know it."

"Probably. And what will that be like this time? Tell me what people are saying."

"All right," Lois said, and she and Delores exchanged a glance. "It's like before, Sam, and you might as well know it. The assholes are saying what they will say, and the rest just think you had to go back to get fixed up again."

"She's right, Sam," Delores said. "You can't let it bother you too much."

"I know that both of you are right, and I keep thinking what George said. All I have to do is make it till June and it's all over."

Lois finished her coffee and went for a walk. Delores and I talked and hugged and kissed on the bench in the below-freezing cold. I wanted to return the love she felt for me, and blamed the drugs that I couldn't, and knew that was a lie. I didn't think I loved her, and never really had, except for those three almost perfect days at the ocean. I'm sure she sensed it, too. We were friends, and I think it was enough.

After they left, I walked all over the hospital grounds for over an hour, and so many questions rose up I couldn't walk a straight line, it seemed, and most of these questions I dodged. I went back to the ward and told the attendant I was having a bad time, and without hesitation he took me to the medications room and gave me an extra dose of Thorazine.

A half hour later, all the questions about Delores and my father, and George, and so many others, receded like images do the farther you walk away from a mirror.

That was the end of my first Sunday with outdoor privileges, and I had to admit I wasn't ready for home; this first visit I could remember with normal people had conjured up so much I couldn't handle.

In certain ways, the more I stayed here the more I liked it. It was a safe routine. The hospital staff did their best to brighten up the place for Christmas with red and green crepe paper, and big paper bells, obviously used in years past. They placed a green plastic tree in the corner by the bumper pool table and hung paper and plastic ornaments on it, icicles, too. In my ward of thirty guys, over half were going home for Christmas, and as the day grew closer, the ones that were staying grew closer and friendlier.

It's hard to admit I stayed away from many of the others because of fear, and this showed me clearly how others felt about me at home. I kept trying to figure it all out, so I could be whole again, or something like it. I decided each mentally ill person exists differently, simply because each person is different, just like normal people, and that mental illness might be seen as a terrible exaggeration of the normal. Excess nervousness, depression, sadness, anxiety, and never purely one of these, rather a mix, like rain and snow and sleet all in one day. Very little sunshine. I decided as I walked around looking at the shabby ornaments, that mental illness represented modified normal. Everyone gets angry or sad, but that was the normal state of things here, at least most of the time, because, here, too, the excesses magnified, like when they put you in a strait jacket and watched you all night long. A person banging his head against a cement wall, paint chips flying.

Christmas was only two days away when Joey called. "Hi ya, Sam."

It took me a second to recognize his voice. "Is that you, Joey?"

"Sure. How ya doin'? Merry Christmas."

"All right. Same to you."

"When can you come home?"

"Hard tellin', Joey." Then, "Who's workin' all my hours?"

"That's somethin' I called to tell ya. I am."

"What? You took my job?"

"Till you get home, you jerk. And with no pay. After you and Delores took off, I talked to Billy. He told me about the money you borrowed. I said if he'd let me work your days I'd start paying it off."

Now I knew what my grandfather meant when he said, "Dumbstruck." I couldn't find words.

"I'll pay you back. Soon as I can. You must be working seven days a week."

"Don't worry, you'll be home soon. You sound good. This is your Christmas present. No pay backs."

"Holy shit. I can't accept that."

He laughed. "You're not in a position to refuse. Friends help friends, Sam. C'mon."

"Thank you very much, Joey, but they won't let me talk much longer." The attendant was tapping the face of his wrist watch. "Drink a beer for me at Christmas."

"They treatin' you okay?"

"Mostly. Bye, Joey. Merry Christmas. Thanks."

"You're welcome."

I lit a cigarette at the desk, then sat on a couch, numb. Then a shiver went through my body, top to bottom. Christmas, something I'd mostly associated with presents and good food. Now this, and Delores and Lois giving up theirs. Sure, Joey and I were friends, and got drunk together, rode the back roads. Once in a while, but not really close. Now this.

People give and give to me and I am unable to match them in return. Why? Am I a selfish bastard?

No. I knew that wasn't true. As much as I wanted to avoid it, these, I don't know, call them inabilities, my thoughts always went back to almost drowning, and my fear of not paying George back, something probably impossible to do. Why couldn't I change? Accept that George saved me, Delores loved me, Joey and Lois were good friends without expecting me to do anything except return friendship? Then I'd go back and think I could have quit school and signed up with George and maybe been with him now. I could have stayed with Delores on Cape Cod and then married her when we were old enough. No. I'd saved my own ass. Maybe even to the extreme of pushing myself into insanity. Could that be possible?

I whispered to myself as I butted out my cigarette, "You are weak and selfish, and not really a friend to anyone." I quickly looked around when I realized I'd said this out loud, then, louder, "Fuck it! I may as well stay here forever," and the attendant stared at me, then asked if I was all right.

Too much of something. Again. I started to yell about George in Viet Nam, my girl's lost baby, and then two attendants had me under the arms and I yelled, "Fuck Christmas," over and over as they led me down the hall and gave me a shot, then led me to my room. They put me in what is called light restraints, straps for the wrists and ankles attached to the bed. I remember fighting those straps and hearing one of the attendants say in the hall, "No more. He's had the maximum dose."

"Don't worry," the other one said, Brian I thought, then I recognized his dark rust red hair as he came in with another needle. He jabbed it in, and the alcohol swab so cool. "Rest, Sam," he said. "Let the medicine work." He patted my arm in the way I remembered he'd done that first night I met him, then grey and black, like old movie film, flickered in my head, and at times I fought, and believed it was death I was fighting against so hard, then too, sometimes I fought against life.

# CHAPTER 39

In the morning the head nurse stood over me and I watched her remove the restraints. "Another bad time, Sam."

"Not ready to go home."

"No, not quite."

"Will you send me to another ward?" Every muscle ached from struggling.

She hesitated. "Not yet."

The way she said it scared me and I could tell the possibility was real.

"Would you like me to tell people not to come tomorrow?" She sat on the bed next to me.

"I don't know."

"Did something about the phone call cause this episode?"

"It's so stupid."

"Tell." She gripped my right hand.

"People are so nice to me and I can't return the favor, the friendship."

"Is it necessary? Do they expect it?"

"No. I want to."

"Then it is your problem, Sam."

I stared at her, then behind us at the new snow on the windowsill. "Yes, I suppose it is."

"You have a serious and complex illness. It took a long time for you to become this ill, and it will take some time to recover. No one recovers quickly from manic-depressive episodes."

"Will I ever?"

"You responded very well to the lithium once, and except for last night's setback you've done quite well again. You see the progress, don't you?"

"Some. Without the pills I'd be a blob or something."

"You may have to take them for the rest of your life. Many people do."

"I want to be like everybody else."

"I'm not so sure you do." She let go of my hand and walked to the window. "It might be more accurate to say that you want to be the best, the best friend, the best worker, son, lover, soccer player." She looked down at me." When you fail at any one of these things you are completely at a loss as to what went wrong."

It made sense.

I sat up and we both stared at the new snow, a light breeze cleaning off the inch or so from the tree limbs.

"A number of things have piled up on you over quite a long time, and perhaps cumulatively they triggered the chemical imbalance in your brain, maybe like ice breaking a forgotten rain barrel, tiny leaks at first, then all at once." She tapped her foot on the hard linoleum. "The psychiatrists wouldn't care for my explanation, perhaps, but they have no concrete answers as to why or when certain people have a manic or depressive phase. It is believed to be passed through the generations in the genes, but why the disease manifests itself now and not later is a mystery." She turned to me again and I sensed she was telling me all this to help me not have to go to another ward. To help me help myself with this knowledge. "The drugs can, and usually do help. You have to take them regularly."

"I worry that what happened yesterday will happen again and again no matter what I do."

"You let yourself go to excess without thinking, like your abuse of alcohol. The drugs help you calm down, but you have to learn how to think about these problems. Don't blindly let them take over."

I put my hands on my knees and smelled sourness from under my arms and wondered why she was spending all this time with me today, then remembered most of the others had probably left. Christmas Eve.

"This might not be the best time, but there is one other very important matter you should think about and compare it to how you have acted in the past." She looked into my eyes and some how locked mine into holding the gaze. She said, "If George dies, will you take the role of 'the best friend ever of a friend that died?'" She made hash marks in the air, "or 'the best mourner.' You've got to think about the possibilities and come up with a plan." She reached out and touched my shoulder. "I'd hate to see someone with your ability and kindness spend time in another ward. And I'm not threatening you, either."

"I know." The thought of George's death pushed in my heart and for a few seconds I could not draw a breath, then I let a long one out.

"Thinking he might die is why I tried to jump before."

"I thought so." She checked her watch. "I'm late for a meeting, Sam. Try to go over what we've talked about slowly."

"Thank you," I said.

She stopped in the doorway. "Try and think of ways to help yourself." Then she walked quickly down the corridor, the sounds of her nylons against one another reminded me of the beach, the rasp of waves scouring the sand. And George so far away that it was a different day. Christmas.

One thing she had said, that I had considered vaguely, but never admitted, was that if George did die I would be the damned best dead friend's friend ever. She helped me admit it, see the wrong of it. Even if it never happened.

I spent the rest of the morning wandering around the ward, staring up at the high ceilings, the shabby decorations, and because there was nothing to hang crepe paper or bells from, everything was along the walls or on three floor lamps, and I wanted to cry. Nothing in the center. Space for crazy thoughts.

Before lunch, the head nurse asked me again about Delores and Lois coming.

"What if I have an episode while they're here?"

"I doubt you will; I'm not saying it isn't possible."

"They saw one. That's enough. I'm weak." I stared at the floor, a hope for sympathy rising from the linoleum, surfacing.

"It is easier to be weak, to succumb to the stress. If you don't fight, you don't win."

"You'll call them?"

"Yes. Go have your lunch."

She walked away. I thought that it helped she treated us like her lost children part of the time. It was obvious she had not enough time to accomplish what she wanted. The others had left for lunch, and I walked quickly through the old men's ward.

The corridors were empty, my footsteps sent back sharp single echoes. It reminded me of walks to the nurse's office in elementary school for a Sucrets, and the few worries of those days, before George saved me. Now your mind is sick and it's Christmas Eve and you're in a mental hospital and George is off fighting a war, a war so few believe in, yet the bodies add up every day. Does George believe in it?

Lunch, and more Christmas decorations, some food-spattered, then a walk in the cold air, the smell of snow, and what, from somewhere a long way off, the whiff of turkey roasting?

Later that afternoon, normal people paraded into our ward in their expensive clothes, and sang Christmas carols for five minutes; then they smiled and waved, so pleased they'd done something nice. They filed out, and I wished I could see the expressions on their faces as they sang to those old men.

We had Christmas cookies and eggnog, non-alcoholic, of course. A good swallow of cold beer would have hit the spot. Beer, the stress chaser, I thought, as I walked down the hall to my room after the last round of pills for the day. I still didn't think, as the head nurse suggested, that I abused alcohol, but used it to help during the worst times without pills.

I wrote George a long letter telling him the truth about the last few days, then tore it up and wrote a short happy note, like the smiles on those people's faces.

At ten the next morning after a try of "Merry Christmas" to everyone, I saw Mom and Dad's car drive past the window I was staring out of. Hadn't the head nurse called? I couldn't trust my eyes as Delores and Lois piled out of the back seat, smiling and laughing at something.

"Merry Christmas," I called from the porch steps across the lawn to the parking lot, and they all yelled the same. Just like it was Christmas.

They'd brought several bags of gifts for me and each other, and I had nothing to give, then I saw one tag that read to Mom from Sam and knew Lois or Delores had done that. We hugged all around, except I shook Dad's hand, and he seemed as nervous as I was in this place; he stared at the high ceiling often.

At Mom's and Delores' insistence we all went to a small stone church on the hospital grounds, and I sat between Dad and Delores, terribly wanting the lightness and warmth the reverend repeatedly described as His love.

We walked back in a clump, all smiles, and even I was lifted by these people I cared the most about, family all, really, so close to me when I thought no one would come. I will get better. Am.

"To tell eases the burden," I said on the top steps I'd hurried up, staring down at them. Then I told them they weren't supposed to have come, and about the restraints of the other night. Dad looked quickly away, and their expressions told they had not been told not to come. Also of how much they cared. I thanked them for coming. "It helps so much," I said, then turned away, walked down to the end of the narrow porch.

Mom and Dad and Lois went inside, and Delores came up beside me. "Do you know why it happened?" Her eyes bright as snow.

"A small step back. Maybe I shouldn't have told."

"No." She buried her head between my right arm and side. "Always tell. We've been through so much."

"It's very hard for you."

"Only because I love you so much."

"What's to love? Maybe you should try not to." I hadn't really meant to say that.

She stared up at me. "Why?" I knew that was next.

"Maybe I don't love you back," I whispered, "not that I don't want to." I looked up at the clouds, obviously full of snow, low and gray and thick. I imagined all their weight falling on me at once.

"Not now," she said. "I think I understand. Let's not talk about this now."

"Aren't you awfully sick of this. It's lasted forever."

"You'll get better. Don't put so much pressure on yourself. Please. At least not about the two of us."

I knew she was right. It was like the veils of gray in the sky lifted, and I grabbed her tight and held her close. "I thought the other day that no matter what happens you and I will always be good friends."

"Yes. Always. Please come home soon."

We walked into the ward. My dad said he didn't think they should stay much longer. The forecast called for six inches of snow.

"It means a lot that you came today, Dad."

"Should have before." He smiled. "I guess I said that to you at the other place."

"Forget it."

Cafeteria workers wheeled in a turkey buffet, and by then most of the patients had at least one guest, and we stood around eating. It was almost normal. I wondered what Christmas was like on the other wards: people without an illness staring at those who did, trying to figure out who was worse off, their son or that one's son, daughters in the women's wards.

After dinner in my tiny room, Delores and Lois passed around all the gifts, and in a flurry, we opened them, then Dad said they really should go. A few flakes now and then drifted across the windows.

We packed up all the gifts and I thanked Mom for the mittens, about the only gift I could keep. She pushed the matching scarf back in the box.

"This has added years on you hasn't it, Mom?"

Dad, Delores, and Lois seemed to stop for a few seconds, then went on packing up Dad's fishing lures, Mom's slacks, and a cranberry mohair sweater I'd gotten for Delores, that Mom must have bought.

As they put on their coats, Mom smiled and said, "It's all worth it, and I mean that. Somehow I think you'll be a better person for all you've been through." Only a mother would think such a thing.

At the top of the steps, I shook hands with Dad again, hugged Mom and Lois. Delores stayed behind with me on the top step, gave me a big kiss, then placed an envelope in my coat pocket.

"What is it?"

"Open it after we're gone. It's a picture Lois took of me." She smiled, and we kissed again; I could see great clouds of exhaust coming from Dad's car.

"Merry Christmas, Sammy," she said, then trotted down the steps, across the lawn and into the back seat next to Lois. I could see all their smiling faces through the lightly frosted windows. Dad drove off, tooting his horn long after they had gone out of sight.

# CHAPTER 40

On that Saturday and Sunday after Christmas, I kept to myself in the nearly empty ward or took long walks and stared at the new snow. It helped like the ocean, so clean and bright in the sunshine, each flake distinct, like the crest of each wave.

For the first time in quite a while I wondered what was going on at school, and if I could catch up and graduate on time. Those signs in my locker and the other evidence of stigma didn't bother me as much now, and I hoped I could ignore it the next time. It was either take what people at home dished out or come back here.

Mental illness is a mystery, I decided, as I walked to the small store for candy bars. A mystery that has to be solved in order to be cured, by drugs, therapy, and thought. I think I'd finally reached the thought part. And knew my soul was also healing. The soul is such a philosophical question. It cannot be touched in a physical manner. Every one has a soul, a force that defines them. I'd lost my soul and struggled to understand that as I slowly recovered.

Chewing a Baby Ruth, I kicked through the snow and thought how people talked about cancer and how it scared them, yet they felt very sorry for the person, and sent cards to the hospital, food to the family's house. Why the fuck wasn't the same true for mental illness? It wasn't like you could catch it. No, you had to hide a mentally ill person; family and friends didn't talk about it. In many ways, that mentally ill person was shunned as if he might transmit it.

The next week went along, and I talked to the doctor as usual and one of the therapists for twenty minutes at OT. Small improvements each day. The doctor said the lithium was at the correct level.

The New Year came and went, and I think each day I piled up a little more clarity, like the time to get better had come, the craziness had worn itself out, or the drugs really had settled in; more and more I thought about home.

The routine helped; I could shut out those old men as we walked through, and the strangeness of the cafeteria had taken on the quality of a freak show, and I wasn't so much of one as I must have been during those two forgotten weeks.

The days, predictable as the clock, not like some time ago, and I spent my time thinking of other things. Although I could not right past mistakes I damn for sure could try and not repeat them again.

Those whippoorwills still bothered me at times. Whip or will. Whip your will, and I leaned more and more toward my will and putting it into a correct perspective and moving on. No more whipping myself crazy, like a grown dog chasing its tail.

I told the doctor the next time I saw her about the whippoorwills and the resolve to control my will and not let stress build then explode and land me in here again.

She held up a tiny hand, her large almond shaped eyes stern. "I've never seen a whippoorwill, but I can tell you for sure that you cannot control every aspect of your illness, Mr. Caster. Try to understand this." She pushed herself away from the desk on silent wheels and stood up, the first time she'd ever done so. A tiny woman.

"The lithium prevents the radical highs and lows of your illness. You will have to take other medications if you are to help lessen the mood swings from time to time."

"You mean like Thorazine."

"Yes, or something milder." She reached for my file, opened it, flipped through several pages. "You were at the maximum dose; in the last two weeks you've come down to half of that." She smiled. "I think your manic episode has mostly passed." She sat again. "We do not like to keep people any longer than necessary. You are soon well enough to go home."

"When?" I stiffened.

"Let me finish. You must always take lithium and it is important you have blood levels taken every two months. See your doctor at the clinic, and," she tapped the desk, "it is crucial that you monitor yourself if you want to stay out of here. They've helped you do that here at occupational therapy?"

"Yes."

"If you feel depressed, or excessively nervous, or have much anxiety, talk to your doctor so he can prescribe something to help. Never let it go for very long. Are you clear on what I'm saying?"

"Yes."

"Good. Let's see. Today is Thursday. You go home for Saturday come back here on Sunday, and on Monday tell me how it went. If okay, maybe you can go home some day next week."

"Okay." I sat, kind of numb.

"You may go now, Mr. Caster."

"Thank you," and I wasn't sure I meant that.

Saturday arrived before I could blink, it seemed. I used everything in me to plan for every possibility. On Friday I spent an hour with a therapist, and I knew she and the others had helped because it all seemed to sink in that I did have control over the situation, and that's what staying mentally healthy was about, mostly, that is when the drugs allowed you to control it.

All the way home, Mom and Dad treated me like a fragile antique glass, and I wanted normal like I wanted simple things: hot dogs and fries, a rest by the river, my own bed.

When we reached home I wished I'd stayed at the hospital. Going back. That had been true for too long. I sat behind the wheel of George's car; he must have worked hard to get it so clean. Always wanting to go back: back to before almost drowning, Delores, abortion, running away, the nuthouse. No more before. I slapped the wheel and a twinge in my arm reminded me of all those glass cuts. I backed the car out and headed for the dirt roads.

It was ten below zero. Then it dropped on me like a bird shit bomb: if I ever go back into that illness so far that I lose time again, I will not come out of it. Ever. I was not guessing. I knew it. I'd end up in one of the back wards, and either not even know it, or when I came out of it be so damaged there would be no return to this, driving a car, thinking seriously. Being free.

Control. I shifted into third, then second, to go around a hairpin turn to the right. I had resisted so many things, and damn the illness, genetic or stress caused; I did not think I was meant to spend my days in a back ward at the nuthouse. I shook my head back and forth slightly, and cursed that blackness, then caught myself wishing it had never happened. I rolled down the window and shouted, "No! No more backwards," and had to laugh, too, because that sounded so stupid, but I still meant it, as the wind froze my face and I wasn't sure if the tears were from the cold, or happy, or from fear of what might lie ahead.

The truth of my situation scared the shit out of me. Live with it. So easy, so hard. So unknown. George might die, and I really did not think I could face that unless I died too.

I headed for Delores' and my spot. Only four inches of snow on the ground, and George's car rolled softly over the fluffy whiteness into the birch grove, their black limbs so distinct against their white bark and the snow. Small limbs lay on the ground like miniature tree fingers, so stark and naked, and I thought of Delores' eyes. Nothing so black and white as the pupils and whites of her eyes. Nothing so gray as what I'd been through, put myself through.

I loved her as a friend I was sure—as a wife, that would have to wait. That didn't seem so awful.

In the silence, the car engine began to tick, then stopped, and in the utter silence of the birches and snow, I imagined a hot jungle, bullets whizzing, choppers blades whipping the air. All those lives going to waste, and not one fucking thing I could do about it.

I smoked several cigarettes, not able to tell if I blew smoke or frosty air and could again see the worry in my parents' eyes as they drove me home—a worry that seemed etched permanently. I gazed at all the birches and remembered all the times Delores and I had come here, and those times weren't about finally making love, or drinking, or laughing, or arguing; they were about getting to know each other, and it meant a great deal to know her. The time had been worth it, and now thinking about it, I wished I'd known that was what we had been doing. It really did add up to something important.

I backed the car around and went to pick her up, and looking back through the mirror, decided that I'd shed a limb or two, and it was probably about time, even if they were quite small.

Did the lithium help me to do that, these clearer thoughts, the therapy? Perhaps. Even more I decided it was a glimpse of whiteness against the black. Learning from the black, the white, the gray. Combinations.

Delores' mother waved from a kitchen window, then Delores was on the steps, smiling, then down them almost bouncing.

"You're late," she said.

"Riding around. Thinking."

She leaned across the seat and gave me a kiss, then I backed out of the driveway, still afraid of her father.

"How's school?"

"Boring."

"I'll keep busy catching up."

She clapped her hands. "When will they let you go?"

"This coming week, if all goes well."

"Sam, you smiled. It's so nice to see you smile."

I looked in the mirror, a real one, and smiled some more, something I'd forgotten; those muscles and skin a smile folded into didn't feel normal.

"I'm ready to come home." I grabbed her hand and squeezed it. "I don't like that place. I did for a while, you know."

"You are home."

I drove to our spot, and Delores was upset about the tire tracks. "Someone's been here."

"Me."

"Oh."

We hugged and kissed, so awkward with bucket seats, and the damn Thorazine wouldn't let me do anything else, no matter how much we both wanted to.

"Don't worry," Delores said. "You won't have to take that stuff much longer I'll bet."

"Damn right. What time is it?"

"A little after noon," she said, after checking her Minnie Mouse watch, a Christmas present to her from me via my mom.

"Let's go to McDonalds over in Elsinore."

"Okay."

On the drive we didn't have much to say, and on the way back Delores fell asleep several times briefly, and I asked if she was okay.

"Yeah. You don't know how relieved I am you are home. I'm just quiet and relaxed."

"I'm a little tired, too."

"You wouldn't want to go to the dance at school tonight?"

"Who's playing?"

"Bill and the Wizards."

"Sure. I think I will. Okay if I drop you home, then I think I'll go home and take a nap."

"Will you come in?" she asked a few minutes later as I neared her house. "Both Mom and Dad would like to say hello."

"Been a long time."

"Just for a minute."

"All right." I turned into her driveway and parked, my hand so clammy it stuck to the frozen door handle.

"Hello, Sam," her father said, and hesitatingly held out his hand.

We shook, and I said hello to her mother.

"I've made some mistakes and I hope you can forgive them, and thank you for letting me see your daughter," I said this all at once, then stared at the floor.

"Been awfully cold," her mom said. "Like some hot chocolate?"

Delores put her arm through mine, and I wanted to tell them what it was like to be mentally ill, to lose so much time.

"Maybe another day. I should go home. Thanks, though."

I backed the several steps to the door, and Delores said she'd be ready at eight.

"Thanks again," I said, as the heavy door clicked, then I kind of wobbled down the steps, my insides quaking, and cursed that, and was happy they'd been nice, but wanted to go back to the hospital, and as I gripped the frozen metal of the car door handle, wanted to fall in a heap and beg for a normal thing to happen. Just one. Anything.

# CHAPTER 41

At home, Mom asked almost the same questions she had on the way home from the hospital, and I wanted to shout I was better, even though you couldn't see the healing like on a scrubbed knee. She couldn't understand, wanted me back to normal in an instant. Mom acted like if they said I could come home from the hospital I must be fine. I had no terms accurate enough to let her in on the slow process of recovery. I was okay, really okay, a part of the time, and that was real progress. And I was learning how to cope with the time I wasn't okay. That was progress.

"Mom, I'll be home for good, probably Tuesday. The doctor says if I take the medicine I will be fine."

"They said that before."

"I stopped taking the pills; I ran out. Do you want me to stay in that place forever, so you won't have to worry about what I do here?"

"You know that's not true."

"I'm sorry."

She went to the counter. "This came after you left this morning."

"From George," I said. "I'm going to lay down for a while."

I propped up the pillows and stared at George's neat printing on the outside of the envelope framed by red, white and blue markings. Air mail.

*Dear Sam:*

*Hope you're reading this at home. Lois writes you're better.*

*Keep it up.*

*More and more often I'm out in the jungle with my platoon. Good guys. You'd like them.*

*Worry about yourself. Not me. And dammit take better care of my car than you did before.*

*Going out for beers now. The guys are waiting. Get better. Or I will drown your ass.*

*Your best friend,*

Some letter writer. Jesus. Jungle. Snakes and all kinds of slimy shit. I couldn't imagine it. I rolled over, the letter still in my hand, and stared out into the cold toward our tree house. No white birches where George was fighting, and I imagined everything over there like an overcrowded fish tank, then dozed off and didn't wake up until Mom called me for supper.

Dad sat at the kitchen table drinking a beer. "Happy New Year," he said. "Forgot to say that on the way home."

"Yeah. Wasn't much of a celebration at the hospital."

"Your mother and I stayed home as usual."

"Let's eat," she said, and placed a plate full of fried chicken and biscuits on the table. Real food.

I appreciated Dad's trying so hard, but it was so obviously an effort.

So hard to talk, even to my own parents, the same things on our minds behind each sentence: is he better?

In the shower I had a deja vu feeling of that first date with Delores so long ago. Except now I was trying to scrub away the hospital smell, and then going to pick up my girl, who'd had an abortion not long ago. We are older.

On my way through the living room Dad didn't say anything about the clothes I was wearing, like he had about that fancy paisley shirt, or how I smelled. Sometimes I think that window tried to lure me in; I pushed that away.

The gym was loud and dark. This was the first time I'd ever come to a dance without drinking, and it all seemed unreal. The basketball rim and the dangling white net appeared suspended in nothing against the clear backboard. Not much chance I'd ever play on this court again.

Delores gripped my waist closer to her. She asked me what I was staring at.

"Oh, nothing," I said, and knew I'd probably looked like some of the people at the nuthouse staring blankly into the distance.

"How is the team doing?"

"Not so good."

A light slap on the back and I turned. Joey. "Hello, Sam."

We shook hands.

"I'm glad you're home."

"Me, too." We'd been talking loudly, and the band ended a song and I'd yelled that last.

"You working hard?"

"Yup. Guess what?"

"What is it?"

"Bought me some transportation." He stood a little straighter, puffed up a little.

"What'd you get?"

"1951 Chevy pickup. Good shape. Only paid two-hundred."

"All right. We'll hit the roads. Maybe soon I'll be paying you back the money I owe you if I can get my old job. Do you think Billy will take me back?"

Delores had walked off with a friend, and Joey and I stepped out into the hall, brightly lit, so we could talk. The band was playing a Stones tune.

"I don't know what Billy wants to do," Joey said. "You know how people get."

"Not Billy."

"It was quite a bit of money, Sam."

"I guess it was. I'll go talk to him." I paused. "So you didn't tell me the whole truth about this when we talked before."

"No. I didn't want to upset you. Don't get me wrong, it might be all okay. Billy hasn't said much to me."

Delores came around the corner. "Can we dance?"

"Sure." We walked into the gym and Delores stepped back and forth on the balls of her feet, swung her arms to the beat of "Street Fightin'

Man" and I couldn't catch the rhythm, and it was like the first time I'd ever danced.

Shit, I'd lost my job probably—and a friend—I'd always thought of Billy as a friend. At least he hadn't pressed charges, and it all came back to what Delores and I had done and how close I'd come to going to jail. It really hit me. For just a few seconds the greyness began, and Delores must have sensed it, too.

She gave me a quick hug, then pulled my shoulders down so she could say something in my ear. "Please stay better. Don't go away."

I nodded, then we walked over to the side of the gym and sat near where we had that first time so long ago, high up in the bleachers, the sound a mass of echoes, and the people smaller. We held hands and listened to the end of the song, and I missed music, especially The Doors, and some of the Beatles tunes, especially "Yesterday" where "all my troubles seemed so far way." I took deep breaths and closed my eyes, and told myself I could take nothing for granted, and the eerie image of those whippoorwills caused a shudder. Delores squeezed my hand, leaned closer.

Between songs I said, "I don't have a real good grip yet, Delores."

"Do you really expect to, so soon?"

"Guess not. Didn't think I'd lose my job either."

"You haven't heard that from Billy."

"No."

Lois spotted us and came up the bleachers.

"Have a seat," I said, and liked it, one of them on either side of me.

"How are you?" She took my other hand.

"I think I'll make it this time, more prepared I hope."

"Good."

The band played a slow tune and we could hear ourselves talk. "Got a letter from George today," I said. "He says he's been in the jungle. How do his letters sound to you, Lois?"

"I don't think he's telling everything."

"Probably be hard to, I guess."

A chaperone, my English teacher, walked along the bleachers four or five levels below and stopped. "Two girls, Sam?"

I held up both my hands with the girls' hands tightly grasped. "Why not?"

He smiled and winked, then walked on. Treated me the same as ever, I thought. "Let's go have a cigarette," Delores said.

Outside I said, "That wasn't so bad."

"What?" they both said, nearly at the same time.

"No one acted like a jerk."

"I told you before, Sam," Lois said.

"I know. There will always be assholes and I should ignore them. I'm starting to understand a lot of things." I knocked my fist against my head. "But I'm thick and maybe playing with a few dominoes short."

We all laughed together, and that rare thing caused a feeling that I really would get better.

On Sunday afternoon, Mom and Dad drove me back to the hospital, and during the long cold ride they barely said a thing. It was like they were just sitting there growing more gray hair.

"You guys don't think I'll ever be normal again, do you?" I asked when we were almost there.

Mom half-turned. "It's gone on for quite a while now and we're afraid you may not be ready to come home yet. We want what's best for you."

"I can see that."

"Time won't stand still," Dad said.

"I want to go forward. I think about that every day."

Dad turned onto the hospital grounds.

"We're just tired, Sam." Mom said, and stared straight ahead, rigid. At my building, I opened the car door while we were still moving.

"I'll call as soon as I know, and my heel skidded against the frozen pavement. Then I closed the door and walked down the same sidewalk I had walked with George, then turned and waved when Dad beeped the horn, and it was all ghostly, especially their faces through the frosted glass. For the first time I knew how I might feel in their position. The shame, the uncertainty, the fear. Your only son on the sidewalk of a nuthouse. Then I decided if this thing was genetic I would never be the father of another child, and it seemed with that a tiny part of me healed over, because the last one had not come into this world and could never experience some of the horrors of its father. I imagined if that child had lived how the years would have passed as I waited and worried that my son or daughter would go crazy, and of course I would see the symptoms in a glance, movement, or statement. And in a tremble of connected thoughts, as I stepped over the threshold and through the hospital door, my thinking spiraled back to my parents and how they might be blaming themselves for what had happened to me. Yet, of course, they had no way of knowing before they'd brought me into this world. Not like you do, I reminded myself.

# CHAPTER 42

I waved to Brian, on duty behind the desk, and he motioned me over.

"Good weekend, Sam?"

"Mostly."

"Put your things away, then come back and tell me about it."

"Okay."

When I came back we talked for half an hour about my parents, Delores, George, and school. Brian said, "I wish I had a special mirror that would let you see how your mind was acting when you first came in, so you could compare it to now." He smiled. "An illness x-ray."

"Believe me, I can feel the difference, almost as if the sick parts have healed and are covered with a thicker layer of skin."

"Good."

Then we played a game of bumper pool, and didn't say anything more about illness, and it was almost like being in a regular hospital, except for a new patient, obviously loaded full of Thorazine, head rolling on his shoulders like it was on the gimbals of a rolling ship.

As I stood waiting for Brian to take a shot, I knew I was growing accustomed to two worlds, at least to a certain degree. It had a strengthening effect; the question was, would it be enough? Brian called my name, and I knew it wasn't the first time, and I quickly took my shot. Did I want him to write a good report so I could go home? Not sure.

After medication, before bed, I sat with the rest of the group and watched television. Limbo, this is it. This ward was where they sorted people. Some stayed, and others went to the worse wards, and I'd been lucky, but still in limbo. Here and home had a grip on me and I could see the bad in both.

More memories to pack away, and this time not for later use against myself. Whipmywill. George might say Wimpywill.

With no ceremony or excitement, early Monday morning the doctor said it was time to go home, and I said good-bye to everyone at OT, and we all laughed and said we hoped to never see each other again. It was obvious some were jealous, like I had been on other days.

By noon on Tuesday I was home, and it was as if I'd finished one thing and had to start another. No say about it.

During the first few days of school, the fact that I was treated differently became something I had to accept, instead of something I had to fight and win. Normal. Though it was probably not a fair comparison, I considered myself a hardened soldier who knew the enemy well, and the tricks to save himself, and also how to stay away from trouble. The not-so normal becoming necessarily normal.

My third day in school, Coach asked me into his office. He wanted to know if I remembered how to make a basket.

I held my arms out and then gripped my fingers. "How's that?" He lifted his foot and tapped the side of my butt with his toe, then smiled.

"Be at practice. We could use you."

"Thanks."

It certainly was nice to know I was needed, even halfway through the season.

I told Delores between periods that afternoon, and she jumped up and down like one of the cheerleaders. "Big game Tuesday. Will you play?"

"Maybe."

"They need you to rebound, Sam. You're the tallest. They've only won two games out of six so far." She leaned against me. "We going out tonight?"

"I hardly have money for gas. I shouldn't have taken that money without asking."

"Why do you put off talking to Billy? You always told me he never stays mad for very long."

The bell for the last class rang. "Pick me up at seven, okay?"

"Sure." I slapped her butt as she walked away, and from across the hall the history teacher raised one hand and waved a finger back and forth. Very normal.

I trotted to my last class of the day and tried to pay attention but kept staring at the sugar white snow swirling in the wind, granules sparkling in the sun. Then I reached in my pocket and gripped the celestine ball Delores had given me for my birthday. I took it out and rolled it back and forth across the lined pad, and the sky blue and cream whites soothed me.

I wrote, no more nuthouses for this boy, then erased it. But I had pressed the pen so hard that the message was identifiable on the next two pages in the notebook, and I ripped those pages out, too. The ripping sound caused the teacher to look my way, then she resumed reading from a text about medieval art.

The guys in the locker room seemed happy to see me, and after I'd run a few laps and stretched, I started shooting and didn't miss as many as I'd figured. When we scrimmaged, I pushed and shoved under the basket for position and took in most of the rebounds. The coach called out my name, clapped his hands, and said, "Atta boy, Sam," and I was part of something again.

After practice, one of the second stringers came over, one of the guys I suspected had written the notes.

"No hard feelin's?" he asked and stuck out his hand.

"Forget it," I said, and instead of shaking his hand, slapped his stomach with the back of my hand. Twinges in my stomach and a few quick goose bumps reminded me how close I'd come to pounding the shit out of him, before.

In the shower and after, while I dressed, memories of the hospital haunted me. All the goodbyes had been positive because home was the goal for everyone, but the knot in my stomach grew as the memories of the safety in that place crowded one behind the other, like water backing up against a dam for the first time. Or maybe like water above a clogged drain.

I left the locker room to several calls of, "Glad you're back. Good goin." I still couldn't tip the teeter totter balance toward home. Here was like driving a race car without a seat belt.

I drove to the edge of town and parked in front of Billy's house. It was an old stone home set back in a grove of dense cedars. I'd only been there once before, and as I knocked, just wanted it over one way or the other.

Billy opened the door. "Hi ya, Sam. Come on in."

Same old Billy? He closed the door behind me, and I turned to face him.

"Thought you might as well fire me face-to-face." Not what I'd intended to say at all. Then, "I deserve it, and I'm sorry," my voice shaking. All those years he'd trusted me, said I was his best worker.

"Don't say any more. Come in and sit."

I said hello to his wife, who was out in the kitchen.

Billy's face was set when he came back with a Coke for each of us. He sat in the recliner across from where I sat on the edge of the couch. The room was expensively furnished, and spotless.

"Did I misjudge you, Sam?"

"I don't know." The Coke backed up all fizzy in my throat and I finally got it down.

"Five years you worked for me, and now this. What would you think if I'd done the same to you?" He slapped the leather arm of the chair. In anger, exasperation? He leaned forward. "Christ almighty, Sam. Running off with a fifteen-year-old girl, and you're eighteen. How could you do it?"

"You're," I stuttered, "You're—it's not about the money, is it?"

"Hell, no." He stood up and paced back and forth in front of the couch. "Are you going to tell me this all happened because of your mental illness?"

"Well. Some. I wasn't exactly thinking clearly. Delores did go along with it."

He stopped in front of me, turned and faced me, shaking his finger he said, "I always thought you were tough and independent. You did something stupid and it's wrong to blame it on Delores or mental illness. I think you were too chicken to run away on your own."

"I gotta go, Billy." I started to stand up and he took a step back, then, "No! You will listen to what I have to say!" His wife came in, and I could hear the sharp sound as she took a quick breath. Billy waved at her, but she didn't move away from the kitchen doorway.

"Billy," I said. "Why does all this matter so much to you?"

"Oh, nothing," he deflated like a popped inner tube, and sat again, and visibly most of the anger left his face, and his cheeks sagged of their own weight. His wife walked away.

"You are one of my best boys. I've always told people that. It's my pride, I guess."

"Twice now, Billy, I've lost time, somehow blacked out living and only tiny bits come back. The medication is working now, and I should be all right. They say I have a disease, and if it is treated correctly I can live pretty normal."

"Well, that's good." He paused. "You mean you didn't do all that stuff you did because you, I don't know, couldn't handle life, or something like that?"

"No, I don't think so. At least not entirely. Maybe it's like a battery that has a weak cell, and you can make it last for a long time with brand new acid, but it will never be the same as a new one. Billy, they call what I have a chemical imbalance."

His wife came to the doorway again and said that supper was ready and she'd set an extra place.

"C'mon and stay," Billy said.

"No thanks. I'm sure Mom is wondering where I am."

As I walked to the door, I decided I still wanted to hear it from him.

We both started to say something, and I turned, my hand on the door knob.

"What?" I said.

"Joey came to me this afternoon. He doesn't want all the hours he's working."

"I'm not fired?"

"If you were, how would you pay back Joey?"

"Good question."

We stood there and all I kept thinking was that a thank you wasn't enough.

"Shake on it," he said.

We gripped hands, and before I knew it I was on my knees, my hand almost numb. Billy laughed. "Do me a favor." He lifted me up. "I don't want to ever say I misjudged you."

"I'll try my best. That's a promise."

He put an arm around me and we walked to the door. "Work out a schedule with Joey. See ya soon."

On the drive home, a point George had tried to make me understand for years seemed finally to hit. A gray area existed, a portion of the unexpected, should be expected, had to be expected, in everything that came along. Even if something seemed straight and clear there were always consequences that might unexpectedly arise. Either from not understanding that idea, or refusing to accept, it had caused much of my grief.

I stopped by the river and stared toward my ice-covered rock and the river, a sheet of thick ice. I had a girl, a team to play on, a job, and a future if I could just keep things in order. George was still in Viet Nam though. Sitting beside the road, I shifted through the gears, first, second, third fourth, reverse; the pistol grip a perfect fit, the purr of the motor a contented cat, and for once I decided I'd do my damndest to live my own life and deal with what came from doing that, instead of all the other stupid things I'd always done. What a fuckin' worry wart. Then I remembered what Gramp always said about worthless things. "Like pounding sand in a rat hole." Made sense. I'd sure done my share, and the rats always found a way out.

After supper I wrote George a long letter, an honest letter, then worked like hell on school work for two hours. The phone rang, and I knew I was late to pick up Delores. I told her about Billy, and that I really just wanted to stay home tonight.

Home. It was strange to be here after having stayed so many places in the last few months. How could home, the idea of it, seem so strange?

I said goodnight to Mom and Dad, and Dad asked if I was home for good. When I looked at him, it was obvious to me for the first time that he had aged, and changed in other ways, too, into a somewhat more accepting type of person.

"Yes, he is," Mom said from where she lay all curled up on the couch. "I believe it and you should too, Paul."

As I rested in my bed, I remembered those times at the ocean, and the brook with Delores, and the river with George, and they all added up to the best times in my life, yes, even when accompanied, at times, by so many horrible thoughts. The water always like oil in an engine eliminating the worst friction, preventing the possibility of a seize up, and it had taken me so long to come to this that a few minutes before I fell asleep, my pillow was wet with tears, and a contentment settled like on those summer evenings when George and I sat in the tree house listening, mimicking the cries of the whippoorwill.

# CHAPTER 43

During the next two weeks of intense cold, I was very busy catching up, studying, working, playing ball, seeing Delores, and like Lois had said, the only people who acted different were the people almost everyone thought of as assholes, whether they were teachers or students.

One, in particular, was the guidance counselor. I met with him the day after we had won my first game by five points. Coach had said I sparked the team, and I imagined what it might be like to play in the manic part of my illness. At times, especially when I stood alone in eerie silence on the foul line, the scrutiny of hundreds of eyes on me, I wondered how many considered they were looking at someone who'd recently been in a mental hospital, and oddly I drew on them for concentration and only missed two of eight foul shots that night.

The next day I sat across from the guidance counselor, and he wanted to know if I'd considered joining the armed forces. I told him I had been looking at college catalogs and I wanted to go. As I told him this, he looked at my file and shook his head negatively.

"Sam, you should go into the service, and when you come out, if you still want college, they'll pay for it, that is if they'll take you with this illness. Believe me."

"If I'm alive."

"By the time you go, the war will be over. I'm quite sure."

"Quite sure doesn't cut it for me."

"Well." He leaned back in his chair. "You know where the college catalogs are. Help yourself." He closed the folder and tossed it away from him.

"Thanks for the advice," I said.

"You ought to follow through a little more on your jump shots," he said. "Good job rebounding."

"Right."

Stigma. It could send me back if I would allow the nastiness it caused to grab a hold. It was like a hate. I hated those who treated me differently, yet knew if I let it show, the stigma would worsen, bring more attention to me. Ignorant bastards!

For the next few weeks while the temperature still dove below zero almost every night, I rose a little more each day. For me everything was new, and sometimes I thought it was as if that second stay at the hospital had been like boot camp, a training perfectly suited, in all its horrors and few kindnesses, to prepare me to go on. I really did think and act clearly most of the time.

Days of routine, busy ones: school, practice, work, nights out with Joey during the week, and Delores on weekends, and I did my damnedest to drink no more than three beers a night. I just didn't want to stop altogether. During study halls I filled out college applications, and by February I'd sent two applications to nearby community colleges, as a kind of insurance, and one to my first choice, Paul Smiths, a forestry school in the heart of the Adirondack Mountains to the north. That was the one I wanted. George and I had talked about me going there when he was thinking about the Army, me ahead of him for the first time at something, and him joining me and us living together when he came home from the war.

Outside, all those summers with George and last summer in the birches with Delores, had convinced me I wanted to be a forest ranger: I'd imagine myself high up in a fire tower scanning for a wisp of smoke, a guardian of the forest. I'd protect it like it had protected and comforted me and Delores.

The birches. Several times in the three weeks since I'd been home, Delores and I had walked through a foot of snow in the below zero cold, mittened hands squeezing, up path to our spot. The birches did not seem as white against the snow, but their black limbs stood out like darkness complete. Our brook was invisible, yet even in this cold we heard an occasional gurgling noise under the snow, and I wondered if its source wasn't warmer than most other springs.

"Be difficult to make love here now," Delores said.

"Do you miss it so much?" The few times we'd tried in the car I'd been unable; we'd discussed it and blamed it on the pills. I was off most of the Thorazine and the doctor at the clinic said I should be off it all together in a month. To be honest, I think I missed getting drunk more than sex.

"I miss the closeness," she said. "That's all. It's plenty enough we're together."

We walked back in the bitter February cold, away from the spot that meant so much for so many reasons, and then I knew, faced the fact that I needed Delores, as much as I wanted her or loved her. In the past six months she had been lover, mother, friend, and perhaps during this time, a mother again. I wanted to tell her, but a small fear inside said she might leave, so I didn't. Yet, ironically, I did know that she would stay as long as I needed her, and I don't think I could ask for any more. As we trudged along in the deep snow, I couldn't give thanks enough for having her to help me through these past four months. My mother, Lois, and Delores; I thought, I've been blessed by the best women imaginable, and the question of why never entered into it one bit.

As February went along I'd quit desiring the routines of the hospital every time some little thing went wrong. I often thought of the little exercises they'd taught me on how to cope with my illness and did a relaxation exercise of tightening a certain set of muscles as hard as I could, holding it, then letting them relax. And like one of the therapists had explained, I tried to dismantle problems to find their cause, then adjust to whatever circumstances were connected with a specific problem.

I began new habits. Joey was still amazed that I rarely drank more than three beers at one time. I gave him half my weekly pay, after some fierce arguing to be sure. I even smoked less, and no pot.

We played our last basketball game on February 17 and ended the season with a five in twelve record, not good enough for sectional play.

That was fine with me, and I went home each day looking for college acceptance letters.

George wrote that he'd been on R and R in the Philippines and caught the clap from a beautiful girl—but that it wouldn't keep him out of the jungle for long. He also wrote that he missed home, his first mention of that in any letter I'd received.

Almost every night that I didn't work, Mom and Dad and I watched the black and white, but nonetheless bloody screen, as the commentators almost blandly described the killing and showed battle scenes; I couldn't help it, I always looked for George.

"Not like where I fought in World War II," Dad said, pushing himself back in his recliner. "Those jungles must be one sonofabitch."

"And that's the way it is," Walter Cronkite said, and I thought, Well that sucks. Here it is February 20, 1971 and my best friend might be killed at any minute. For what? No one in America seemed certain of an answer to this question. "Shit," I said. "I'm going for a ride."

"You okay?" Mom asked from the couch, half asleep.

"Yes." I stood in the living room doorway. "You know I should be hearing from at least one of those colleges."

"You applied pretty late. It may take a while."

"I want to go."

"You should."

"I will." I smacked the door jamb. "Even if I have to just take a few classes the first year and work to pay my way."

I drove for an hour to all the old places, listening to *The Beatles, The Doors,* and *The Rolling Stones*. Those musicians and the things they had to say always made me feel better. Especially Morrison when he sang, "I been down so goddamn long that it looks like up to me." Yes sir!

The next day at work, a little after supper, George's mom drove up to the pump island. I walked up to her window, expecting her to want the usual weekly five dollars worth of gas, about the only time I saw her.

"It's awful, Sam."

"What?" He's dead.

"They've listed George as Missing in Action. They came to the house and told me." She wiped her face with the palm of one hand. "What am I going to do. My son."

She gripped my forearm and pulled me down toward her.

My throat felt like I'd swallowed a tennis ball and I could barely speak. "Shit," I muttered. When things are just starting . . . No. I can't be sucked in by those thoughts from the beginning of this.

"Did they say anything else?" Her breath smelled of garlic and beer.

"Someone from Albany will call tomorrow."

Torture. Beating. Suffering in a bamboo cage. For the first time since I'd come home the blackness creeped all around me, spreading like ink through a roll of toilet paper. I leaned forward against her car, my knees on the frozen black top.

"No!" I said very loud.

She gripped my arm. "My oldest son."

"We have to wait and see," I said. "They might have found him already while we are here worrying."

"You're better now. That's so good." She let go of my arm.

"Yes."

Till now, I thought, weirdly wishing for Popeye strength, wanting a can of spinach in my back pocket to help at a time like this. Pop it in the air, take a big gulp, super human power.

"I'd better go," she said. "I had to come and tell you. It shouldn't come from anyone else."

"I'll stop by after work." I stood up and rubbed my knee caps.

"Good."

She drove forward a few feet, then stopped. "I need some gas."

"Back up a little." By now I was almost numb with cold, my fingers like icicles. I put in five dollars worth. She paid me, and I watched her old Chevy go down the street, salty and dim in the street light glare.

My brain was a stone. I leaned against the pumps and let the cold freeze my hands and face. All the little tricks I'd learned in therapy would not work. The balance I'd achieved with the lithium wavered like two equal weights on a teeter totter in a howling blizzard. I said to myself, you can't do anything about it. Hope and pray and keep yourself together. He'd want that. He'd be thinking about that. He knows I know. If he was still alive.

No body. That's how much the cold numbed me. At least twenty below. MIA. That meant no body to the army. A number. Missing. They didn't know. Probably didn't give a fuck either. I had to go inside. Standing out there was like fighting a battle with icicle swords: shattered ice crystals instead of blood. My soul weakened.

I walked around the station, and the numbness and blackness came and went like someone opening and closing a curtain on a starry night. I kicked an empty five-gallon metal pail across the garage, then I chased it and kicked it and chased it some more until finally the clanging and banging brought me into something I could understand. And as if Lois stood right beside me I heard, "Don't you become one of the assholes!" Then I yelled that out as loud as I could, kicked the battered pail one last time, and sat, more like collapsed, into a stack of tires, my ass way down, shoulder and knees level with each other. Then I saw George in this same position, what, maybe six months ago, and I'd thought I was going to have to help him out of the stack. Boy, he'd bitched me out that day.

It won't do any good to sacrifice yourself for George when it can't do him any good, and I remembered what the head nurse had said about my wanting to be the best friend of a dead friend ever.

Deep down there was absolutely no doubt that if I went back to the hospital in the shape I had been in before I would never come out again. Of course, I'd been doing so well I'd left the Thorazine at home the last few days. So I got up again and kicked that dented can all over the garage, intent, like a cat chasing a rat, then I started to curse at the top of my lungs. Left foot, Bang! "Godammit!" Right foot, Bang! "Fuck!" Left foot, Bang! "Shit." Then James Morrison's voice came into my mind, "Run Run Run," and I pushed that away, and finally, stopped, out of breath, sweaty and exhausted. All I could think about was torture, and if that was happening to George I wished him dead. Imagining that's what he would want, too.

# CHAPTER 44

I waited on two customers while trying to decide what to do; then I called Delores, and when I told her, she thought I'd lost my mind again. She really seemed to think I was hallucinating and I told her to forget it. I said, "You call George's Mom then. Goodbye!" My anger poured like gas from the nozzle: pumping. Where's the match?

Then it came to me that Delores, too, may have reached her breaking point, and she knew if what I said was true, she was in for another long and terrible heartache with me at the hospital. I couldn't do much about that right now.

My dime tinkled through the maze of metal curves. "Hello, let me talk to Lois."

"Sam?"

"It's better I tell you more than anyone else," I said, heard her breath catch. "George is MIA."

Silence.

"I'll be right there. You at work?"

"Yeah. Almost ready to close." Just telling her helped.

I walked around the station, and the toes on my left foot throbbed; then I filled another bucket with hot water and soap and began to mop.

Lois came in and smiled a little crooked.

She leaned against the cinder block wall, and I swung the mop back and forth in a pendulum motion. She told me that George had said before he left that capture was his worst fear, and as if I'd been sprung from a diving board those words put me back to the day I almost jumped out of the window. Keep up George or those cowboys will catch us.

"We've got to help his Mom," I said. "And his little brother."

"Yes, I'd forgot about Albert. Jesus."

She came over and hugged me, the mop still in my hands. I saw her footprints on the clean wet floor, so tiny, and I stared down at her, at her full breasts and thought what George would give to lean against them now.

"How are you?" she asked. Hugged me again, tighter.

"Strangely," I said, over the top of her head, staring out the frosted garage door windows, "I think maybe all I've been through has been preparation for something like this. Like if this happened before other things I'd be put away forever, but now I'll get through it."

Lois walked around and around the car lift while I shut off the outside lights and gas pumps, then I started in on the floor again. She just kept walking. Slow and intent.

I came back to her after I'd locked the safe and the door and shut off the lights above her. Soft light from the street came in, the only other light from the soda machine. Oddly her features reminded me a little of George in profile, and I blinked quickly to see if my mind was flipping again. No. The curve of her left cheek and the way her lips were pursed were definite reminders of George. George. Where are you now? I should have gone with you.

Lois walked up to me and stopped. She placed only her forehead against my chest, arms hanging limply at her sides. More tears fell in a pool at our feet, mixing with flecks of red paint and the used oil of a thousand cars. A salty rainbow pool.

"I can't stand it," she said. "I've got to know."

I sensed her terrible need and uncertainty like she had mine in past times.

"We have to believe they will find him, might already have. Don't wish him dead. You know how tough he is."

"What about you?"

"Callouses, Lois. More and more, thicker and thicker every day, like ice on the river."

"Hold me, Sam. Please hold me."

Later, "It's okay, Sam. Isn't it?"

"Yes, I think it is."

The phone rang. Delores.

"I'm sorry."

"Did you call George's Mom?"

"No. Of course not. I don't think I could go through again what we've been through."

"I understand." And I really did. I thought, she's fifteen and been through more than most people ever face in a lifetime.

"Lois is here."

"Let me talk to her."

I mopped over where Lois and I had been, then walked outside in the cold, picking up papers, cigarette butts and small twigs. The thermometer read fifteen below, five degrees warmer than earlier, and like a thick wide rubber band my mind expanded and contracted, but within certain boundaries, and I could almost sense the lithium, as if it set up a barrier to the wildest thoughts. Without it I'd be slugging down whiskey, crazy as the day those whippoorwills flocked around me.

Joey drove his clunker in from across the way and rolled down his window. I tried to light a cigarette and couldn't flick the wheel on my lighter. Hands numb as stones.

"How goes it, Sam? Cold enough for ya?" He shut off the motor.

"Got a lighter in that thing?"

"Yup. It's so goddamn cold the tape player won't work." He handed me the lighter and I touched its hot orange to my cigarette. "George has been listed Missing in Action."

"Oh, no."

"Come in where it's warm."

As we came in Lois hung up the phone and said, "Delores is awful sorry."

"I guess I should be used to people expecting me to act crazy." All three of us stood on the clean floor in the garage, and I knew I'd have to mop it again.

"Can't we do something?" Joey asked.

A florescent light buzzed over the oil display out by the cash register, and I could feel the cold seep into the garage and realized how much I'd been sweating.

Certainly a Thorazine night. I walked across the garage and picked up the five-gallon bucket.

"What happened to that?" Joey asked.

"We had a little argument. I won."

"Oh," he said. "When you heard."

"God damn fucking war!" Lois shouted. "Let me see that can." She almost kicked it out of my hands, then started in around the garage, and we could see it was doing her some good.

"Ferocious," Joey said.

It made me laugh and I shouted, "If George could see you now, Lois. It's the strangest game of kick the can I've ever seen." She stopped.

"I feel better," she said, and with one more kick, the can skidded into a corner. She came over and put her arms around me again. "We can't do anything," she said. "We've done all we could tonight."

"One thing," I said. "We must do the best to get through it and help each other. We have to."

"I hope you can do it," Joey said. "It could be a real sonofabitch."

"Let's put it this way. If I don't, you'll be visiting me in the hospital for the rest of our lives."

"No," Lois said. "George will come home." And she got a stubborn look on her face, just like Delores did in the worst of times. She smashed me in the chest with one fist and Joey in the same place with the other. "I know it," she said, as the air rushed out of us.

# CHAPTER 45

Up and down, inside out, outside in, but still in control. That's what I told the doctor two days later about George being MIA.

"That's very good to hear, Sam." He leaned back in his swivel chair. "How much Thorazine have you taken since George's mother told you?"

"One whole one. That first night, or I'd never have slept."

"You've done well. This war is a horrible thing."

"Sometimes I wonder who I am because of the pills."

"Tell me truthfully," Dr. Randall leaned forward. "Would you want to fight this illness without medication, again?"

He was right, and it had to be that way. Pills forever, or the hospital. Yet I couldn't stop the urge to want life unassisted. It sucked – necessarily sucked, I decided.

"Can I ever try without them?"

"It's doubtful. Think about your reaction to your friend being missing."

"They prevent intense emotion." Part of me wanted a reaction free of drugs, yet I knew what that might mean.

"Perhaps you should think of it as unreasonably intense emotion."

"How does the lithium work?"

"Scientists aren't sure."

"That figures. Does your profession know anything for sure? Or is it more like the army's way, you do the thinking for your patients?"

Dr. Randall stared at me.

Then like a breaking wave I went on, "Like sending men to occupy some dinky little village, and some are killed, some wounded, left to rot in the mud, and some are listed as missing and who knows what the fuck really happened." I stared at him. "For what and for who?"

"I can't answer that." He swiveled in his chair and faced the window. "You've learned, haven't you, that some questions have no answer?"

"Always my problem," I whispered.

He faced me again. "What was that?"

"I said I've always wanted answers no one had answers for—like when I almost drowned—ever since then I've owed George and wanted to pay back. Can't. Even though I'd have done the same thing for him and not expected anything in return. Still, maybe, if he never comes back . . . I just want to see him again."

"Don't let this get out of hand. You're not making sense, Sam."

"I have the lithium, now."

"It's not a cure-all by any means."

"You're right." I took a deep breath and the water in my eyes would not come out, and I could see Delores' eyes, brimful.

"Come and see me tomorrow." He flipped to the next page on his calendar. "Tell the secretary four o'clock."

"I'll be okay. I have to sit and think quietly more often."

"I want to help you through this," Dr. Randall said.

"This is such a sonofabitch. I have to go see his mother. I hate it. I don't know what to say."

"I can't tell you what to do. Except one thing," and I held up one finger like he was doing, then we both said, "No drinking."

I took a long drive in the dying afternoon light and didn't stop till I reached that high bluff overlooking the Hudson River.

Most people back in town had probably heard about George and I figured they were waiting for me to lose it again. Not this time. I knew I could not sacrifice my whole life for something: friendship, George's death. No one's existence depended that much on another's, no matter how much it may seem to. And for the first time, as I stood on the edge of that bluff, the river a thousand feet below, I caught a glimpse of how alone each one of us exists, no matter how much we'd like it different. I stared out over the river, a jagged channel chopped through the ice for ships, water almost black, ice glaring translucent in the setting sun, and I wanted to jump very badly. God, it's a long long ways down. What will I think of on the way. I stepped one foot out over the edge, perfectly balanced on a sun cleaned rock.

I'd never do it.

Would I have done it that night if Dad hadn't grabbed me?

I think so. Absolutely another person. Cowboys coming hard on us. I stepped back, and spit over the edge, knew it would evaporate long before finding earth again. Control. Balance. If I can think and learn from all I've gone through, I can exist, survive. And though I tried, I couldn't quite make all the connections between the experience of mental illness and now.

I arrived home late for supper and Mom was waiting; she was waiting for me to take another trip away from her, I was sure.

I gave her a big hug. "I'm not going back."

"Good."

I patted her shoulders. "Worry as much as you want. I'm not going back."

Dad came in from the living room. "What's this?"

"A hug," Mom said.

"Did you save me any supper?" I asked.

"Your mother was worried."

I wanted to say, 'I almost jumped off a cliff,' and too clearly could imagine the expressions on their faces, and knew I couldn't tell anyone, not even Delores. "I'm doing the best I can."

"It's terrible what happened to George," Dad said. "He knew it was a possibility when he signed up."

"I know, Dad. I'm sure the recruiter told him that. Let's not argue."

"No," he said. "Let's not."

He went back in the living room, and I knew I would never see things cut and dried like he did. I'd always look underneath. I really did believe that sometimes there were answers to things that appeared unanswerable. Not understanding can be crucial.

I wanted a beer; my mind ached. Shit and damn.

I took a Thorazine after supper, and an hour later I was in bed asleep.

A little after two in the morning, I woke up and stared through the cold panes of glass at the points of stars, so bright on this moonless night. Probably twenty below again, and hot where George is. The Thorazine in me drew a dim curtain over the pain. Maybe I would be the best mourner a best friend ever had.

I paced up and down in the living room. Since Tuesday I'd known he was missing, and now it was Thursday, actually Friday morning, and Tuesday seemed like yesterday, like it would always be yesterday. The Beatles' song, "Yesterday," and the hurt was so intense I walked bent over, and admitted, too, that part of me liked the pain. That was sick. A symptom of my worst sickness coming back.

Over and over I paced silently up and down, treading the carpet, and I began to whisper on each foot fall: "won't go back, won't go back." Over and over. So cold out and warm in here, my head like blank slides on a dark wall, the images going from white to shades of gray as each slide is changed in an unending change of sameness. The window lurked to the left, so inviting. Except nothing was chasing me this time.

Why aren't the pills working? More like a Band-aid on a severed leg stump. In my room, I swallowed another Thorazine, then went back to the living room and sat in Dad's recliner.

I just wanted you to know. Everybody. The whole world. Ignorance. Hating. Hating to wait.

Waiting for Thorazine. It works. No one can doubt its power. Like a curtain ending the perverted play in my head: a glass shattering leap into the cold. It worked. Kicked in and my flesh sagged on its bones.

I got up and paced, and the steps became more measured, deliberate as the medicine drained the stress and insanity like an open faucet. My mind more baby-like, the thoughts simple and flat, limbs like weights without motion, or labored motion. Weights attached everywhere.

"Yesterday, oh yesterday, came suddenly." Good old McCartney, I thought, then went back to bed, snuggled down under the covers.

When Mom woke me up for school, I could barely get out of bed, and the sun sparkling on the snow outside almost blinded me. Will I forever be without George?

"No more nuthouses," I whispered through a mouthful of toothpaste.

George's car barely turned over, then caught and the tuned exhaust system bellowed out plumes of white fog. I waited for the oil pressure to rise and remain steady, then eased out the clutch and the wide tires gripped the icy driveway. Just another day at school.

They'd get no satisfaction this time. Mick Jagger strutting up and down the stage. The tape deck had the slows because of the cold and the car rolled easy over the frost heaves along the river. I patted my pocket. Yup, the pills were there.

The morning passed, then the afternoon. Lois and Delores not knowing what to say at my more or less normal behavior. All waiting.

It could be days or weeks or months. Or never. We all knew that.

"Lois is falling apart," Delores said in the parking lot after school.

"She loves him," I said. "She's finding out how much."

"Do you tell how much you love someone by how much it hurts?"

"That's a part of it, Delores."

"I must love you quite a bit."

For a brief instant, I could see her on that metal table, legs drawn up in stirrups, and the hum of a machine that had the power to remove life, vacuum it away.

"I owe you so much," I said.

"No. Don't say that."

"You've given up so much for me."

"No, for me, too. I didn't do anything I didn't want to." She turned and walked away, and as many times as I'd seen her that day this was the first I realized she was wearing my favorite skirt, those little tiny shiny threads of purple glinting in the afternoon sun.

I called her back and we went for a drive along many of the roads we'd travelled. I wondered what she'd think about us in twenty years. Later, we held hands for a long time in front of her house and clips of our times flashed by: especially the details of that night she came walking from the house with her suitcases, running away. Like George said, I was one lucky sonofabitch.

We kissed, and she smiled, I thought a knowing smile of something I could not grasp. Then she opened the door. "Goodbye, Sam."

As I pulled onto the road I said, "Jesus, where in hell is the balance?"

I waited in the doctor's office for twenty minutes past my appointment, and caught myself thinking, probably some other nut taking up my time. Then it came to me that the other people in the waiting room were nuts or recovering nuts. Actually though, you couldn't tell. Not like black and white. So, if I'd be quiet about my mental illness in a new place no one would ever know. Why didn't one of those colleges accept me?

Memories of George, the big ones, passed like seasons, blending into one another like leaves on the ground. Would there be any more?

The receptionist told me to go upstairs.

"Afternoon, Sam."

"Hello." I sat in my usual place, a chair centered in front of his desk, still warm from the last patient.

"No news."

"None."

"Anything you want to talk about?"

"I'm fighting it. It comes, and we fight, and I take some Thorazine and we beat it."

"Not such a terrible system. My sense is that your mind is very powerful, emotionally and intellectually, and you may always struggle with these questions. About life, illness, truth. But if you learn how to handle it, or fight it, you may be fine. A great success, actually."

"It's a see-saw. I think he'll come home, then I don't."

"Normal, don't you think?" He steepled his fingers.

"Suppose so."

"What next?"

"Fight."

I closed my eyes and leaned my head toward the floor. Dr. Randall didn't say anything for the longest time.

"Can I go now?"

"Yes." He handed me a prescription slip to have a blood level drawn on Monday.

Downstairs I walked out into the cold.

George's mom wasn't home from work yet, so I waited in the car and turned the motor on once in a while for heat. When it was almost dark she drove in and I got out to meet her.

"Hi," I said, and George's brother looked at me, then stuck out his right hand for a shake. "Hi ya, Albert."

"Any news?" I asked.

"No. You'll be the third to know after us. Come on in."

"I couldn't visit the other night. Tough shape," I mumbled.

"It's okay. I thought as much." Then she told us she'd had a visit from the DOD and a Sergeant. They told her with the war winding down they were hopeful of news about George.

She fixed us coffee, and I looked around at the small kitchen, red and white checkered wall paper, old gas stove, and blue linoleum. She handed me a cup before she said another word. Albert had gone to his room. Her silence unnerved me. We sat next to each other at the kitchen table.

"I don't know what to say," she said. "I don't want to upset you. You see I think of you as the closest thing to George I have left." Several tears fell into her coffee, oiling the top with a dark rainbow. "I look at you and see him."

I sipped my coffee and the cup was slippery in my sweaty hands. "You have Albert."

"He's so young. He thinks it's all a game of soldiers. I saw you and George grow up. Your special friendship."

I couldn't think of what to say.

"Thanks for stopping." She stood up and clearly wanted me to leave, then she sat down again.

"He'll come back," I said.

"Maybe and maybe not." We sipped more coffee.

"You're doing better."

"Yes. I definitely am. The medicine helps. I think more now before I go crazy."

She gave me a strange look.

"I mean I think more, and because I do, I don't go crazy."

"Oh."

"It's tough to explain."

"You're better."

And by the faraway look on her face I could tell she was thinking George probably wasn't.

"I should go home to supper."

"Stop by again."

"I will. Please call if I can do anything."

"Other people have said that. It means most from you. Nothing, though. Not a thing can be done." The phone rang and we both jumped, an automatic prayer for good news.

"Hello," she said.

"Oh, hi, Lois." She waved, and I left.

For the next week, like the layers of pond ice thickening and cracking, or on nice days thawing a little, then re-freezing at night, I grew more accustomed to not knowing. In a way it was such a big thing, this not knowing, I mean, becoming accustomed to it like a normal person would be quite an accomplishment. Maybe. I had to get used to it like I had to not understanding so many other things. Normal?

Of course, I couldn't tell how much the drugs helped, or having such good friends and parents. I think they were all surprised I didn't fall into little jigsaw pieces again and end up in the hospital. I figured three strikes and you're out.

As the weeks passed winter melted into early spring, and still no word of George. I took less and less Thorazine, saw the doctor every week, then every other week, and just kept right on a going past when the leaves came out and the May flowers bloomed. Lois adjusted. Delores adjusted. Both carried weights. They had helped me know love as something lasting, an accumulation, shared, staying together through good and bad. Delores and my relationship settled like the heavy snows of winter flattening leaves; now most of the romance gone, but something stronger in its place. An accumulation compressed.

More than anything else, every time the mental illness did try to win, I'd fight with every trick I'd learned, and especially think of those stinky old men and the terribly sad atmosphere of the cafeteria. It all helped snap me back into trying extra hard to think more clearly.

Life settled into a series of fits and stops, starts and glides. At times, as I looked back it was as if those whippoorwills really had been trying to tell me something, that my life in many ways was like their song: so repetitive for one thing, and always singing in the dark, always afraid to see the truth in the bright light of day. I had to break out of my endless whippoorwill pattern.

I stood by myself next to the brook in the grove of birches, fresh, fully opened leaves blowing in the warm breeze. "Whippoorwill," I called, "Whippoorwill," up into the leaves, past them toward the bright blinding shafts of hot sunshine. "Whippoorwill."

# THE END

THE END

# EPILOGUE

It was in the beginning of my second year of college at forestry school when George's mother called and said George was coming home in a week. He'd be at the base hospital at Fort Drum, and we could see him. I told her I'd come home the next night and we'd drive over together. His Mom said they'd told him George had to go through debriefing and certain assessments. I just wanted him home, evaluations or not.

"He isn't dead!" I yelled, and my roommate gave me a strange look, like I was talking about Jesus or something. Then he realized I meant George.

"That's great."

I had never given him up.

I went outside and took a long walk in the woods behind our dorm, and the year and a half of waiting collapsed all the way back to the time I'd seen him at the train station. Then, like a thousand prism colors twirling, the days fell upon themselves and I relived our childhood together, and I didn't think of the bad or sorrowful times, except for the briefest seconds. No black. The days of my sickness were over. No, I knew that was not true. I kicked among the bright fall leaves, and it didn't matter so much what we'd been through. It mattered we were alive.

I was certain that no matter what horrors George had been through, like me, he would survive. Mental illness or war, I thought, what an unbearable dilemma.

I came to the top of a hill and stared down at a small, almost perfectly circular pond below. River water. Brook water. Ocean water. The sleek stillness of the pond glistened in the fall sunset.

The will to live, no matter how weak or deranged, could always survive with the help of friends.

There must always be friends.

I hurried down to the pond through thick underbrush to see it up close. The pond's water was clean and spring fed, fresh to the taste, and it smelled rare and earthy. Valuable. Water dripping from my chin, I leaned out over the water, stared down into it. My reflection smiled all the way through me. George is coming home. George is coming home. And I knew in the deepest part of my heart that I'd never go back again.

# ABOUT THE AUTHOR

Timothy Strong holds a master's degree in English and Creative Writing from Binghamton University, where he was mentored by Larry Woiwode. Tim's poems and short stories have been published in *The Alabama Review*, the *Mississippi Review*, *Blueline*, *False Grief*, and *The Awakenings Review*. An entrepreneur, he owns and manages the BirchBark Bookshop, offering over 75,000 used and rare books. He lives in the foothills of the Adirondacks.

# NOTE FROM THE AUTHOR

Word-of-mouth is crucial for any author to succeed. If you enjoyed *Whippoorwill Chronicles*, please leave a review online—anywhere you are able. Even if it's just a sentence or two. It would make all the difference and would be very much appreciated.

Thanks!
Tim

Thank you so much for reading one of our **Coming of Age** novels. If you enjoyed the experience, please check out our recommended title for your next great read!

*The Ghost of Jamie McVay* by R.G. Ziemer

"Ziemer weaves a tale that will make your heart race."
-Tina O'Hailey, author of *Absolute Darkness*

View other Black Rose Writing titles at
www.blackrosewriting.com/books and use promo code
**PRINT** to receive a **20% discount** when purchasing.